THE OTHER

R Lawson Gamble

for Sarah
My fellow
Los Aloman!

R Lawson Gamble

First paperback printing 2013

Cover Design Copyright © 2012 By Digital Donna

ISBN-13: 978-1482535082

ISBN-10: 1482535084

To My Readers: Lynn, Jonathan, Nancy, & Leslie;

and To Ann

who never questioned my decision to write instead of work

PART I: JOHN ROUNDTREE

ONE

John Roundtree's house sat hollow-eyed and alone at the edge of town, not a town so much as a few dusty buildings clumped on either side of the state road that passed through on the way to more important places. His dusty old pickup out front with the cloth showing through the tires hadn't moved in years; weeds grew high around it and lizard tracks disappeared under it. Nobody knew what John Roundtree did anymore. Few people saw him outside his house in the light of day and those who did guessed from his red eyes and wild hair that he didn't get much sleep. They whispered around that John Roundtree spent his nights communing with evil spirits.

John Roundtree wasn't always like that. Used to be he built things with brick, fancy walls and such. He was a real artist with brick. At first he worked with his own sun-dried clay bricks and then when the fancier imported bricks became cheap enough he started to use those and he would build beautiful things. He lined up the bricks so the fancy designs matched and the wall looked almost like a solid piece of hand decorated stone. Back then he was in demand all over the Reservation and beyond. Most of the people in town had a Roundtree wall or patio somewhere on their property.

But it was a long time since Roundtree built a wall. It was a long time since he did much of anything, for that matter. Not since the night his son died during childbirth. After that, he didn't come into town anymore, maybe just once or twice a month to buy flour or a little sugar at the dry goods store. A rumor started floating around that Roundtree, crazed with grief that his son was stillborn had left his young wife to bleed to death.

After that residents of Elk Wells talked of a man-like creature they saw at night. Sometimes it appeared on a lonely road, they said, striding across it or running along with moving cars before it disappeared in the darkness. About the same time sheep herders out on the mesa started to complain of lambs gone missing in the night and nothing left the next morning but pools of blood. A herder told of being awakened in the night by strange sounds and looking out to see a tall figure standing at the pasture fence, solitary against the moonlight, chanting and staring back at him. The townspeople listened to these stories and they thought of John Roundtree. So when the hunters found the body of that little girl up on the mesa they naturally figured Roundtree had something to do with it.

The hunters noticed the circling birds against the rose-tinted sky above the rim rock and saw where the flat rays of the early morning sun glinted on something that didn't belong there and the three of them walked that way. When they came close ravens flurried into the air and flapped and scolded at them and a vulture stood awkward on scaly red legs and glared before giving way reluctantly and unfolding its long wings to staggered into the air. After that they saw the body. They came up to it together and stared down at pale skin festered and burned and soft blonde hair that lifted and fell in the breeze and a baby face with wide unseeing green eyes. She lay there on the hostile desert sand like a broken doll.

They thought at first the girl had been killed by an animal, maybe a mountain cat or a bear. Her little frock and the flesh under it had been torn open as if by a claw and her head was twisted at a funny angle and her neck broken, like it all might been done with one powerful swipe. You couldn't tell if the face and the arm wounds were where the vultures and ravens had started in on her or if it was something else that had caused them. The guide Eagle Feather guessed as how the little girl couldn't have been lying there more than a couple hours on account of how much was still left of her.

It took almost an hour for one of the hunters to climb back down off the mesa and drive in to town and then another hour to return with two Navajo Nation Policemen. The Navajos walked over to the little girl's body and studied it for a few minutes. They looked around at the ground where she lay and put a plastic poncho over her and cordoned off the area with yellow tape off a dusty roll. One of cops spoke on the radio while the other had a cigarette and then they all stood at the edge of the bluff where they could see the sun glint off the windshields of the cars far below and waited there for the FBI agent to arrive.

It was late morning when a puff of dust first materialized in the direction of town and moved slowly toward the mesa. It grew into a white pickup truck pulling a horse trailer and it came up and parked next to the other vehicles. The men watched as a tiny figure emerged from the truck and went into the trailer and reappeared leading a horse. The sun burned down and they watched the figure move methodically from horse to truck and truck to horse until at last it lead the horse beyond the parked cars and out of sight beneath the mesa rim. When they next saw him he was walking toward them and the horse he led had a full pack behind the saddle and a rifle in the boot. The man's shirt was spotted with sweat and his tanned face gleamed under the dirt-smudged brim of his hat. Sky-blue eyes took in the scene and a mouth that most times seemed about to smile looked grim.

The FBI agent came to Eagle Feather and shook his hand, then nodded at the two Navajo Police. He glanced sidelong for a moment at the two hunters who stood off a bit before he walked over to where the tape fluttered around the girl's body. He studied the ground outside the tape for a while and then stepped over it and looked down at the tiny shape outlined under the flapping black plastic. Kneeling, he reached over and gently pulled it back.

"Aw, damn," he said quietly.

Eagle Feather stood near the yellow tape, watching, his face an empty page. "Sucks when they're so young." The slight breeze lifted his long black hair that hung down beneath the battered felt hat with its solitary ragged feather that jutted from the band. His eyes usually twinkled but they were solemn now.

He'd known FBI Special Agent Zack Tolliver for ten years, ever since the agent came to the Rez. Back then, Zack was a young man fresh out of the Academy, assigned to assist Supervisory Special Agent Ben Brewster who was the Four Corners Indian Affairs FBI liaison for the Reservation. Zack'd leaned on Eagle Feather from the start. Since then they'd worked together through the good and the bad. This was the bad.

"What the hell was she doing up here?" Zack wondered. Eagle Feather didn't have an answer.

The Navajo Indian Reservation in Arizona is huge and empty with few roads and lots of heat. For an FBI agent it was a place that offered no social opportunity, just lots of boredom interrupted by brief moments of sudden violence. The rookie agents who'd been assigned to assist Agent Brewster in the past hadn't stayed long. It wasn't that Ben Brewster wasn't a good man and a good officer. He did all he could as best he knew how to assist the Navajo Nation Police in a job that required constant vigilance in a hostile environment, where drunkenness was the easiest escape and violence the first solution. But it wore him down. After Zack arrived with his steady patient ways and bulldog tenacity Ben began to lean on him more and more. These days with retirement close Ben tended to stay in the office and handle the paperwork and let Zack respond to the calls and make his own decisions out in the field.

Zack looked up from the ground near the body and over at the two Navajo policemen who stood relaxed but attentive at a respectful distance.

"Left heel worn to the inside?" he asked quietly.

"Over there." The younger policeman Jimmy Chaparral nodded toward one of the hunters.

"Vibram, like new?"

Lané Shorter, florid faced and stocky, pointed to the hunter with the shiny leather boots.

"And two official issue leather soles."

It was a statement, not a question and both policemen looked at their feet. Zack grinned and said to Eagle Feather, "Add your high-tops and I get five. That's all I see here..."

"Seems strange, alright."

"You work trail better'n me. Did somebody brush-wipe here?"

"Maybe, but if he did, he's damn good."

"Know anybody that good?"

"Not around here."

Zack stood and hitched his belt. He took his time and looked all around at the horizon then up at the sky. "Dropped her here, maybe?"

"Nope. No impact marks, no bounce, no rotor wash from a helicopter. Anyways, she'd a been more broken up."

Zack glanced over at the two hunters and then back to Eagle Feather. "You been with these boys all along?"

"Yup. Pulled 'em out of bed this morning and walked 'em in front of me. That one" -he pointed to worn left heel- "came on her first, then puked over there."

"Hmm." Zack looked over and caught the eyes of the two policemen. He waggled his finger in a circle. "We need to scout up some sign," he said. "There's got to be somethin' here. Jimmy, Lané, E.F., let's do a search. We'll walk in a circle all in a row; inside man goes outside with each revolution. Let's see what's been left for us." He turned to Eagle Feather. "Why don't you tell your two sheep shooters to stay put 'til we've finished."

Eagle Feather went over to speak to them.

The four men lined up and moved forward in a crazy slow dance, kneeling, peering and twisting and reaching down to feel indentations in the dirt or to move dry leaves and ground cover. The dance went on for near an hour while the two hot and unhappy hunters sat in their appointed spot in the limited shade of a Mexican Broom bush and watched their hunting day evaporate into dry air.

The human chain worked its way steadily out from the where the body lay until Eagle Feather raised a hand. He knelt and looked at something on the ground. The two policemen held position and stared and sweat gleamed on the back of their necks.

Zack came over and stood next to Eagle Feather. He looked down and said, "Bear."

"Maybe. Maybe not." Eagle Feather studied the ground. His finger traced the indentations of five fat toes and a large round pad. "Big foot, big bear, but not so heavy. In soft ground a bear this big should make a deeper print. Look here. The print is deepest in the middle and less deep on the outside. It should be an even depth across the forefoot." Eagle Feather sucked in his breath as if tired out from all the talk.

"Anyone else see tracks?" Zack called out.

Lané Shorter was at the outside of the row. He squatted down and scanned the ground in front of him.

"Over here," he called.

They all came over to him. In the soft dust was a track almost identical to the first. Jimmy Chaparral stepped off the distance between the two tracks.

"He's got a long stride."

The men scattered out. The call came right away that another track was found and after that another. All of them were similar to the first one, some closer together, some further apart.

"Notice anything funny about these tracks?" Zack asked after a while. He scratched his head, his hat tilted back. "Look, here you got a long step, then a short step, short step, long step, short step, short step. But all the tracks are imprinted the same, real even. This print over here that comes after a long step should slope back 'cause of the angle of the leg, but it doesn't."

"Could be down on all fours," Shorter suggested.

"But if he is," Jimmy Chaparral joined in, "the stride on a bear this big should be longer at the long steps. And even then, there should be more slope to the print."

"And the tracks from the rear legs should imprint different from the tracks of the front legs," Eagle Feather agreed quietly. His next words were emphatic. "Two legs," he said, certain. "It's walking on two legs."

They all clustered together and stared down at the tracks, careful not to look at each other.

At last Zack spoke what they all knew. "Not a bear."

Everyone stood quiet, eyes to the ground. One after another they looked up and nodded.

Zack pushed it. "What, then?"

All eyes went back to the ground.   The question hung there. Jimmy Chaparral turned and walked away along the tracks.

Zack spoke a little louder, pushing it harder. "And don't give me any shape shifter witch stuff."

Shorter looked at him. "A Yee Naaldlooshii can turn into an animal to hide," he said. "This could be a bad witch, a Skinwalker." His tone was stubborn.

Zack opened his mouth to respond but right then Jimmy called to them. "I've got blood."

The men gathered around and looked at the new print Jimmy was studying. He pointed to a small brown blotch where a long claw had pushed into the dirt. Zack took a sample bag from his pocket and carefully scraped the bloody sand into it.

Shorter walked a little further on. "Over here," he called out.

"More here." That came from Eagle Feather, who'd moved ahead of Shorter. Now they saw there was a distinct trail of blood along the bear tracks. The sun was at its zenith and the ground baked. Zack rose from studying yet another print, his shirt hot against his back. He placed a blood sample safely into a Ziploc bag.

"So," he summarized, "we got foot prints of a bear that isn't a bear. The bear tracks go away from the little girl but not toward her. There's blood in the tracks but we don't know if the blood belongs to the little girl or to someone or something else. We don't know who the girl is, where she came from, or what she was doing here. We don't know what the bear, which isn't a bear, is. And we don't know why the blood trail increases going away from the crime scene instead of the other way around. But we do know one thing: we've got a killer on our hands." He looked at the Navajo men. "A human killer."

They avoided his eyes.

"Jimmy, you and Lané take these samples and go back to the crime scene," Zack said. "Take some good pictures of the tracks on the way back. Secure the scene when you get there and radio for a forensics team and full support from my office. And men..." he said quietly, "I see no need to mention the color of that little girl's skin. So long as the media doesn't know the victim is a white girl they won't come swarming over us. It'll buy us time." He shook his head sadly at the implications.

The expressions of the Navajo men didn't change.

Zack looked at Eagle Feather. "Can you go on a bit with me? Your sheep shooters be okay?"

Eagle Feather nodded.

Jimmy pulled a compact camera out of his shirt pocket and the two Navajo Nation Policemen started to photograph the prints. Zack and Eagle Feather moved on along the bear tracks, quicker now, and changed lead from print to print. Sometimes they'd lose the trail of prints on the hard sandstone surface but then they'd rediscover it further along. Often small droplets of blood guided their way.

"He doesn't try real hard to hide his trail."

"No, seems like he doesn't care if we follow it."

Further along in the sandy soil they found one clear impression after another. Here the tracking was swift. Zack was out in front when there was a different track. The bear print was changed.

Zack stared at it and felt the hair on the back of his neck stand up. The print he saw there in the sand wasn't a bear any more; it was the barefoot print of a man.

"Oh, shit!" he said.

TWO

Lenana Fitzgerald sat squeezed into a too small chair at the dispatch desk in the single room office of the unassuming Navajo Police station in the center of Elk Wells. The sign hanging outside read Navajo Nation Police and that title was repeated in grand arching calligraphy on the dusty office window. Lenana's desk was strategically placed to guard the outside door. A sign next to her nameplate read Information. Behind the sign were a central dispatch radio unit, a desktop computer, the telephone, and a stack of files. One file lay open in front of her now, its papers scattered by frequent swipes of her beefy forearm when she reached across the desk to press the talk button on the dispatch radio.

The other two desktops in the office, by contrast, were bare, the chairs empty. A small formal nameplate on each desk identified the two Navajo Policemen: Lané Shorter and Jim Chaparral. Their barren surfaces proclaimed the perpetual absence of the men who occupied them, constantly on patrol or responding to calls. The gun rack on the back wall held the standard complement of two businesslike shotguns and an AR15 assault rifle. The men would be carrying Glock 22 forty caliber handguns strapped in their holsters but they relied on their batons to deal with the drunk and disorderly citizens who took up much of their duty time. Two bullet-proof vests hung on the wall despite Navajo Nation Police policy to wear them at all times when on duty, but as Jimmy Chaparral often pointed out, "We're always on duty", and besides, they were just too damn hot to wear.

Lenana didn't mind that the two men were gone much of the time. She could handle pretty near anything that came up, like yesterday when she wrestled an out-of-control- high-on-drugs teenage boy to the floor and pinned him there with her ample body while she telephoned his father to come get him. Truth be told, though, there wasn't much for her to do since most of the calls were handled on the spot by one or the other of the policemen and nobody demanded that records be kept, not for the usual drunk and disorderly or spousal abuse responses...there were just too many of those. Lenana would sometimes get a little walk-in business, like permit requests, no-trespassing signs, or simple complaints, that sort of thing. And, yes, the email log had to be checked from time to time, but mostly she could sit and sip coffee or visit with her friend Katie from the café next door.

Fitzgerald was not a common family name on the Reservation nor was Lenana in any way Irish. She had acquired her surname courtesy of an actual Irishman who bestowed it upon her impulsively one day and abruptly disappeared by the next. At first Lenana clung to the name for romantic reasons but after she found that her acquired name gained faster responses to her calls outside the Rez she kept it, as she liked to say, for professional reasons.

But not every day was uneventful and when tensions increased, as her two police colleagues discovered, Lenana remained cool and professional. Now, though, both of her capable hands were occupied; one gripped the telephone and the other held the talk button on the radio transmitter.

"Lané, come in. Where did Zack go? His office is all over my butt." A pause followed by a burst of static came from the radio dispatch unit. From the neglected telephone in Lenana's right hand a tinny voice carried on, unfazed. The phrases 'Monument Mesa' and 'Zack & Eagle Feather' and 'send forensic team' and 'Jimmy Chaparral in one hour' were scrawled on a scratch pad near the radio, barely legible. Another loud burst of static came from the radio and Lenana turned her attention back to the tinny voice still speaking in the telephone handset.

"I don't know what the hell is going on up there," Lenana said. "I'm not getting any response at all now. All I can tell you is that Jimmy is due back here any minute. I'll have him call you the second he gets in."

Lenana hung up the telephone. As if on cue, the radio sprang to life.

"Lenana, do you read me?" It was Jim Chaparral. "Lenana, I'll be there soon. Listen, don't talk to any reporters. Got it? No reporters."

"What's going on up there, Jimmy?"

"I'll tell you all about it when I get there - damn - sorry, ran a front tire into a hole. Listen, Lenana, start digging around for any missing little white girls in the area...no, make that in the state and maybe in Nevada...and California. See what you can find. I'll be there soon. Out."

"Little white girls! What the...Jimmy, how old? What description? Jimmy...?" There was no response but static. The telephone in her hand rang loudly. "Navajo Nation Police, Elk Wells. No, I told you, I don't know where Zack is; I presume he's up on the Mesa with everybody else. Sorry sir, but I just told your assistant the same thing. Don't you people talk to each other there? Jimmy should be here in five minutes and I'll have him call you. Yes, I promise." Lenana put down the phone.

"Jesus!" she said. The phone rang again. Lenana put it to her ear wearily, but suddenly sat upright. "I'm sorry". She spoke warily. "I don't know what you're talking about. You might try the police station over at Tuba City."

When the front door banged open and Jimmy Chaparral finally walked in Lenana was still on the phone. Jimmy dropped like a stone into the chair next to her desk.

"What a day," he groaned.

Lenana liked Jimmy. He was the most personable of the policemen who passed in and out of this office, a man at ease with himself and not afraid to share his thoughts. Now, though, slumped in the chair like a potato sack, all he shared was fatigue and a whole lot of anxiety.

"I've never had to deal with anything like this before," he said. "We've had shootings and knifings and all kinds of aggravated assaults but nothing like this." He looked up at Lenana. "How are you doing with that missing child search?"

Lenana had her own concerns. "That call was from the Tuba City

Times. How the hell do they know about this already?"

"The Times? Who knows? Nobody on the mesa could've called them; there's no cell service up there. Maybe Zack's office leaked it."

"Well, they're calling every five minutes. As to missing kids, I haven't had a lot of time to research but I did come across a couple of possibles. There's this one: five days ago in Reno, Nevada, a six-year-old girl abducted from her family's backyard, right out of a kiddie pool, for God's sake. Blonde kid, fair skinned. It's an active investigation. And here...an eight-year-old Hispanic girl walks down the street to the corner store in suburban Phoenix, two days ago. Vanishes. And I'm just getting started on this. But I'm gonna need more details."

"Here, give me the one about the blonde girl. Who has it, Reno Central? The girl up on the mesa is somewhere around that age and she's blonde. And give me the name of that reporter in Tuba City. I'll try to get her off our backs for a bit."

Jimmy took the notes Lenana passed him and walked wearily to his desk. It wasn't long before that pristine surface was littered with files and papers and covered with sticky notes and coffee stains just like Lenana's desk.

THREE

Zack stared at the barefoot print in the sand, as clear and unmistakable, as it was unlikely.

"Could be a man in a bear suit...."

Eagle Feather shook his head, his grin tight and humorless. "You wish, white man. Look here. The print follows right in stride like the bear went from all fours up on his rear legs and then without missing a step turned into a man. Look how the impression of the human print is exactly the same depth; the weight's distributed exactly the same as the bear print. How does he manage that? No, no, it's a bear that became a man, or a man who had been a bear. You take your pick."

Zack could not accept this conclusion. "Okay, we know that's not possible, so we need to find a more reasonable explanation. Whatever he is, he's leaving sign that we can follow, so we will."

"Yeah," Eagle Feather said. His face showed no emotion. "He's leaving sign, maybe too much sign."

"As if he wanted us to see this...this transition, trying to spook us, maybe?"

"Spooks me," Eagle Feather said. "I don't know how he did it. He's either very, very good, or-"

"Whoa, we're not going there yet," Zack said. "Whatever you all may be thinking about witches or Skinwalkers or things that go bump in the night, I'm not buying. This is a man, not a ghost. He may be clever, but he's a man and a man will leave a trail and where there is a trail, we can track him."

"We can track him." Eagle Feather's reply was confident.

"Okay then." Zack went on, relieved. "This trail is gonna be long, hot, and hard. He's likely in a cave or holed up in an Anasazi ruin out there somewhere" -he waved toward the distant higher terrain- "or could be he had a vehicle waiting on a road beyond the mesa and could be anywhere by now. Whichever, I'm going back for my horse and rifle and then I'm going to attach myself to his trail like a flea to a dog and see what happens. You go back to your sheep shooters, shoot some sheep, earn your bucks and then come find me. I'll cut you a check for your help. Fair enough?"

"Fair enough."

The two friends turned and walked back along the prints together in silence, each engrossed in thought. When they arrived at the crime scene they found Eagle Feather's two clients obediently waiting in the shade of their bush, passing a water bottle back and forth, food wrappers ringed around them. More caution tape had been strung around the body and Lané Shorter stood near it, working his radio. He saw Zack approach and said a few last words and put it away. Then he took out a notepad and pawed through it.

"Messages for you, G-Man. Forensics is on their way." He ticked that note off with a stubbed pencil and went on to the next. "Ben wants you to call, said something about his boss being on him for information." Lané looked up from his notebook. "Chaparral's gone back to the station to tell Lenana what's happening. He's gonna try to keep a lid on this. He'll lead the forensic team here." He added, "I get to stay here."

"Thanks, Lané." Zack glanced at the policeman. "You okay with that? Somebody's got to guard the crime scene; it's important. I need you here to brief the forensics agents. I'm going back to follow the suspect's trail while it's still fresh. You know that lady, Libby Whitestone, with the tracker dogs? Ask her to bring Big Blue out here. We're gonna need him on this one."

Libby Whitestone worked a small ranch just outside of Tuba City. A widow with two grown boys, she bred horses for her living and trained bloodhounds to track missing persons and criminals as a hobby, a pastime that was very useful to local law enforcement. Big Blue was her best dog. Together, Libby and Big Blue had proved themselves locating people in the vast empty Navajo Reservation.

"Eagle Feather's taking his clients off to shoot sheep and he'll catch me up later," Zack told Lané, turning away.

"Call Ben," Shorter reminded him.

Zack turned back to him, speaking softly. "Do me a favor, Lané? Just pretend I haven't come back yet. I'll call him after I've got something to tell him."

Shorter stared for a moment and then nodded.

Zack walked over to his horse standing patiently behind dropped reigns. He dug a large water bladder out of the pack behind the saddle and poured some into his cupped hand, drank it up and poured another handful for Diablo. Then he returned the bladder to the pack, carefully tightened up all of the pack straps and gathering up the reins led his horse out on the stove-hot mesa, back along the trail of the enigmatic footprints.

When Zack had gone Eagle Feather went to collect his clients from under their bush. The sheep hunters peered miserably out from under its inadequate shade when Eagle Feather approached.

"You boys still up for the hunt?"

"Hell yes!" they blurted in unison.

"We won't find nothin' worth hunting up here anymore. Even if the killer didn't scare away everything on four legs, the rest of us trampling around here has."

"Killer?" One of the hunters caught him up. "I thought you said you found bear prints."

"Yeah, that's right. A killer bear is what I meant," Eagle Feather said. "We'll just scamper on down to the car and drive over to Ute

Butte. It's forty minutes down the road and I know just where to find some sheep up there. We'll load up some cold ones along the way. Gather up your trash first."

While the hunters collected their scattered wrappers Eagle Feather stood watching Zack and his horse disappear far out on the mesa. He grinned to himself, remembering Zack's reaction to the barefoot print. He knew most white people had trouble with the thought of spirits, let alone the idea that a man could learn to transform himself into an animal. White people depended entirely upon logic for their sense of security, he thought.

Eagle Feather had spent time working toward his Masters in Anthropology at Arizona State on a Reservation Grant program. There he'd been exposed to leading edge neuroscience and had listened with interest to his professors talk about the right hemisphere of the brain, which they presented as coding the 'big picture' -- imaging, creativity, spirituality -- and the left brain which supplied detail - the 'trees' of language and analytical processing. He figured this was something his ancestors knew all along. There are two worlds, they believed, this world and the spirit world. No Diné - the Navajo name for themselves meaning 'the people' - would be surprised to know that a man has two brains. How else could you live in this world and the spirit world at the same time? Not even his college professors could fully grasp that idea. Eagle Feather saw that his clients were ready to go and turned to lead them back down the mesa path.

On the shade-less barren plateau the mid-afternoon sun baked down on Zack's shoulders and his soaked shirt clung to his back like a hot compress when he bent over. He crouched and stood repeatedly, working his way slowly and patiently along the line of human footprints leading straight as an arrow through the creosote bushes and Bear Grass toward the far off swell of hills, purple and shadowy in the distance. He kept Diablo short-reined up close with his left hand; the leather and horsehair smell of the animal was a comfort to him. Whenever Zack felt anxious he liked to talk to Diablo, explaining things to him. He did that now.

"He's walking easy here, a nice biped stride now that he doesn't have to pretend he's a bear. See the forefoot push-off and the deeper imprint of the toes? The minimal heel depth? This man is used to walking long distances, probably runs, too, and he's used to going barefoot. See the spread of the toes, how they splay and dig in individually? He's a natural walker, using every part of the foot, not bunching everything up like if it was used to being stuffed in a boot."

Zack knelt and examined a dried blood pool. "Here's more blood," he informed Diablo. He came out of his crouch and the meager bit of shade that the horse provided. He worked the water bladder out of the depth of the pack where it would stay a bit cooler and leaned against Diablo to think.

"Let's go over this thing again. Here is what we've got: we've got no tracks or sign within a hundred feet of the girl's body. Then we've got these carefully arranged bear tracks for the next half-mile leading away from the scene. Then he gives that up and goes barefoot, his natural way, still moving straight off. We find the first blood three hundred yards away from the body in tracks going away from the scene and the blood amounts actually begin to increase the further away he goes. Which makes no sense. Why does the blood quantity increase when he's leaving the murder scene? His own blood, maybe? Bleeding from his nose from excitement, maybe? No, there's too much of it, and he's walking strongly. Well, I guess we'll have to wait to see whose blood it is, after the lab tests it."

Zack sighed and went on with his thoughts. "So, let's go with what we know, which is that our only suspect is walking away making these tracks. If we want answers to our questions, we'll just have to keep after him."

Zack tucked the water bottle back into the pack, re-cinched the straps and took the reins up again. He was hot and tired. He looked out over the terrain ahead. The flatness of the land and the lack of any growth taller than a creosote bush offered him good visibility. Farther out he could make out a copse of trees growing where the ground swelling up gained enough altitude to cool the air. His quarry could be out there, waiting and watching. He looked back where he'd come, feeling a little unsettled. He was a good five miles from the crime scene and his colleagues. It had taken more than two hours to get here. He'd have to decide soon whether to camp out or to turn back. Once it got dark, he couldn't track anymore. He was out of radio range now, his cell phone was useless, and there was no way to check in with the office. That SAT phone that Ben Brewster kept promising him still hadn't come. He sure could of used it now.

"Ben's going to get some serious pressure coming down on him if I don't report in for another ten or twelve hours," he said to Diablo. "But if I leave now, whoever we're tracking could sneak back out here and clean up his back trail tomorrow; if he's still around, that is. He can't do much about it in the dark, though, so maybe if I stay on his trail he won't chance it tomorrow."

Zack moved ahead, his mind made up. "If I'm him, I'd get out of here tonight seeing that this stubborn FBI agent is sticking to me like burrs on a shaggy dog."

All of Zack's muscles ached from constantly bending and crouching, and he was hungry. He told himself as soon as he reached that first stand of trees he'd look around for a likely camping spot and then he'd heat up a nice big packet of noodles.

FOUR

Linda Whittaker, FBI Forensics Specialist, M.S. Biology, Ph.D. Pathology stopped to catch her breath on the steep mesa trail for the fiftieth time, or so it seemed to Jimmy Chaparral. She turned and looked back at him, her brow creased with annoyance and her nose wrinkled up like something smelled bad.

If she complains again I'm going to leave her here, Jimmy thought.

"I just don't get why...the agency wastes...time and federal money... and resources for me to have to come out here...to do your job for you people," she complained, working hard to catch her breath. "You're a sovereign nation...you have your own police force...you have your own facilities...so do your own investigating."

Agent Whittaker was a no longer young woman who was very much out of her element. She went on. "Your people are always carving each other up. You know that as well as I do."

Okay, that's it.

Jimmy spoke calmly. "Mostly only middle-aged white women," he said, "when we can get them off by themselves." He spoke the words straight-faced but he instantly regretted it when he saw alarm rise in her eyes.

Jesus! She really believes it. Jimmy spoke quickly in a more conciliatory tone. "As sovereign nations go, we're below third world. If it weren't for the casinos, your taxes would be paying for our food and clothing and all our other needs. We just don't have the resources you seem to think we have."

Linda resumed her slow climb without further comment, switching her tool case to the other hand. She wore a wide brimmed hat that Lenana had found for her but it left a lot of unprotected white skin exposed to the sun. Linda was very unhappy. She hadn't asked to be assigned to the remote, god-forsaken FBI office at Tuba City but they needed a good lab technician and she was the best available, or so they told her. It seemed a wise career choice at the time - be helpful, be a team player, and wasn't it supposed to be just a temporary assignment? But enough was enough. Right now, she couldn't wait to get back to LA.

Jimmy moved slowly up the dusty trail behind her trying to ignore the pendulum-like swing of her wide bottom at eye level. He had been surprised back at the Police Station when insistent taps sounded on the front door where no one ever knocked and he was even more surprised to see a solitary female standing there who claimed to be a forensics agent, the sum total of the response to Zack's request for FBI support. She was a very unhappy agent at that, and started in right away complaining about potholes in the road and how difficult it was to find the tiny office. "Why don't you have a bigger sign?" she'd griped and when Lenana wanted to know when the other agents would be arriving Linda had disclosed that she was it, the only agent that would be coming, a thought that set her off again, saying "What did you expect all the way out here in the middle of nowhere?"

Well, Jimmy thought, Zack wanted to keep the lid on this case. Now it seemed the only people not interested in it was the FBI. The woman had identified herself as Agent Linda Whittaker and she stood awkwardly looking around the office as if she expected to find the body right there on the floor. She had reached a whole new level of unhappiness when she learned that she would have to make another lengthy drive followed by a strenuous climb up a mesa to get to the crime scene.

After the long siege of complaints from the unhappy woman, Jimmy's customary patience and good humor were exhausted. He couldn't wait to drop her off at the crime scene. Lané will be perfect company for her, he thought. Complaining to him would be like bitching at a post.

The remainder of the steep trail up the mesa was every bit as unpleasant, the final ignominy a necessary assist with the palm of his hand placed on Linda's ample bottom to propel her up and over the last steep section.

But they arrived at the crime scene at last and Linda caught her breath and at once transformed into an entirely different person. Jimmy understood for the first time why she was valued by the agency. She immediately barked a series of orders, organized a perimeter check, did a blood trace and then directed the careful removal of the plastic that covered the small body. Lané Shorter had to dig for his notebook just to keep track of the rapidly dictated flow of detailed observations. A constant assembly line of sample bags were filled with minute dirt particles from little shoes and with fibers from the socks and the frock, with hair and fiber from the panties, and with samples of skin residue and other substances from around the wounds, from the rest of the body, and from the ground under and around it.

"One large deliberately perpetrated wound, probably fatal, on the upper abdomen just below the rib cage, one powerful slashing thrust with four or five sharply articulated instruments, an animal claw or a gardening tool. Other superficial wounds perpetrated post-mortem, likely by scavengers. Death occurred elsewhere, the body was transported to the scene and abandoned, already bled out. No surface signs of molestation, panties intact, seem to be undisturbed," she intoned into her recorder as she worked.

"Here, you, the big fellow," she said, indicating Shorter. "Help me turn the body over." Lané and Linda gently rolled the girl's body onto its side revealing the desert dust compressed beneath. Something glinted in the compacted dirt. Linda scooped it up. It was a locket of some kind with a gold case and chain.

" Must have been torn off the girl's neck or else dropped or placed here," Linda commented. The locket went unopened into a plastic bag and joined the samples already in Linda's case. "That might help us identify the victim," she observed to no one in particular. She straightened up, stretching her back and looked directly at the two policemen for the first time. "I'll need to take these samples back to my lab. There's nothing else to be learned here. Did Agent Tolliver finish his observations? Did you got photos?"

To their nods she replied, "Okay, you can remove the body and transport it back to my lab now." She took a large black plastic bag from her kit, unfolded it and passed it to Lané Shorter. Then she looked around the barren mesa top where Desert Spoon cacti had begun to cast their long shadows like oversized cartoon clones of themselves across the sand and shuddered.

"Where is Agent Tolliver, anyway?" she asked?

At that moment Zack was entering the first stand of juniper trees that marked a higher elevation. It was the acrid but refreshing scent of pine that broke his concentration and alerted him that his surroundings had changed. He rose slowly and painfully from his crouch, stretched, and looked around. Ahead, a mat of dried juniper needles littered the sandy soil; it would make tracking a little more difficult, he thought. Worse, shadows were beginning to deepen with the rapid sinking of the sun. It was time to quit for the day or risk losing the trail altogether. Zack dropped Diablo's reigns at the first level spot he could find within the thin grove of trees. He found the water bladder and shared it with his horse.

"I hate sleeping on the ground," he complained to Diablo. "It's never quite level enough to get a decent night's sleep." Diablo nodded. Zack looked around, then sighed and set about setting up camp. First, he removed a short vaquero-style horsehair rope from his saddle and circled it around his sleeping area. He knew it was probably just a myth, the belief that a horsehair rope would prevent snakes - or was it scorpions? - from crossing into his sleeping area but he always did it anyway because it comforted him. Then he removed the large pack from the back of a grateful Diablo and leaned it against the base of a nearby tree within handy reach of his roped sleep area. The rifle in its scabbard went inside the rope along with the blanket and saddle that would become Zack's bed and pillow for the night. He set up a makeshift hobble for his horse just at the edge of the clearing with enough length for Diablo to move about to graze but not to run. Not that he was likely to run away, but a bear or a mountain cat could spook him.

"We're camping dry tonight," he explained to Diablo, keeping him informed. "There might be water somewhere around here but we've got plenty and we don't want to risk destroying any sign by stumbling around in the dark."

Diablo whinnied his understanding and Zack went off to gather up dry grasses for his mattress and pine needles to kindle his fire. He got the fire started using his lighter and shaped a small pyramid of short dry pieces of juniper branch over it. The fire flared up right away and settled into crackling and snapping. Zack found his package of noodles and heated them with water in his tin cup. He lay back on his saddle to enjoy the moment. By this time the sun was down to just a shiny sliver along the rim of the hills and in the encroaching darkness the flame created shadows that grew into phantasms leaping and playing on the nearby trees.

It was cool enough to enjoy being close to the fire. Zack settled in nearer the flames' warmth and pulled the saddle blanket over him. He tried not to think too much about who or what could be somewhere out there in the shadows that grew dark and mysterious around him.

Nightfall was also enveloping the little town of Elk Wells but no one in the Navajo Nation Police station had noticed it. The building was an island of light along the deserted street, a ship alone on a dark sea. The local police contingent of two had grown exponentially, swelled by reinforcements from nearby districts until there was literally insufficient room to contain all the people and the excitement and energy that threatened to burst apart the tiny office. After a coffee cup had spilled on Jimmy's desk and someone had jostled Lenana's writing arm for the ump-tee-ump time, Lenana finally laid down the law and sent everyone without a specific job outside to wait on the sidewalk until all decisions were made and actions decided. The little girl's body lay on a cot in the single jail cell, the only space available, wrapped in the black body bag and waiting for its final destination to be determined. Linda stood nearby, trying to be heard on her cell phone. Jimmy Chaparral and Lané Shorter were at their desks, each on a telephone, talking and scribbling notes while they peered at their laptops. Lenana kept trying to hang up her desk phone but it rang the moment it touched the cradle. She picked it again and started to speak then stopped and listened and then without replying she clamped her palm over the phone and called to Jimmy in a loud stage whisper.

"It's the press. They got the word somehow that the victim is a little white girl."

The room grew quiet. No one needed to be told what this news meant. The press would soon be swarming over Elk Wells like the Sioux over Custer at Little Bighorn. And when the press arrived, the investigation would be slowed to a crawl.

"How can they know already?" Jimmy griped. "The only people who know are those of us who were up on the Mesa and saw her. And Eagle Feather said he'd keep his clients quiet."

"If Eagle Feather said he'd hush the hunters, they didn't talk," one officer remarked.

"So that leaves you, Lané, and you, Lenana, and Zack, who can't tell anybody anything yet, and me and…" His eyes swung to Linda Whittaker where she stood near the jail cell still speaking into her cell phone. She suddenly became aware of the silence and abruptly halted her conversation and looked up. Everyone was staring at her.

"What…?"

"The press seems to have the information that the victim is a white girl," Jimmy said. The growing redness of her face told all. "I guess I must have mentioned it to my roommate. I had to tell her I'd be home late tonight…" She stood there looking miserable.

After a poignant moment, Jimmy spoke decisively. "Its water over the bridge now," he said. "We've got to work quickly. Linda, you'll have to make arrangements for the body right now. You two"--he waved at two men near the door--"put the body in the back of my pickup and pull the tarpaulin over the top. Take Linda wherever she wants to go. Linda, the Tuba City lab is out of the question, the press will be waiting there for you. Find another place. You can do it as you drive along. Call Ben Brewster, he'll have some ideas." He turned to the others. "All of you listen, please. From now on, I'll need to be the only spokesperson for this office. Ben Brewster will be the one who speaks for the FBI, at least until Zack comes down from the mesa. Direct all questions to me or to Ben. Tell the press nothing."

During the ensuing activity he spoke quietly to Lenana. "We'll need a ruse to decoy the press. Let's try this: write "little girl" and "Antelope Mesa" on your note pad. Leave the pad visible on your desk as if they are notes you just jotted down from a radio call. With a little luck, the reporters will jump to conclusions and scurry off to the wrong mesa on a thirty-mile wild goose chase. That will buy us some time."

Jimmy turned to his subordinate. "Lané, set up a continuous guard over the trail up Monument Mesa. No one goes up that trail. Keep it low profile, though. There's likely to be news helicopters buzzing around looking for any unusual activity. The last thing we need is the press to find the crime scene and especially those bear tracks."

FIVE

Zack awoke abruptly, his eyes open wide. The blackness around him was complete, thickened by the deeper dark of trees that he sensed rather than saw. The fire beyond his feet was a tiny glow smothered by the night's mantle, illuminating only itself. Zack raised himself up on an elbow and strained to see, trying to recollect what awakened him. A sound still echoed in his head, the sound that had jerked him from sleep not by its loudness but by its nature, a sound that didn't belong, a snake-like hissing sound like gas escaping a shaken soda bottle. He could hear it yet, indistinct, out of place, wrong. The night was still...too still. There were none of the usual night noises, no insect whirring, no rustlings. Above him through a frame of twisted dark limbs he saw scattered stars in a lighter sky. But a silent impenetrable blanket of darkness hung all around him. Where was Diablo? Zack stared hard in the direction of his hobbled horse, looking for the comforting shape of the animal against the darkness. His straining eyes saw only more layers of blackness. There was no sound of shifting hooves, no snuffling, no breathing. Was Diablo asleep? Or...?

Now you're being silly, Zack thought to himself. You've let this idea of Skinwalkers get to you.

He rose up to a sitting position, but he couldn't bring himself to call out to Diablo, to shatter the delicate stillness. He strained his eyes and his ears. To his nose came the sweet scent of pine and the smoke smell of the smoldering fire and, yes, there was a faint but reassuring scent of hair and sweat, the smell of Diablo, but...there was something else...something that didn't belong, something musky, over-sweet smelling, like rotting fruit. Zack's heart beat faster. An imbedded instinct hijacked his brain and sent his hand groping for his rifle and he lifted it slowly to cradle on his arm, the safety clicked off, ready. His eyes searched, his nose worked to pinpoint the fetid odor, faint but permeating. It was all around him now in the darkness, growing stronger. His pulse raced wildly, the hair all over his body prickled.

Why doesn't Diablo move? He waited; the surrounding darkness seemed to hold its breath, to wait with him. Then he saw them, had they been there all along? Were they just in his mind or before his eyes, that pair of glowing red points in the blackest black of the trees, those cruel red eyes looking into him and through him, intent, predatory eyes. He looked at them, tried to focus on them, tried to see a shape around them but the more he stared the less he saw and only by looking away could he then see the eyes, see them sufficiently to aim his rifle at them but there was no outline, no darker layer of dark around them to give him a sense of what manner of creature owned these eyes that bore into him, held him, terrified him, and did not move.

Whatever it is, it must be tall, he thought, for the eyes were high above the ground, maybe six or seven feet but it was hard to figure, hard to guess against the height of trees and bushes blended together by blackness. Zack fought his fear, fought against the acute sense of helplessness that threatened to overwhelm him and raised his rifle slowly. It doesn't matter what it is, he told himself, it doesn't belong here. He leveled the rifle, tried to ease the pounding of his heart, he held his breath and then released it and squeezed his finger on the trigger, slowly, incrementally, tried to keep his aim right between those two red eyes.

Then they were gone. Startled, Zack released his finger just before firing, the rifle still aimed at the now empty shadows. The night hung heavy, dank, soundless. An unusual smell remained. Zack sensed a presence yet. Rising to his knees, his eyes intent on the concealing darkness where the eyes had been, he shifted the rifle into his right hand gripped like a pistol and leaned forward to grope with his left hand along the ground toward the fire. He felt the firm roundness of a protruding branch and pulled it from the glowing embers and in one quick motion stirred the fire into sparking life and raised the smoldering branch above his head, whipping it about until the sleeping embers stirred into flame. He swiveled his head around, searching the suddenly illuminated glade. The nearest trees reflected back the light and chased the grotesque shadows away, revealing their secrets.

Where those eyes had been, there was nothing. There was no sound other than the loud crackle of the newly stirred fire and the pounding of his heart. Zack fed the fire all the fuel that remained and it settled into a bright and steady burn and brought the comfort of light dancing reassuringly on the surrounding trees. Zack settled back into a crouch and rested his rifle on his knees and waited. He desperately wanted to go find Diablo, to assure himself that his horse was there, that all was as it had been. He wanted to convince himself that those eyes had been his imagination run wild and not some threatening creature thing beyond the firelight. But if he left his position near the fire he must become vulnerable to whoever or whatever might be out there. He knew his only course was to wait, to keep the fire bright, to stay alert and ready to shoot.

Zack had passing thoughts about the irony of crouching here in a Mexican standoff with his own imagination. Yet deep inside him an intuitive warning bell still sounded and his entire being resonated with it. This is real, it told him. Don't let up. The soundless darkness wore on. Zack grew cramped in his squatting position but couldn't give in to the discomfort. He must remain in this position so that he could spin quickly in any direction. But his legs and knees began to ache and his feet became numb. He tried to keep the blood flowing by bobbing up and down and stretching in his crouch.

Time passed. How long? An hour? Two hours? He didn't know when it was he smelled the juniper and the sweet pine and the musky dry grasses once more. Or when he began to hear the insect sounds again. Or when the permeating fetid odor had begun to dissipate. But still he dared not close his eyes. He fought sleep, drifted in and out, his lids drooped, snapped open, floated down once more.

Suddenly, a presence behind him. He tried to turn, to face it...his legs wouldn't move, his limbs wouldn't function. The rifle in his hand was lead, he couldn't lift it. In desperation he fought to raise it, to shoot...

"Whoa, careful there, white man!" A familiar voice. "Are you trying to shoot your toe off?"

Zack's eyes jerked open. The filtered rays of dawn gave a glow to his surroundings. "Eagle Feather?"

"I'm not going to let go of this rifle until I know you're awake."

"What the hell..." muttered Zack. Looking up, he saw Eagle Feather grinning down at him where he sat still trying to pull the rifle out of Eagle Feather's restraining grasp. Zack released his grip.

"I guess I dozed off."

"I guess you did."

"How did you find me?"

"When a white man decides to fill the entire sky with smoke, he isn't too hard to find. Eagle Feather looked over at the large fire, just beginning to die down. "Get cold last night?"

Zack looked around, trying to put the night into perspective in the new light of day. "Let me get a pot of coffee going and I'll tell you about it." He cocked an eyebrow at Eagle Feather. "You must have gotten an early start. How'd you track me in the dark?"

"I didn't! Big Blue did." Eagle Feather waved his arm back in the direction they had come. "After we gave the boys a chance to shoot a sheep yesterday and got them home with it, the day was mostly gone. I got a couple of hours sleep and headed back up here. Libby Whitestone and Big Blue were at the trailhead setting up camp, thinking to get an early start in the morning. Since I was going on she decided to join forces and we came up the trail together. It was dark when we started out, but I could get us to where I had left off and then Blue did the rest."

"Why not wait until morning?"

"Thought maybe you could use some help sooner." Eagle Feather studied Zack's face. "Seems I was right."

"Where are Libby and Blue now?" Zack asked, looking around.

"They're out there. Before we came on this grove of trees, Blue's scent trail split and it had him running up this way and then back to where he'd started, then off yet another way. Whatever we're tracking meandered around a lot. I saw enough smoke coming out of these trees to pollute Phoenix so I sent Libby and Blue following one scent trail and I came on and found you squatting there dead to the world, gripping your rifle like a drowning man clutching onto driftwood!"

Zack winced at the image. He had the fire stirred fully to life. He scooped coffee into a filter bag and poured water through it into his dented and blackened coffeepot, then put it into the fire. The cobwebs of the night slowly cleared from his brain. He saw those red eyes very clearly in his mind.

"You don't think it's risky for Libby to be out there by herself?" he asked and almost as soon as he spoke, another thought came him. He leapt up abruptly.

"Diablo!" he exclaimed. "I forgot all about Diablo!" He looked across the glade where he had left his horse hobbled. The early morning sun angled its bright yellow rays across the trees into the meadow where Diablo had stood when darkness fell the night before. No horse stood there now. Zack reached the place in long strides, then suddenly stopped, his shoulders slumped.

"Oh, no," he murmured. "Oh, no, no, no."

From behind him Eagle Feather saw the reason. Diablo lay on his side, his long face toward them on the soft sand, his eyes open but still. A fly buzzed near his nostrils.

Zack sank down where he was and put his head in his hands.

Eagle Feather stared down at the horse. "Okay, Zack!" he demanded finally. "What went on here last night?"

There was no response from Zack. He remained silent, his face hidden in his crossed arms. At that moment there came a loud rustling sound in the mesquite, moving rapidly toward them. A large animal emerged and hurtled itself at Eagle Feather. The huge bloodhound planted two great forepaws on his shoulders and sloshed his face with a large wet tongue. Eagle Feather tried to hold him off.

"Hey, Blue," he said. "Take it easy." The sounds of more movement came from up the slope. A woman come into view and moved toward them, pushing her way easily through the deer grass and skirting the creosote bushes. Her hands were protected by fingerless leather riding gloves. She wore a battered straw hat, wide brimmed against the sun, and a sleeveless T-shirt under Farmer John coveralls. Her face was brown and weathered from an active outdoor life, etched in equal measure by humor and a distant sadness. She took in the scene as she approached and exchanged a glance with Eagle Feather, and then looked down at Zack who barely acknowledged her presence.

"I should have kept him next to me," he whispered hoarsely.

Libby studied the prostrate animal. Then she said, "This horse is alive. Aren't you going to do anything to help it?"

SIX

Linda wiped away a tear with the back of a rubber-gloved hand. Not normally overly sentimental, she was unsure whether her sudden rise of emotion was due to sadness for the abuse so obviously suffered by the little girl on the table or if it was simply her own lack of sleep. She turned her face back to the digital recorder.

"Multiple abrasions and significant trauma to genital area. Specifically, abraded labia minora, torn hymen, and abraded and swollen labia majora suggesting frequent and repeated forced coitus..."

Linda's voice broke slightly here and she stopped abruptly. Yesterday had been a very long day followed by a short night. The decision to move the girl's body to the Prescott facility wasn't made until close to midnight. Although the regional FBI office at Flagstaff was closer and held jurisdiction, it was thought the press would know that as well and turn up in force. Once the decision was made she had driven to Tuba City to grab some personal things before setting off on the longer drive south to Prescott. Once there she caught a few hours sleep on an associate's couch but rose again before daylight, grabbed some murky coffee from the machine dispenser and began her examination, buoyed by a promise from the night clerk going off duty to send along Danish and a fresh coffee. She'd been at it now for two hours or more. The promised Danish and coffee had come and gone long since but the exterior exam was finally complete. She had just shifted position from the foot to the middle of the dolly and had her tools positioned for the first chest incision when the double doors to the sealed room whooshed open.

Linda glanced up to see Ben Brewster, her senior FBI agent from Tuba City. She reached up to turn off the voice recorder.

"Thought I would check in on you. You must be pretty tired."

"Thanks, Ben. I'm not my most perky right now, but I'm good enough," replied Linda, suspecting the real reason for his visit. There must be a lot of pressure coming down on Ben for quick results.

Ben looked down at the body. "Jesus! She was so young!"

"That's been everybody's reaction, but we get past it," Linda remarked, hoping the tear in the corner of her eye didn't show.

"Learn anything new?"

"Well, yes and no," Linda replied. "It was obvious at the scene that her neck was broken and equally obvious that she had suffered a massive wound to her torso from some claw-like instrument, strongly suggestive of a large animal such as a bear. The remaining scavenger wounds are quite clear. Other hemorrhaging and markings on her body are older, such as the bruises on her thighs and pelvis, which likely came from repeated sexual aggression."

"Oh, Christ!" muttered Ben.

"Yes, molested by the bear, no doubt," quipped Linda dryly. "But the bigger news appears to be the cause of death. We had assumed initially that the torso wound came first followed by the broken neck, maybe from falling or from the weight of her assailant landing on her, but what I'm seeing here from blood flow evidence suggests the reverse, that her neck was broken first...in fact, long before the torso wound had occurred, maybe by as much as twenty four hours or more."

"So that means..."

"Yes, that the torso wound was done post mortem to create the illusion of an animal attack." Linda pointed with new eagerness to the little girl's neck. "Do you see those faint impressions, those bruises? Thumb and fingers, in just the right place, front and back. The bastard just snapped her neck like a twig. That's her cause of death, right there, but that's not official until I do the internal to eliminate the possibility of drugs or poisons."

"OK, so let's see..." Ben ticked off the sequence of events. "The girl's neck is broken by someone, she is transported to the scene over a period of twenty four hours or so, then somewhere along the way she is clawed with an instrument to suggest a bear, then she is dumped in an area that is remote yet right next to one of the more commonly used trails in the area and tracks are left to try to further promote the bear idea. Is that about it?"

"That's the way I see it," responded Linda. "And don't forget that she had been repeatedly assaulted over a longer period of time prior to that..."

But Ben was already walking toward the door with his cell phone to his ear. He turned back to Linda as the doors whooshed open for him.

"Great work, Linda! We're very lucky to have you! Call me as soon as you learn anything else!" And he was gone.

Despite her anguish Linda felt a sudden warm feeling, a feeling almost forgotten in recent years, and she turned back to her work.

Two floors above Linda's basement laboratory Ben put his feet up on a cluttered desktop and listened to the voice in his cell phone that had been glued to his ear ever since he left the Lab. He was in the temporary FBI office in Prescott, maintained for the benefit of agents who found themselves in need of office space and modern facilities when operating in the area. Approached from the street, the building appeared to be offices, many for rent, but extremely high utility fees and expensive monthly rents discouraged would-be renters. The FBI administrative office with responsibility for this part of Arizona was actually located in Phoenix and that was where Ben's superior, currently speaking authoritatively into his ear, was located.

Ben listened patiently, took a deep breath, and replied. "OK, here are my two top concerns. First, as you say, the old barely hidden prejudices of both the Navajo and non- Navajo are going to surface once it's learned that the victim is a little blonde white girl. Things could get real nasty, especially in the hands of the press. Second, the reaction of the Navajo to a murderer who according to the tracks our boys found appears to shift form from man to animal might be just as concerning. Once the people on the Reservation start to believe that there is a Skinwalker around any information flow we hope to receive will dry up like old corn. The ancient beliefs run deep out there and none of the Navajo are going to line themselves up to be targets of evil spirits. The problem is, I don't know who knows what. By now the word could be out on both counts, for all I know!"

Ben listened again, then sighed and explained. "Yes, sir, it is the actual creature from mythology. The belief is widespread. Similar creatures can be found in many cultures around the world. Anthropologists call them shape shifters but to the Navajo they are Skinwalkers because they literally inhabit the skin of their animal familiar and possess its powers by their magic."

Another pause. "Yes, sir, the Navajo indeed think of them as witches and this could become a witch hunt...Yes, sir, I will do all I can to prevent that. Special Agent Tolliver is still up on the mesa and there's no cell signal up there. We've been out of contact almost twenty-four hours now. Best-case scenario...by the time I hear from him he's got it all wrapped up with the culprit in tow ...Yes, sir, I know. Don't worry, you'll know as soon as I know."

Ben pulled his phone away from his ear, checked for messages and put it in his pocket. He sighed deeply before he reached across the desk to the landline phone and pulled it toward him.

SEVEN

"Alive?" Zack stared up at Libby with awakening hope. "Alive?" he repeated, blankly. Her words slowly penetrated his dulled brain. Then he moved next to Diablo and supporting his head held a palm up near his nostrils. Yes, it was true; he could just feel the warmth of Diablo's breath.

Libby came and knelt next to Zack and felt along Diablo's lower jaw behind the cheek to find the external maxillary artery. "I feel a slight pulse," she said. Pushing Zack's hand aside, she pulled back the horse's lips. "Blue gums; we need to increase his circulation. EF, I need blankets, ponchos, anything you can find to warm this horse. Zack, bring as much water as you can. We need to hydrate this horse at once. Quick now!"

The men hurried off to their tasks. Libby moved her hands expertly over Diablo, examining every inch of him, whispering to him in quiet tones, calming him. The animal responded magically to her voice and touch; there was a slight tremor and eye movement.

Eagle Feather was back with Zack's trail coat, a poncho, and the saddle blanket. At Libby's direction he spread them over the stallion. Zack came rushing back with the water bladder. He knelt and poured a generous amount into his hat. Then they raised the horse's head just enough for his tongue to reach the water, Zack cupping the liquid in his hands to help him

Libby had completed her examination of Diablo from nose to tail on his upper side and began to feel under his raised neck. Suddenly she exclaimed and when she brought her hand out something was pinched between her fingers. She carefully dropped it into her other hand. They all leaned in to look. In her gloved palm lay a cactus spine, its tip red.

"This was deeply imbedded in Diablo's neck," Libby said. "Now how do you suppose that got there?"

The men studied the thorn closely where it lay long and straight on her palm. Eagle Feather grunted his surprise. "That's a spine from the Pigmy Barrel Cactus," he said. "Most cacti spines curve, at least a little bit. The Pigmy's spines are among the few that don't. They were prized by my ancestors for use as needles. But the Pigmy Barrel Cactus isn't common." He glanced around. "I don't remember seeing any around this camp."

Libby studied the spine closely. "I think it's coated with something," she said. "Look there, part way down the shaft. Do you see that slight change in color and sheen?" She had a sudden thought. "You know, this horse might have been drugged."

Zack looked at Diablo, who seemed to be responding to his treatment and had even taken some water. "I've got sample bags in my kit," he said. "I'll get that spine analyzed as soon as we can get out of here."

Zack was all business now, appearing to recover as quickly as his horse. "There's coffee boiling in the pot that's just going to waste." He gave them all a weak smile. "Let's grab a cup and then see where we stand."

The trio moved over to the fire, leaving Diablo to recover undisturbed. They all found cups, filled them from the steaming pot and made themselves comfortable.

It was Libby who raised the question this time. "You had a visitor last night."

"Sure did," Zack agreed. Libby and Eagle Feather looked at him curiously, waiting. "I'll tell you all about it," he said. "But first, tell me what you've learned this morning."

Libby looked at Eagle Feather. He was staring into the fire so she began. "First, you should know that when Blue came to the place where the bear paw prints changed to human foot prints he gave no sign, meaning that as far as he was concerned it was all the same scent. Second, we are tracking a human, and I say that because Blue tracks him the way he tracks humans, slower, more careful-like. Then when we got near here" -Libby gestured back the way they had come- "Blue found where he had come back to cut your back trail, maybe while you were setting up your camp. He must have been waiting near these trees to see if anyone was following him and when he saw you comin' along he doubled back to try to learn something about you. I'll tell you this; he knows his stuff."

Zack felt uneasy, realizing how careless he had been.

"His next move," Libby said, "was to go up that slope east of this grove. He settled in up there, looks like. I found a round depression and the grass knocked flat like a deer bed. He must have rested there a few hours. His next trail came down here the way Blue and I just came down."

She pointed back up the slope and looked at Zack.

"He came right down to your horse, Zack. Didn't you hear anything, any noise from Diablo?"

Zack shook his head slowly. "No. Something woke me, but it wasn't Diablo. I have a vague notion of some sort of swooshing sound as I woke up, like air from a punctured tire or something but I never heard a thing from Diablo."

Eagle Feather looked up quickly. "A blowing sort of sound? A short burst?"

"Short and fast. Like this..." Zack pursed his lips and puffed quickly through them.

"Now, that might explain it." Eagle Feather looked at each of them. "Diablo didn't have time to nicker. He was shot with that drug tipped cactus spine; darted before he could make a sound. That's got to be strong stuff on the tip of that spine. Be careful how you handle it."

"How do you know all this?" Libby demanded.

"I should have figured it out sooner." Eagle Feather frowned, upset with himself. "That's another reason the Ancient Ones valued the Pigmy Barrel Cactus spine; because it is straight they could shoot from blowpipes. They used to make them from hollow reeds, to kill small animals," he explained. "The weapon wasn't common, it was used mostly by shamans who knew how to make the poisons that they smeared on the spine tips." Eagle Feather looked at each of them in turn and spoke quietly. "We could be dealing with one who follows the Witchery Way. This could be a powerful Navajo witch."

"So why didn't this powerful witch drug me too instead of running off when I started waving my rifle around?"

But even as he asked the question, Zack knew the answer. If this man or witch or whatever had wanted him dead, he would be dead right now. That must not have been his intent.

Zack turned to Libby. "Where did he go after he drugged Diablo?"

"Big Blue can tell us that after breakfast."

Just then they saw Diablo struggle to his feet, shedding the coats and blankets. Zack went to him.

"Seems like he's better," observed Eagle Feather, watching. By the time the coffee pot had been emptied and rinsed and Zack's camp packed up, Diablo did indeed appear to be his old self. Zack watched warily for any sign of distress when he cinched the big pack on the horse but Diablo's recovery appeared complete and he moved his head up and down, anxious to get started. Zack thought about this drug, the temporary nature it, and then he thought about the little girl and wondered if the drug might have played a part in her demise.

Libby put Big Blue on the long leash and the dog was pulled her back up the hill they had come down earlier. Standing next to Diablo, Zack found himself watching Libby climb the steep slope, her movements effortless, her still girlish form lithe and strong. Zack admired Libby. He always made sure to hire Blue when he needed a dog because he was the best and, well... he had to admit he enjoyed Libby's company. She seemed to sense his gaze and looked back at him suddenly and smiled. Zack felt a sudden blush. Feeling foolish, he abruptly leaned down and scooped up Diablo's reins to follow them.

When he arrived at the top of the ridge above his old camp Zack found Eagle Feather still hunting for sign. Waiting there, he paused to look back the way they had come. He could see far across this tumbled land to the distant buttes and mesas that framed it, standing out in bold relief against the brightening sky. It was still early morning but the emerging sun created a world of glowing yellows and golds that warmed the cold corners of Zack's mind, left over from his night fears, and he could feel new confidence rise in him. He looked down on the tree grove that had sheltered him during the night. Yes, this ridge must have provided an ideal observation point for the bear-man to watch Zack and his camp. And the deep sand underfoot would assure little noise when the killer had approached Zack's camp in the darkness. Zack shook his head again his carelessness.

Eagle Feather was pointing to a partial print with toes etched in the sand. "He's still barefoot," he said. "Look closely there at the toe prints. See how each toe digs in independently working like your fingers would if you were crawling along on all fours? This man is more at home without shoes than with 'em."

Eagle Feather went on. "After drugging Diablo and scaring Zack" - he paused to grin at Zack's obvious discomfort- "after that, our man came right back up the slope and just sat here. See how Blue just kind of circled around this one spot? Our man must have been real confident that Zack wouldn't follow him here in the dark and he just waited. He probably didn't move from here until he heard us coming along."

Then as an afterthought, "And he didn't rush off then, either; see how his prints are even with a slight forefoot indent? He simply walked away, very calm."

"Alright, alright," exclaimed Zack, feeling a touch of annoyance at the admiration Eagle Feather seemed to feel for the killer. "So Superman walked away, he didn't fly away. That means we can follow him."

Eagle Feather looked up at Zack, his face blank. "That's a fact," he said. Then turning to Libby, he said, "Let's turn Blue loose for a bit."

Libby leaned down to Big Blue and whispered into his long floppy ear. "Go, find!" She removed his leash.

Immediately Blue put his nose to the ground and trotted along the ridge to the north. Eagle Feather followed, his nose almost as close to the ground as Blue's. Then came Libby and finally Zack, leading Diablo. All of them were seasoned trackers and observed the courtesy of walking to the side of the trail to allow those behind to make their own interpretations, except for Blue, of course, whose large pug marks went right down the middle. The progress of the humans was slow and before long Blue had moved on ahead and out of sight. Eagle Feather set the pace for the rest of them, slowing frequently to study a print more closely or to scout around for some other sign. When Blue had been out of sight over five minutes Libby pulled a silent whistle from the center pocket of her Farmer Johns and blew it.

"Now he'll wait for us," she said.

"Ask him to bay so we can establish a direction," Zack suggested...."and I won't mind if his bellow makes Bear Man a little nervous."

"Sure." Libby blew a different sequence into the whistle. At once, far up ahead, Blue's voice went up.

"That's a great dog." Eagle Feather said.

Libby smiled proudly. "He's my best."

"He seems to be swinging around to the north-west." Eagle Feather got back to business. "There's a ranch road over that way." He started to move ahead.

"Wait," said Zack suddenly, bringing everyone to a halt. "We should be thorough. When I came into the tree grove yesterday I was following his trail. You found where he had gone after I set up camp, but we didn't complete the link from his original trail through the grove to the point where he backtracked me."

Eagle Feather knew his friend. "You're going back."

"Just for a moment. Why don't you two rest here a moment and I'll just go connect the dots."

Eagle Feather nodded his agreement. Without a word Libby reached out for Diablo's reins.

Zack smiled his thanks and turned back. When he reached the shade of the Junipers he found the barefoot prints he had followed the day before and followed them on through the grove. Emerging from the trees he glanced ahead and saw the steep ridge they had ascended from the other side. The tracks went up the slope. Zack followed. Part way up the slope was a level bench and beyond it the steep angle of the slope resumed. At this this natural resting spot Zack turned and looked back. From here he could see out over the tops of the trees to the flatness of the mesa beyond.

Zack looked out, imagining himself the hunted man, trying to understand his thoughts. He looked down at his feet. The barefoot prints were clustered in the dirt on this natural shelf, pressed in deeply and layered one on the other as if the maker had waited here a long time. Zack looked toward the back of the bench. Something caught his eye. He looked closer. There among the barefoot human prints he once again saw the prints of a bear.

EIGHT

Lenana stared at her friend. She might have expected this from others on the Rez, but not from Katie.

"Who told you the little girl was killed by a Skinwalker?"

"The whole town knows."

No doubt, Lenana thought.

"And we all know who it is, too," Katie went on.

"Look, Katie, we got to go real slow here." Lenana chose her words carefully. "Innocent people could get hurt if we're not careful what we say." She added, "I didn't expect this of you."

Katie looked offended. "It's not me. I'm just reporting what people are saying. I'm not starting anything; it's already started!" Katie looked away.

"Katie, do you believe in these things? In shape-shifters and witches that can suddenly appear and then disappear?"

"My parents believe it. And so did their parents. I know the people outside the Rez say these things don't happen, that these things can't exist. But what do they know? They're not us; they haven't been raised like us. They live far away from this land in cities with bright street lights and TVs and concrete sidewalks."

Lenana stirred more sugar into her coffee. She'd taken a much-needed break from the craziness that was her office to grab some breakfast at the café with Katie, as she often did. She didn't want to leave Jimmy alone there; he'd stayed at it pretty much all night except for a couple of hours of sleep at his desk. But he'd insisted, saying that a normal routine and the appearance of business as usual was the best way to keep people calm. But from what Katie was telling her, things weren't all that calm.

"What are people saying?" she asked quietly.

"Everyone knows that John Roundtree began studying witchcraft after his wife and child died. He stopped working. He never even finished the last job he was on. He stopped coming around town in the daytime. So how does he live? What does he eat? People see a light on in his house late at night; they see shadows moving from room to room. He's still there. Some people told me they've seen someone coming and going from his house at night. If it's John Roundtree coming and going, where does he go? What does he do? You tell me." Katie looked rebelliously at Lenana.

"There's never been a complaint against him," Lenana observed calmly. "In all that time we've only had the normal complaints about the weeds and broken bottles in front of his house, that's all. And he's always sent in his tribal fees on time. Hardly a basis for an investigation." Lenana was feeling a little defensive despite herself.

"I'm just telling you what people are saying, like you asked."

Later, back in the office, Lenana waited for a lull in clamor of the telephones to report the conversation to Jimmy.

He looked despondent. "I know. I've heard it too. Some of our most upstanding citizens are insisting I go out and arrest John immediately. To tell you the truth, although I know that their reaction is rooted in fear, I think there might also be just a teensy bit of plain old curiosity." He smiled humorlessly. "But, as I keep telling 'em, we do not have just cause for legal action and until we do, we'll simply follow the chain of evidence, which" -Jimmy checked his watch- "I certainly do hope shows up in the person of Zack Tolliver before very much longer."

That said, Jimmy looked at his notes. "What have you got from

Linda Whittaker over in Prescott?" he asked. "Could our victim be the Phoenix girl?"

"Its too early to tell just yet. But the Phoenix girl doesn't seem a fit. And the Reno girl had been well cared for right up to the time she disappeared five days ago. Linda says that the abuse our mesa victim sustained had been going on a long time, probably several years."

"Wherever our mesa girl was over the last several years wasn't a good place. So theoretically, she might have been abducted several years ago. Let's move our search back accordingly, and given the potential time frame, we'd better widen our search area as well."

"So basically unlimited...?" asked Lenana.

Jimmy laughed. "Well, let's leave Interpol out of it for now and hope we get lucky..."

"Did I hear that law enforcement on the Navajo Reservation operates on luck?" The new voice floated in from the front door, which had been propped open in the vain hope of some airflow and to prevent the continual banging from everyone passing through it. The pleasant vibrant voice came from a young woman who now leaned casually against the door jam. A wide brimmed straw hat tied under her chin couldn't keep long strands of wispy blonde hair from wafting across her face. Their first impression was of a charismatic woman with very white teeth and intense green eyes. Her warm smile was intended to offset the directness of her opening sally. Her voice, like the rest of her, projected silky confidence. Looking up, Lenana had a feeling she had seen this woman somewhere before. "Or do you actually employ some sort of methodology?" the woman went on in her teasing tone.

"Who's asking?" responded Jimmy. He looked up wearily from his desk. The ruse he had asked Lenana to employ as an attempt to misdirect the Fifth Estate toward Monument Mesa and consequently away from the office had worked for the most part, but a few reporters had hung back in town hoping to glean news from the efforts of others, and they were making a nuisance of themselves.

"I'm Melissa Mann," the woman announced, as if expecting an

immediate response to her name. "But you can call me Melissa." She stepped into the office and looked around. "So this is the heart beat of the Navajo Nation Police?"

"This is it. Can we assist you in some way?"

"I'm sure you can. Who is the little blonde girl whose body you found on the mesa? Who killed her, and why was she dumped way up here? That will do for starters."

Melissa moved smoothly past Lenana's guardian desk to perch familiarly on the corner of the empty desk next to Jimmy.

"Help yourself," Jimmy said pointedly.

"Thank you," said Melissa, with another smile. "So...?"

"If we did have the answers to any of those questions, you certainly would not be the first to hear them."

"Now that's pretty harsh...and we've only just met." Melissa pouted flirtatiously.

"Lenana here will update the press if we learn anything of significance," replied Jimmy, ignoring Melissa's advances. "You can get it from the news feed, like everyone else."

"Well ...Jim, is it?" She leaned forward and read his nametag. "You will find that I am not like everyone else."

"Here you are just like everyone else."

Melissa's confident smile never wavered. "Well, Jim, I go on the air tonight to begin my first segment of a series about this crime. The next few nights I'll devote a portion of my newscast to your progress. If there is none, I'm afraid that's what I will have to report. Frankly, this crime promises to be a sensation; a little blonde girl killed and dumped in an Indian Reservation..."

Then quickly she asked, "How was she killed, again?"

"What makes you think she's a blonde girl?" Jimmy parried.

"Ah, you don't think we know that? Blonde, white, between eight and ten years old, severely abused..."

Jimmy grew angry, despite himself. "Now just how do you know she was abused?" he demanded.

Melissa laughed. "I didn't," she teased. "But I do now."

Jimmy looked away, annoyed with himself for falling into her neatly laid trap. He tried to restore his composure.

Lenana, who'd been studying Melissa, suddenly burst out, "Why, you're the anchor lady for Channel 4 Evening News out of Flagstaff!"

Melissa looked down at her with a condescending smile. "That's right. Would you like to add anything to what your boss just contributed?"

Lenana smiled pleasantly, her response automatic. "We have no information to disclose at this time."

"Well, okeydokey then, I'm gonna go have a look at the crime scene and take a few pictures." Melissa stood up and stretched languorously, completely in command of her audience. She walked slowly back toward the door.

She turned to look at Jimmy. "Any special route I should take to get up there?" she asked, her eyes twinkling.

"The crime scene is closed to reporters," Jimmy said, not falling for it this time.

"Well, you can't blame a girl for trying. We'll talk soon, then. Tune me in tonight...I'll share what I've got with you, even if you won't share what you've got with me." Melissa gave a saucy laugh and slipped out the door.

Jimmy looked at Lenana in discouragement. "How can she know all that? And what is it she knows that she hasn't told us?" He let out a heavy sigh, and then answered his own question. "Whatever it is, I suppose we'll learn all about it tonight during her broadcast."

Jimmy was lost in thought for a while. He looked at Lenana. "You've got cable, right?" Lenana nodded. "Do me a favor, watch her news show tonight. Call me on my cell if she mentions anything about bears or Skinwalkers or suggests a cause of death. Maybe we can learn something we don't already know."

His next words were angry. "The people around here are stirred up enough without a TV newscaster stoking their fears."

After another pause he muttered to himself, "I suppose we can expect her to tell the entire world tonight that the poor little girl was white and blonde and had been abused."

NINE

Zack stared at the bear tracks and felt a surge of fear. Almost immediately it was replaced by rising anger. This perpetrator, this foul murderer was trying to intimidate him, trying to force his insidious way past Zack's emotional defenses by making him believe that he was up against some sort of supernatural power. Zack didn't know how he was managing it, those eyes last night, this footprint thing, but he wasn't going to fall for it. This had all been carefully planned, Zack was sure. This madman had plenty of time to work it all out, knowing someone would follow his tracks after the victim's body had been found, and he'd had his little surprise all set and ready to go. Well, Zack wasn't buying, that's all. If the perpetrator thought he could scare Zack off with his theatrics, he was sadly mistaken. It was only making him angry and more stubborn. The guy had probably expected a Navajo to track him. Well, Zack wasn't Navajo and he wasn't superstitious - and Bear-Man had better watch himself because Zack was going to keep right on coming.

After a few deep breaths Zack followed the bear prints up the slope a ways. Soon they were replaced by human prints once more, the toes dug deeply into the steep sandy soil for purchase leaving more of a depression than a track. He saw that the trail was taking him in a loop back toward the grove toward the area they had already tracked so he left it there and cut straight up the ridge to the top and followed it there until he caught up to Libby and Eagle Feather. He decided not to tell them about the bear prints he had found. Why bother? It wouldn't help anything and would needlessly complicate the situation. And he had other questions to answer.

"Tell me this." Zack spoke his thoughts out loud. "If this guy wanted to stop me, if he wanted me dead, he had his chance. Why didn't he take it? And why hasn't he bothered to conceal his tracks? From that first bear print back at the crime scene even a greenhorn could have followed him." He went on in a rush. "And here's another thing that sticks in my craw. This crime happened early yesterday morning. He had all the time in the world to get clean away before the body was discovered, well before we got on his trail for the first time. Why did he move so slowly? What was he waiting for? It's almost as if he wants to play with us."

Libby was examining Diablo's pulse to reassure herself of his recovery while Zack was speaking. Suddenly, she gave an exclamation. They looked at her.

"Maybe I can answer your first question, "she said. She was looking closely at the saddle. "Look here. I think Bear-Man did try to hurt you." She pointed to a corner of the stirrup.

The men crowded in to look. There, camouflaged by the darkened leather a cactus spine protruded, standing straight and stiff. Only the sharpest eye could notice it.

"It looks just like the first one, "Libby said.

Eagle Feather inspected it closely. "Uh huh, it's a Pigmy Cactus spine and it's stuck real deep into this leather. It didn't get here from rubbing up against it, it was thrust into the leather with a lot of velocity." He looked at Zack. "Did you use your saddle as a pillow last night by any chance?"

Zack nodded, feeling a slight shudder as he remembered where his head had lain on the saddle, right next to the stirrup.

"That must have been the strange puffing sound I heard, the sound that woke me," he murmured. "It was because it was coming right at me."

Eagle Feather gave a grunt. "Maybe he was trying to stop you."

But Zack was following his own train of thought. "That must be why he stood there for so long, just watching me. He was waiting for the drug to take effect. He couldn't see that he'd missed." Zack pulled out the spine with some difficulty and looked closely at it. There was the same varnish-like coating of some substance coating the business end. He dropped the spine into a fresh specimen bag, labeled it, put it away, and then looked at the others.

"This proves he's not infallible." Zack's words were soft but held angry determination. "Let's go. I doubt he's still out there but if he's stupid enough to want to keep playing with us, I'll end it."

He pulled his Winchester from its scabbard and with the rifle in his right hand took up Diablo's reins and fell in behind Eagle Feather who, without saying a word, took up the trail once more.

TEN

The newsroom of CBS Television Channel Four was cavernous, a modern well-lit facility occupying the entire fifth floor of its parent building in the heart of downtown Flagstaff. Surrounded on all sides by floor to ceiling solar shaded windows, it offered stunning views in every direction, an advantage completely lost upon those buzzing about within this visible beehive of a place, crawling in and out of the honeycomb of cell-like cubicles to the drone of a hundred conversations. At the very center, and removed from the general tumult were several glass enclosed cells and in the center one, queen-like, Melissa Mann stood, for to sit would feel too much like a permanent rest.

"I'm telling you he totally reacted when I said the word 'abused'. I'm certain that's the case, but I need at least one other source of confirmation before going live with it." She looked down at a twenty-something well-manicured crew cut man with his notebook and pen poised. "Art, call around to all our usual FBI sources here and over in Phoenix. Find out where they took that girl's body. If we can find the forensic pathologist who's working on the case we can go to work on him."

Art nodded. He immediately jumped up off the couch and scurried out the door.

Melissa turned to the other couch occupant, a woman in a trim suit with a carefully constructed enameled hairdo that seemed a purposeful contrast to the whisping casual hair look of her boss.

"Let's begin with the Mexican cartel piece," she directed. "Move Jerry's personal interest tape to just before the special. When you end the regular news be sure to leave four minutes for the tape and me. By the way, did Pete do the copter fly-over to get those aerial shots as I asked?"

"Yes. Right here." The woman put down her pad and took up a file next to her on the couch. "There are five shots here, but Pete wanted you to look especially at this one." She held up a large color photo and pointed to a spot in the lower left hand corner. "Look very closely at this area just beyond the cliff face. See that yellow bit? Pete thinks it might be police tape."

Melissa studied the photo carefully and flipped it over to look at the back.

"Monument Mesa? All the other news sources are saying Antelope Mesa. Do we have a picture of that one?"

Her assistant flipped past several other photos and took a paper-clipped group out of the file. "These show all possible locations for a crime scene on Antelope Mesa." She handed the photos over to Melissa, who studied them one by one.

"There doesn't seem to be any road leading in to this mesa. Any trail up it would have to be very long. Didn't we hear that the hunter who reported the crime said it took him an hour to get down and another to get back up again? I don't see anyone getting down and over to the town and back from this mesa in less than four hours." Melissa looked again at the first picture. "That does look like police tape," she said slowly. "What else could it be?" She made her decision. "Have Pete prepare the tapes of Monument mesa. We'll use that tonight. If we're right, we just might hit a nerve." She gave a little laugh, remembering. "I certainly managed to do that this morning."

It was Lenana glancing out the open door of the police station who saw them arrive, three large white Tahoe SUVs parading up the street with ceremonial slowness and parking directly in front of the building without regard for lined spaces, each vehicle emblazoned with the familiar Navajo Nation Tribal Council logo. Jimmy came and stood at the window with her to watch the vehicles disgorge their dignified and imposing occupants one by one.

"Isn't that the Council Speaker?" Lenana asked. "What brings him out here, I wonder?"

"I'm pretty sure I know." Jimmy moved to the door. "Get ready for company." Jimmy and Lenana greeted the dignitaries at the door. First to enter was a district representative who was a second cousin to Lenana. They greeted each another warmly. Jimmy knew him from time spent in official meetings. Then the Council Speaker entered followed by his retinue. He rarely visited the district and almost never came to Elk Wells. Lenana's cousin made all the introductions after everyone was standing in the tiny office. Lenana found chairs for everyone and hurried over to the café next door to arrange for coffee and pastries.

After the requisite polite small talk about the weather, the corn crop, and the sheep population the Speaker cleared his throat and adopted a more serious tone.

"Is FBI Agent Tolliver here?"

"He's still in the field and has been out of communication since yesterday morning," Jimmy replied.

"Then may I infer that you have no specific knowledge as yet of what, if anything, he has learned about the death of that little white girl up on the Monument Mesa?" the Speaker asked.

"That's true," Jimmy said.

"Not," the Speaker went on, "that the fruit of his efforts should necessarily determine the course of action of the Navajo Nation Police, understanding that the FBI has no real jurisdiction on the Reservation and functions solely as an invited collaborator and liaison?"

His words, despite a rising inflection toward the end, were clearly not intended as a question.

"That's true," Jimmy said again.

The speaker went on almost without pausing for Jimmy's reply. "My office has received many concerns from the people of this district in the past twenty four hours. They are fearful." He looked at Jimmy with a humorless smile. "You and I, Lieutenant Chaparral, are experienced and educated people. Our jobs require us to spend time with people who are not of the Navajo culture and who do not share our perspectives. You and I understand that there are people who are unable to see beyond the veil, who do not allow themselves to understand that things do exist that cannot be explained by science or logic. People, specifically, who are not of Diné descent."

The Speaker paused to clear his throat once again. He was an old man, maybe eighty or eighty-five years of age, but who really knew? His face was leathered and deeply lined from a life spent exposed to sun and wind but he had magnetism and projected great inner strength that held his listeners.

"You and I are destined to live in both worlds. You and I know that witches do walk this land, and that there are many kinds of witches, in fact. Our objective, therefore, when encountering a witch is not to question its existence but to determine which kind of witch it is, whether it is a practitioner of the Witchery Way, or a user of Curse Objects, or a practitioner of the Frenzy Way. We need to determine this to safeguard our people."

The Speaker looked sternly at Jim.

"I am told that you have found evidence of a Skinwalker. I am told that the creature responsible for the death of that little white girl flew several hundred yards away from the scene without leaving sign and then left the tracks of a large bear while making his escape. Is this so?"

Jimmy was momentarily shocked. He sensed the eyes of every person in the room on him, Lenana included. He knew that serious implications would be drawn from his response. The Speaker apparently had extremely detailed information and he would not be put off. The room waited.

Jim spoke clearly and carefully.

"We have attempted to withhold certain details of this case for the obvious reason that they might...that they likely would provoke concern. The evidence, as you just described, does indeed appear to suggest an active Skinwalker. But we cannot discard the possibility that an intelligent perpetrator deliberately left those signs for the very purpose of causing alarm and fear in the community in order to distract us from the true criminal. Agent Tolliver is up on the Mesa right now tracking the killer. He expects to find the real culprit or to find evidence that leads to a conclusion other than the presence of a Skinwalker. We are waiting for his report and for the FBI forensics report from the crime scene and autopsy before drawing any conclusions. We will be able to say more after Agent Tolliver returns."

"If he returns," replied the Speaker.

"I'm sorry?"

"If he returns," the Speaker insisted. "If indeed we are dealing with a Navajo witch with sufficient power to become a Yee Naaldlooshii, a Skinwalker, we must conclude that should Agent Tolliver succeed in finding this creature (or worse, be permitted to find it) he will be in the gravest danger. I do not expect that Agent Tolliver has bullets dipped in white ash or that he has taken any of the other necessary precautions to safeguard himself from a witch's magic. Special Agent Tolliver has been gone more than twenty- four hours, you have said. When had you intended to conclude that he would not be returning and to act upon that assumption?"

"Speaker, Eagle Feather is with him."

"Ah...!" The Speaker looked thoughtful. "That does make a difference."

"Eagle Feather went to find him early this morning," Jimmy elaborated.

"He was not with him during the night, then?" Jimmy shook his head.

After another moment, the Speaker shrugged. "This does not

change things." He addressed himself to the assembled group.

"Navajo Tribal law has been broken. Navajo Spiritual law may have been broken as well. We must intercede."

The Speaker paused to sip from the coffee that Lenana had placed near him, and then went on.

"The people of this town speak of a man named John Roundtree. Do you know him?" He looked at Jimmy.

"Yes," Jimmy replied. "And I know the stories. But there is no evidence to link him to this case, none at all."

"Now speaks the person of whom I spoke before, the person who employs the thinking of those who live beyond the reservation, the one who needs to see evidence and to follow a logical train of thought before drawing his conclusion. But now I address myself to the person who is of the Navajo, whose roots are of the Diné. To become a â€ Ãįntâ€ Ä ¯Ä ʾhnii, to have reached the level of supernatural power that allows one to assume the form of an animal for evil, this shaman must have studied witchcraft. To do so, he must have access to all the secret rites and spells and materials that are used in the Witchery Way. Such access is not common, but it is possible for one with relatives who have practiced witchcraft and who already are in possession such things. John Roundtree's grandfather, as you may or may not know, was such a person."

The Speaker paused for effect. Then he raised an outward palm.

"But there is more. To gain this power, a human being must not only gain this high level of witchery practice but must also commit a cultural taboo, specifically the taboo of killing an immediate member of his own family."

Jimmy Chaparral looked confused. "To my knowledge, John Roundtree's parents died of natural causes, he had no siblings, and we know that his wife and child both died during childbirth. No doubt he's just a very bitter man who has withdrawn socially, who has no commitments, no schedule to follow and no longer distinguishes between night and day for his activities, whatever they are."

"Yes," repeated the Speaker with a thin smile, "Whatever they are..." Then he went on. "People say that John Roundtree's wife need not have died. People say that after she delivered her stillborn boy she lay bleeding heavily. People say that John Roundtree in his despair and anger left her to bleed and then to die."

The Speaker looked hard at Jimmy and sighed as if carrying the weight of the world. "That would certainly fulfill the cultural taboo on the order required. That would certainly constitute killing an immediate member of one's family."

Everyone in the little office leaned forward during the Speakers words. They were silent. The Speaker allowed the silence to linger on for a time. When he spoke it was with authority.

"The first request I make of all of you is very simple. It is a solution when a Skinwalker's identity becomes known. It is the Navajo Way. We must all together say aloud the name of this witch three times. If John Roundtree indeed is not a Skinwalker, no harm will come to him. But if he is, he will sicken and die within three days. Either way, we"--he waved his arm to include all there gathered--"will be able to report to the people to whom we are responsible that we do understand the danger and that we have acted swiftly in the traditional way. It will go far to still the fears of the people of this town and of this district."

Everyone nodded in agreement. Jimmy felt relief at this decision. He had expected to be asked to perform a much more difficult task.

The Speaker stood and slowly raised his arms above him with palms outward. "Skinwalker, Witch, we know you and we name you." As he began to pronounce the name John Roundtree, everyone in the room joined him in chanting each syllable deliberately. The speaker turned to face the four principal directions each time he spoke.

"You are John Roundtree, John Roundtree, John Roundtree."

In the silence that followed the Speaker slowly resumed his seat. The name John Roundtree seemed to linger on in the room.

He turned to Jimmy.

"Lieutenant Chaparral, you must go to the home of John Roundtree this afternoon and bring him back to this station and place him in a jail cell. The people fear him and if he is free to roam in the darkness tonight there will be an incident. We must avoid that."

Jimmy felt his stomach clutch. These were the words that he had dreaded. Although he could see wisdom in this action, he could not support it with the law.

"I have no evidence," he repeated lamely.

"You must find a way." The Speaker's tone was kind, but firm. Jimmy nodded. The Speaker stood to leave.

His retinue quickly stood at the signal. His next words were for all of them as much as for Jimmy. "We act as we must with courage and with conviction. Our faith is in you, Jim Chaparral."

After they had gone, Lenana looked at Jim. "What will you do?"

Jim stared out the window at the departing SUVs. "I really don't know," he confessed.

ELEVEN

The tracks gradually descended from the ridge top at the western edge of the escarpment. They found Big Blue part way down resting in the shade of a boulder near one of the prints. Bear Man seemed to have made no attempt to conceal his tracks after leaving Zack's camp. He had moved swiftly after that, apparently intent upon putting distance between himself and his pursuers. Libby could see from Blue's behavior that the scent was hours old by now.

"See the deep forefoot strike and the longer distance between each print?" Eagle Feather went into his teaching mode. "Our barefoot man is running, now that the terrain is easier. Not running scared, running easy and steady."

"He seems to be headed toward the old MacPherson Ranch road," Libby said.

The men nodded in agreement.

Zack walked around Diablo and slipped his rifle into the scabbard. "Doesn't seem likely I'll get a chance to use this." He scratched the day's worth of scruffy beard on his chin. "We haven't seen any more blood. In fact, there hasn't been any blood since leaving the tree grove."

He went on, thinking aloud. "You know, there never really was all that much blood, considering the depth of that wound in the girl's abdomen." Then thoughtfully, "Wouldn't be if the wound was post mortem."

Eagle Feather listened but didn't respond.

"Your Bear Man is full of surprises," Libby commented.

"Too many," muttered Zack.

Libby clipped Blue onto the long lead and waited for Eagle Feather to lead out. They moved quickly now. The trail was easy to follow. Bear Man was running along comfortably, his prints clear and obvious, leading the trackers down the gentle slope toward the flatness of the valley floor that spread beyond the escarpment. Here grey bundles of sagebrush bunched at the bottom of tall candelabras of old growth saguaro that stood separated from one another by rivulets of red-brown sand. It was mid-morning now. Sweat soaked their hatbands and thin streams of perspiration rolled down their backs.

"We're about a mile from the Ranch road," Eagle Feather said after a while. "Looks like he's making a bee-line for it. If he were still out here, I'd see him."

Zack knew this was true. Eagle Feather's eyesight was legendary. Hunters he guided told tales of how he could distinguish rams from ewes among boulders at such a distance that the hunters couldn't even see the boulders.

Zack checked his cell phone. "I've got a signal now." He punched in a number. "I guess the Tuba City cell tower is in range...Zack here," he announced abruptly as the call was answered. He listened for a moment with an expression of wry amusement. Audible from the phone came the rise and fall of an emotionally charged female voice. "No, Lenana." Zack cut in. "We didn't catch him, but we did learn a little more about him. Now that I have your attention, would you please call that new forensics specialist assigned to my office, what's her name, and ask her to search the victim for a cactus spine stuck in her skin, or the mark where one had been, most likely somewhere on her neck? I'll call her later with more details. I've got some blood samples and other evidence for her too. And Lenana, please have my truck and trailer brought around to pick us up on the MacPherson Ranch road. We're, oh, maybe five miles south of Route 160. Have you got someone to do that? The keys are in it. We'll be waiting by the road. I'm expecting we'll likely lose this guy's trail when we get there but even if we don't we'll need to come in for supplies. Oh, and please call Ben for me. Tell him I'll give him a call just as soon as I get back to town. Is Jimmy there? No? Ok, I'll catch up with him later. Thanks, Lenana."

Zack rang off.

They reached the ranch road just a half hour later. On the dirt surface they found evidence of recent traffic, maybe three different sets of tire tracks, Eagle Feather thought. Blue followed Bear Man's trail right to the middle of the road where the physical prints disappeared but the dog never hesitated and turned abruptly north and followed the scent down the center of the road pulling his handler along behind. Eagle Feather and Zack, still leading Diablo, fell in behind and the procession continued this way for maybe half a mile until just as suddenly Blue turned off the road and began casting about with his nose, apparently trying to regain the scent. Here they found fresh tire tracks where a vehicle had been left by the side of the road. Zack and Eagle Feather squatted to study the tire tracks.

"These tires are bald," Zack observed. He pointed to a portion of the tread impression. "That looks like a patch."

"Right here the tire is worn down to the fabric," Eagle Feather added. "We won't have any trouble recognizing this tire if we see it again. Fact is, I don't know how it got this far without going flat."

"Another question is where did it go once it left here?"

Blue and Libby were making wider and wider sweeps attempting to recapture the scent. They stopped a hundred feet to the north.

"I think Blue's got something here," Libby called back.

Blue was at the shoulder of the road. The men joined them and saw tire prints where a vehicle had backed onto the shoulder to reverse direction. Now it was headed south, back toward Route 160. They walked slowly back down the middle of the road.

"Well, I think that's about it for now," Zack said. "We might as well keep walking in this direction since we have to go that way anyhow. It could be a while before my truck gets here."

Libby fell in with Zack. She reached over to stroke Diablo's neck. "He doesn't seem to have suffered any lasting effects."

"No, thank God. But I'm keeping an eye on him for a while anyway."

"Are you still living out at the old Browne place?"

Ten years before when Zack first arrived from the Academy, he leased an old ranch up near Page, Arizona, on Ben's recommendation. It was a perfect location, near enough to the Reservation to respond quickly but also close to the south shore of Lake Powell and all of the recreational and social opportunities that the tourist mecca offered. The old ranch was a fixer-upper, for sure, but once he'd cleared the barn of snakes and ground squirrels it was just right for his small string of trail horses, a necessity for any FBI agent working the road less plateaus of the reservation.

"I'm still there. I might never leave, after all the work I've put into the place."

"You've managed to hang on to this job longer than most." Libby looked sideways at him with a smile. "I've watched rookies come and go quickly over the years. What's your secret?"

"In a word, patience." Zack smiled to himself as he thought about it. "I'm in no rush to get here or there. I live in a place where each evening the surrounding buttes are brushed in colors that only God's own hand could paint and each morning at dawn I'm treated to a brand new display, no two ever alike. Just that show alone keeps me there."

"You're quite the poetic soul."

"I think we all are but most of us rush around too much to find it."

"You whites are afraid to know your inner selves." Eagle Feather had been listening behind them. "What you've just discovered is something my people have known ever since we emerged up the magic reed and into this 'glittering' world."

"Okay, Mr. I'm-in-touch-with-the-earth-and-you're-not."

Zack grinned back over his shoulder at Eagle Feather. "Is this your way of telling me I should be listening to your Skinwalker theories?"

Eagle Feather's response was solemn.

"The Ancients would tell you that the shadow world is always with us, whether we want to acknowledge it or not. The advantage in accepting it is that later you won't be surprised by it. If you consider the power of spirits as a possibility you will always have both halves of the truth in front of you. This Bear Man might be just an evil man who happens to be a very skilled hunter and tracker and a man who lives intimately with nature, or he could be more than that. He left a lot of signs. Were they mistakes? Or was it all planned? A man who gives his soul to become a Skinwalker is still a man, not a spirit, but he has great powers. I know all these things are possible and no matter what we find, I will still follow the signs wherever they lead."

"You're suggesting I keep an open mind, then? Sure, I'll do that, but I won't shy away from bringing a cruel child killer to justice just from fear of ghosts and goblins, either."

"Blue is a proven spirit tracker so no worries there," Libby said, trying to lighten the mood, and both men laughed.

"We believe that animals see humans and spirits blended together," Eagle Feather said. "They've got the best of both worlds."

Libby resumed her thread of questioning that Eagle Feather had interrupted. "Why haven't you married yet? You must be, what, thirty-five or so? You've got that big old place and you must make a decent wage, even on a government pay scale."

"You don't mind being direct, do you?" Zack wasn't sure how to regard her blunt question. "No deep dark secret there. It's the same thing you always hear. I just haven't stumbled upon the right woman yet. And not too many women that I know of would care to live so far from the nearest shopping mall." But now Zack's attention was turned far down the road.

"Looks like my rig might be coming."

Where the laser straight road merged with the shimmering mirage lake on the horizon they could see a growing speck followed by a round cloud of dust.

TWELVE

Melissa Mann looked at Art in amusement. "A what? A ghost? That's what they believe killed that girl?"

Art looked down at his notes. "It's called a Skinwalker. It's more of a Navajo witch, actually, but it is super strong, able to fly, and they believe no one can stop it." Art glanced up at Melissa, grinning. "They really believe this. The people on the reservation are in an uproar about this, right up to the highest administrators."

"This just gets better and better! Who is your source for this?"

"A reporter with the Tuba City Times, Cindy something, who was able to coax the story out of one of the Navajo policemen. He told her that they found bear tracks a hundred feet from the body; that the Skinwalker had landed there after killing the girl and flying off! The policemen were frightened of this thing. They all really believe it. And every resident of that town will be locking all their doors and windows tonight."

"This is great stuff! Find me someone from that town…what is it? Elk something? Someone who is willing to talk about it live on the air and then get a satellite feed down there. We'll broadcast right from that town tonight, right on the main street. Let's see…it will be seven p.m. when we go on the air so it should just be getting dark as my interview begins. It'll be a sensation!"

Melissa felt new energy surge through her and paced the small office, her brain humming. "Did you find the FBI forensics people who are working the case or where they took the body?"

"Nothing yet. I've put out inquiries to all my usual sources but the

Feds are keeping this one close to the chest. I'll keep at it."

"Do that. And see if you can get a line on where that little blonde girl came from in the first place. There must be a missing child report somewhere; use the news info blogs and all your personal networks, make lots of promises. And get me some details on this shape changing thing-a-ma-jig they all believe in. Let's get all over this one right now!"

Melissa turned back to her notes, her face flushed with excitement. She noticed that her hands trembled slightly and smiled. This could be it, the one sensational story that would make her career.

"Zack just checked in."

Jimmy Chaparral was there in the doorway, back from the café next door, his fourth coffee of the morning steaming in his hand despite the rising heat of the day. At Lenana's words he looked up abruptly and placed the suddenly forgotten coffee down on his desk.

"Where is he?"

"He's out on the old MacPherson Ranch road, about five miles from Route 160. Libby and Eagle Feather are with him. I just sent Luke over to fetch his rig and go pick them all up."

"Does he have any news?"

"Maybe. But he wants to talk to you in person. He kept it kind of low key on the phone."

"Is he coming directly here?"

"Sounded like it."

"Good. Should take Luke, umm, a couple of hours, then. That's time enough to walk over to John Roundtree's house and scout around a bit. I don't like to be told how to do my job but I should at least see if John is over there." He sighed. "I've got my radio; call me if Zack checks in again." At Lenana's growing look of alarm he added quickly,

"Don't worry, I won't confront Roundtree until I've checked in with Zack."

Jimmy took a shotgun down from the rack and started toward the door, then remembered his cup of coffee and turned back with a shy grin and picked it up.

"I need this more than the gun," he joked, and walked out.

THIRTEEN

"That's not my rig," Zack said. He was watching the ball of dust and the vehicle in it grow bigger. "It's not pulling a trailer and it's coming much too fast."

"Nobody but ranchers use this road," Eagle Feather said. "It takes you all the way down to Route 264 but you need four wheel drive to get over the pass. By that time you might as well have driven to Tuba City and back around. Not much point."

"Doesn't someone still live up at the old MacPherson place?" Libby was staring at the approaching car. "Maybe they're simply coming home with the groceries."

"They're coming home mighty fast." Zack said. They stood and watched the vehicle grow rapidly larger.

"This could be our guy." Eagle Feather said what was on everybody's mind.

"Could be at that." Zack made his decision. "Let's not take any chances. Libby, take Blue over to that mesquite bush over there and just tuck in behind it. Eagle Feather, take my rifle and cover me from off the road over there. Take Diablo with you. I'll see who this is."

Eagle Feather took Diablo's reins and walked a safe distance from the road. He pulled Zack's rifle out of the boot and laid it across the saddle. On the opposite side of the road Libby held Blue close and partially concealed herself on the shady side of the mesquite bush while Zack took a position at the side of the road. They waited. They didn't have to wait long. The vehicle rocketed toward them, skittering from side to side from the violent heaving of its springs as it bounced in and out of ruts. It appeared as if it must lose control at any moment. Blasts of dust issued from its churning wheels and enveloped the entire rear of the vehicle in a red-brown cloud. The truck kept up its reckless speed even as it neared Zack. He stood his ground and waved at the vehicle to stop but it only increased its speed and kept coming directly toward him. Through the dust veil Zack saw it was a white SUV, the type used by most ranchers and oilmen in the region. He looked hard at it as it neared but the windshield was impenetrable. But when it was almost upon him Zack felt as much as saw two glowing red eyes fixed on him and there came a familiar odor, foul, musky and dank, the odor from that fearful night. Some strange but powerful force held him rooted where he stood, directly in the path of the oncoming vehicle. Panicked, Zack struggled desperately to free his mind of the disabling power until at the last possible moment he came free of it and dove toward the shoulder, not a moment too soon, and not before the big fender struck his boot and spun him all the way around. He landed on his side on the sandy ground with enough force to drive the air from his lungs, his foot instantly numb. The truck raced on and was lost from view in its own dust cloud receding far down the road. Eagle Feather kept the rifle trained on the vehicle but it never slowed and then it was gone, save for the red dust settling lightly around them like thistle down.

Libby ran to Zack. He was sitting up, sweaty and dust caked, his hat gone, testing his foot inside the boot, pain creasing his face.

"Here, don't move too quickly," Libby instructed him. She knelt to help him remove the boot. "You landed hard."

Eagle Feather replaced the rifle in the boot and hurried over to them. "Why didn't you move sooner, man?" he asked. "You looking for government compensation for an injury in the line of duty?" But his joking was shaky.

"That was our guy," Zack said, and he was not smiling. "I'm fine, I think," he said to Libby, "just bruised. Help me get this boot back on and then let's go see if Blue can pick up a scent from that truck, if there is one to find."

Zack struggled upright. He looked at his scraped palms as he spoke to Eagle Feather. "We need to go check those tire tracks and see if they match anything...if he's left any, the way he was chewing up the road."

"Whoa, hoss, hang on a moment, take a deep breath. Let Libby look you over. The scent and the tracks will keep."

He waited for Zack to settle back down. "You had a good look at that truck, at least until you decided to leave the scene. Did you see anything?"

"No. Well, yes."

"Well, which?"

"Just an impression." Zack was suddenly reluctant to talk about his sense of the red eyes and the feelings that had overcome him moments ago, feelings like the ones from the previous night. He wasn't sure why, but he somehow felt that speaking of it openly might give more credence than he wanted to give to the whole Skinwalker thing. He decided to keep quiet about it for now. Instead he said, "I had a feeling that the driver of that truck knew me, almost as if he expected me to be here by the side of the road..." Zack finished lamely. He shook his head in disgust. "I'm letting this guy get to me."

Libby finished her examination. "You seem fine. Like you thought, just some bruises. But you'll feel it in the morning. You'll need ice on that foot as soon as we can find some."

Libby looked from one man to the other. "Now let's talk about what we're not saying here," she said. "I'm not up to speed with your entire investigation but let me give you my perspective. Since beginning to track the killer with Eagle Feather early this morning I've seen bear prints that led away from a remote crime scene and then transformed into bare human prints that suggest a man who is extremely knowledgeable in outdoor skills, stealthy beyond normal abilities, and entirely comfortable padding around the desert in bare feet. And here is a no-nonsense FBI agent talking about impressions and strange feelings. We've got a suspect who can leap long distances, who can run fast enough to outdistance human and canine pursuers, who can project impressions and feelings on to people just by looking at them.

Now if it were anyone else I'd say you two are talking about a Skinwalker, even if you don't admit it. And even if you're not, everyone on the reservation is going to think so. What is it they say? A Skinwalker's eyes glow in the dark like an animal? That they take on an animal's powers? That they avoid the light? That when they lock their eyes on yours they can absorb themselves into your body?"

Zack looked up at Libby. "How the hell do you know all of that stuff?"

"I've lived on and around the Reservation all my life," she pointed out. "You've only been around here for ten years or so. I've worked closely with the Navajo and I listen and I learn." She smiled. "Fact is, no Navajo is ever going to talk to a white FBI agent about these things."

"I would," said Eagle Feather. "I tried to, but the stubborn white FBI agent wouldn't listen."

"Okay, okay!" Zack said, frustrated. "I know the stories. I know about Skinwalkers. But I can't base an investigation on a myth, a will o' the wisp. There has to be a process, we have to eliminate what we know is real before we tackle what we think isn't real. So let's start with some real evidence. Did anyone get a license plate number or anything that might actually be useful?"

Libby shook her head.

Eagle Feather said, "Lots of dust, no markings, just a plain white Chevy SUV truck, could've been anybody."

"Then let's get back to looking for a scent and some tire tracks, OK?"

They all went back to the road and searched. Libby released Blue and he put his big nose up into the air and trotted immediately off in the direction that the SUV had gone, pausing to sniff about here and there, then moving on again.

"Blue thinks it was Bear Man driving that truck," Libby said.

Eagle Feather crouched down and peered down the roadway. Zack limped over to get Diablo and led him back to the road, then stood there to watch Eagle Feather work.

After a time Eagle Feather walked over to him. "Can't find much. He kept those wheels churning and never left a single clear track. He was probably intending to destroy all his previous prints as well. That might be why he drove back here. But what I can tell you is that the truck that just came through here is not the same one that had been parked here last night."

Meanwhile Libby was staring back down the road where the white SUV had first appeared. "Not again!" she said.

The two men turned to look. Another ball of dust had appeared far down the road.

FOURTEEN

Linda took another hard look at the mass spectrometer reading. Yes, a clear marker for 7- aminoflunitrazepam was present. She had not expected this. Post mortem blood test evidence in clinical forensic situations seldom yielded useful results for her, generally because her subjects seldom reached her table before drug degradation had long taken place. Therefore Linda had not been particularly surprised at the lack of blood evidence for poisons or drugs in this small victim. She had done a hair strand analysis. No poisons and apparently no drugs. But a closer look had suggested a potential positive for the metabolite and now the more accurate and specific mass spectrometer had confirmed it.

Linda was aware that 7-aminoflunitrazepam is the degradation product of flunitrazepam or rohypnol. In fact, the quantity indicated in this hair strand suggested a potential dosage in the range of 500 ug/L or so, usually a fatal amount. But this evidence was still insufficient to establish rohypnol as the cause of death, but for that matter she was unable to rule out the child's broken neck as the cause, either. However, this surprising revelation did help to confirm a hypothetical history endured by this child, one that she was slowly constructing, a story of sustained brutality followed by murder.

Another tear squeezed from Linda's eye and she wiped it away in annoyance. She stared again at the spectrometer results and then pressed the print button. All evidence samples and test results would now be carefully preserved and safeguarded. Too many evil people had escaped their just rewards because of a small slip at a moment like this and Linda was determined that the animal responsible for mistreating this little girl would never escape. She had just bagged the tested hair sample and was locking it away when her cell phone rang. She cradled it against her shoulder as she worked.

"Hello. Oh, Officer Chaparral. He called? I see. Did he catch the perp? Any leads? I see. What was that? A cactus spine? Somewhere around the neck? Did he say why? No, huh? OK, I'll take a look. Have him call me when he gets in, would you please? I've got something for him as well...no, nothing you can use at this point, just some cause of death possibilities, as yet unconfirmed. OK, thanks. Bye."

Linda hung up with her mind racing. Cactus spine? Zack couldn't be concerned about a tiny prick from a cactus among all the wounds that covered this girl's body. He was looking for something else, maybe something administered by the spine somehow. Linda walked over to the table and once again examined the girl's neck, this time much more closely. Now she concentrated on the hairline on the back of her neck, which was usually covered by her long blonde hair. As she searched her brain raced ahead. It would not require a deep injection to administer the rohypnol. A prick just under the skin would do for a non-dilute solution. And that's all it would take for it to show up on the spectrometer reading. Linda drew in her breath suddenly. Just above the hairline in the very center of the back of the girl's neck was a tiny red dot exactly the right size for a cactus spine. Linda reached for her scalpel and took a tiny sample of flesh at the entry wound. She would test this sample and compare it to her other results but she had no doubt about what she would find.

The lowering but still hot sun shimmered off the pavement of the empty road as Jim Chaparral walked slowly along it toward the home of John Roundtree. John lived a quarter mile west of the town center and his house was the last one you came to before you were out of town. All the other houses clustered closer in, bunched together as if trying to disassociate themselves from the Roundtree place. Or maybe that's more a reflection of how I feel right now, Jimmy thought, counting each of them off to himself as he walked. His thoughts turned to the people who lived in them and how they would likely react to the thought of John Roundtree as a Skinwalker. He smiled walking by Jack Hodger's trailer, thinking how the old man would probably pile chairs up against his thin metal door tonight to keep the witch out. Then he came to the Hogan of the Keeners, a very traditional Navajo family, and he thought how that solid wood door and all of those sturdy wooden shutters would be closed tight tonight. Susie Keener would probably sleep stretched across the doorsill of the children's room.

Unless he, Jim Chaparral, did his job as tribal officer and law enforcement agent, he thought. The Speaker's message was clear. Modern law enforcement techniques were fine for outsiders but in the end there was just one way to deal with a Skinwalker. And the Speaker expected Jimmy to handle it.

He saw the nose of Roundtree's old pickup truck poking out long before he reached the Roundtree place. It sat where it had always sat at the end of the long weed infested drive. He came to it and beyond it saw the house, set back from the road. It had been a fine looking building once, with its low wall and a fancy gate - like a formal announcement at the road. The wall was typical Roundtree, ornamental yet solid, but now covered in red dust from broken bricks and burrowing insects.

Jimmy paused by the old pickup and dropped two shells into the shotgun he held broken over his arm. He snapped the gun closed and walked on to the front gate and stood and waited the traditional few minutes to be noticed, not really expecting anyone to come out. The stone walk to the house was a cracked and overgrown with weed and blown sand eddies encroached. Tumbleweeds rolled here and there on the dry baked lawn. He walked slowly toward the house. Lizards skittered crisscross out of his way. The house itself had been constructed of wood to suggest the traditional octagonal Hogan shape although much larger and so subtly done that at first glance the building appeared almost round. It had a single story with a high gently sloping roof. There was no porch, just a heavy wooden front door with two wide steps as an entrance. The place looked run down, the windows dirty and cracked, the ornamental, once elegant edging along the exterior panels was weathered and splintered. Spider webs laced the roof corners.

Jimmy held the shotgun casually but handy as he approached the door. He cleared his throat and felt his heart race. He called out in the traditional way.

"John Roundtree, are you in there? It is Jim Chaparral of The Folded Arms People, for the Red Running into the Water Clan, of the Bitter Water People and The Badlands People. I wish to talk with you."

There was no response, no sound or movement from within. Jimmy felt a nervous flutter in his throat and chest.

"John Roundtree, I do not wish to disturb you, but it is necessary that I speak to you. I am here on the official business of the Navajo Nation Police."

Jimmy shifted his feet as he waited. The sun's heat was amplified in the reflective doorway. He slowly became aware of a sick-sweet odor around him, maybe something that had died under the building, he thought. Still there was no response from the house, no rustle, no creaks, no movement. Silence hung there. Jimmy rapped louder, this time using the barrel of the shotgun, three strong thumps that he could hear echo inside the walls. The sickly sweet odor seemed to stir at each thump. He waited. He called out again.

"John Roundtree, I believe you are in there. If you will not talk to me now, I will have to come back later with a warrant and enter forcibly. I wish only to ask you some questions. I mean you no harm."

No response. No sound.

Finally, "I am leaving now, but I will walk around your grounds. If you do not wish me to do this, you should tell me. I am armed. If you decide to come out of your house you should call out first so that you will not be shot."

Jimmy took a step back and listened and waited. Nothing. He began his walk around the building. He came to a window that was painted in dirt and cobwebs and decided not to try to look inside, he didn't want to present his face as a target should Roundtree decide to blast away from the darkness within. Dry brush littered the side yard and as he came around to the back he saw what once must have been an elegant patio, now cracked and covered in weeds. The back yard itself was large, blending eventually into an area of tall grass where bricks were stacked, now crumbling with plants growing between them. There were several places where short walls were begun as if for practice. Further along an entire building was started in brick with walls that reached only to waist height as if suddenly abandoned. Well-traveled ruts were visible leading out among the brick piles, probably worn by frequent trips with the heavily laden pickup. This must be John Roundtree's brickyard, Jim thought.

He turned the corner beyond the patio and returned by the far side of the house. Here he found another dirty, cracked window and more splintered and weathered facade and then he was back in front. He called to Roundtree once again and listened at the entry a final time. Then he crunched across the dust patch that was the lawn toward the old truck.

Part way along a new sound came to him. He stopped in his tracks, stood still, listened, his back to the house, the shotgun awkwardly cradled over his right arm. He wanted to turn and bring the gun to bear but he made himself wait quietly for the sound to repeat. And there it was, a musical hollow sound like pebbles falling on a dried gourd, somewhere near the house. He turned slowly, listened and then he saw it. A slight breeze stirred and the small wind-chime suspended at the rear corner of the house moved again, swaying in the breeze, and made the sound. Funny he hadn't noticed it before, he thought. He stared at the house. The dark empty windows stared back. When his quickened pulse returned to its former tempo he continued on to the pick-up.

Weeds grew tall around it. The vehicle itself was covered in a hardened dust coating indicating many years inactivity. The windows were streaked with dirt. Jimmy walked behind it and looked at the ground behind the tires. To his surprise and dismay he saw what he had hoped not to see...the truck had been moved. Recently. Someone had attempted to return it to the exact place in the depressions it had made over time but the tires overlapped just enough to be seen by a sharp eye, an eye that was looking for it. Jimmy inspected the grass behind the vehicle. Again it was as he expected. Weeds flattened by the truck's passage were pushed back up again in an attempt at concealment. The faint smell of gas and oil clung like fog to the tall weeds. Someone had driven the truck.

FIFTEEN

They watched as once again a dust cloud and the vehicle causing it grew in the distance but this time it moved more moderately, and its shape was different.

"That's your rig," Eagle Feather said. "I can make out the trailer."

Libby let out an audible sigh of relief.

Eagle Feather's observation was soon confirmed and Zack's truck and trailer pulled to a dusty stop next to them on the empty road. The man driving it climbed from the cab to help Zack remove Diablo's pack and saddle and load it in the pickup bed. Zack wiped the horse down well and led him up the ramp into the trailer for a reward of fresh hay and cool water. Then Zack, Eagle Feather, Libby, and Blue all joined the driver in the spacious king cab for the trip back to town. The air conditioning felt immediately wonderful.

After riding in restful silence for a time, Zack shared his thoughts. "I'll need to meet with Jimmy Chaparral and make a couple of telephone calls to see where things stand when we get there. Lenana said the pressure to get this case solved right away is coming down hard from all directions. Libby, it seems to me our next move will have to involve John Roundtree. We can settle the question of his involvement in this thing by walking Big Blue around his property. If Blue recognizes a scent there, we'll get a warrant and search the house. If he doesn't react at all, it will mean our man was never there, case closed for John. Very simple. Do you agree?"

Libby nodded.

"If Blue doesn't get a scent we have nothing. Bear Man jumps in his truck, drives past us with a smirk, and nothing we can do about it," Eagle Feather said.

Zack looked at his friend. "I guess that's true."

They all sat in silence thinking about it.

"This ranch road, it runs all the way over to connect with Highway 264, isn't that what you said?" Zack asked.

Eagle Feather nodded.

"No turnoffs other than the MacPherson Ranch, no way out until he gets to the end after what, maybe 35 miles? And isn't it pretty slow four-wheeling in some places?"

Eagle Feather nodded again.

Zack made a decision. "Let's see what FBI resources we can stir up." He spoke briefly into his cell phone, giving a series of directions and file numbers. He finished and put the phone away with quiet determination.

"That'll take a big chunk out of my budget, but it'll plug that hole," he said. "I've dispatched a helicopter from Flagstaff. It should reach the southern terminus of the MacPherson Ranch road well before that SUV can get there. All it needs to do is fly back along the road until they come to the vehicle. When they do, they'll report to us, and we'll take it from there."

Libby was smiling. "Then we've got him no matter where he goes."

"Well, don't count your chickens. If it turns out that Bear Man isn't John Roundtree or that neither of them is driving that white SUV we're still left out in the cold. But it's something to try."

When they arrived in Elk Wells they found the peaceful little town that was snoring quietly in the sun when they left in a state of turmoil. The main street looked like a Fourth of July parade, clogged with unfamiliar vehicles including several trucks with news station logos and satellite dishes on the top. They turned into an alley behind the Navajo Police station to avoid the mob but when they stepped out of the truck several reporters spotted them and surged forward and pushed microphones in their faces, firing questions. They shouldered past them and escaped into the office. Once the door had slammed shut behind them they found Lenana with her phone to her ear and sticky notes plastered all over her computer monitor. It sounded like a telethon with telephones ringing constantly and several policemen Zack didn't know speaking rapidly into them.

Lenana hung up her phone as they entered and gasped in relief. "Thank God you're finally here."

"Where are Jimmy and Lané?"

Lenana threw her hands up. "Lané is standing guard over at Monument Mesa at the trailhead to protect the crime scene from reporters. They've been crawling over every square foot of these mesas trying to find it. I don't know how many sun strokes and rattle snake bites we've sent to the Tuba City hospital already."

"And Jimmy?"

Lenana shook her head in dismay. "The Council Speaker and his entourage were here earlier. He laid it on Jimmy pretty hard. Told him it's his responsibility as the Navajo Nation Policeman in charge to settle the John Roundtree problem in the Navajo way. Right after that Jimmy picked up a shotgun and headed for Roundtree's house. That was over an hour ago. I'm worried sick."

Without a word, Eagle Feather strode over to the back wall and took down the other shotgun.

"I guess it's time now," Zack said. "Libby, you'd best go get Big Blue. We'll all take a walk up to Roundtree's house. Lenana, please call the Speaker's office and tell him we need a warrant to search the Roundtree premises, ask that he time stamp it an hour ago, scan it and send it here by email. He's the one who set all this in motion so the least he can do is make it legal."

Zack pulled out his phone and called his office. Ben answered almost immediately, his voice loud enough to be heard by everybody in the room.

"Zack, where the hell you been?"

"I've been chasing a ghost all over the mesa. We tracked the killer back to the McPherson Ranch road but lost him there. But everything's unfolding right now. Ben, this guy is tricky. He came real close to stopping me for good up on the mesa. We haven't identified him, but everyone here is convinced it's John Roundtree, that brick mason whose wife and kid died several years ago. Worse, they think he's a Skinwalker, so now the whole town is in an uproar. The Tribal Council got involved and I've just arrived here to find that Jimmy Chaparral has already gone over to the Roundtree place by himself and hasn't been heard from for more than an hour."

Zack was walking toward the door as he spoke. "I'm going over there now to back up his play. We're taking the tracking dog to either confirm or disqualify Roundtree as our suspect. We've got to move fast in case Jimmy's got himself into trouble, I'll get back to you as soon as I can...Oh, by the way, I just spent five grand on a helicopter."

Everyone heard Ben's loud protests just before Zack put away his phone. Zack looked back at Lenana. "Get some policemen to cordon off John Roundtree's house for a hundred yards in each direction. No spectators, no reporters."

Eagle Feather was waiting in the street outside the station. Libby appeared around the corner of the building with Zack's rifle, leading Big Blue. They joined up in the middle of the street and walked side by side through the center of town, people giving way, Big Blue tugging them along.

"Feels like we're headed to the O.K. Corral," Zack remarked.

"Wouldn't miss it," Libby said, laughing.

SIXTEEN

Linda spoke as deliberately and clearly as she could. "I don't know what Zack found up there on the mesa, but he learned somehow that the perpetrator was administering drugs by injection, possibly with a cactus spine. After his call I reviewed the corpse topically and found a possible entry just at the hairline. I tested it and got a positive result. I never would have found it on my own. So here's what I've got. Time of death is very approximate but it was at least 48 hours ago or could be much longer. She was drugged first, and then her neck was broken, deliberately and expertly. The large abdominal wound, as we surmised, was done postmortem to try to misdirect us. The good news is she never knew what happened. The bad news, her death was probably a relief. Indications are that she was abused for months or even years prior to her death."

Linda caught her breath. "But the real news is this: I've positively identified the drug he used as rohypnol. It's a potent tranquilizer that produces a sedative affect...amnesia, muscle relaxation, a slowing of psychomotor responses. We know it as the date-rape drug. But this is a very pure strain, an un-dilute.

Ben, this guy knew what he was doing. First, you don't find this quality of the drug on the street corner. He would have to get it imported directly from Mexico or some similarly unregulated location. He used only the un-dilute for a specific reason; he knew it wouldn't leave much trace. The victim had no physical signs from restraint, no wrist or ankle bruising, that kind of thing. I'd guess she was kept under the influence of the drug continually. Most of the time she'd probably forget the abuse...she'd forget everything, in fact, even who she was." Linda grew emotional again and stopped. "Maybe that was the good news," she added wistfully after a moment.

Ben said, "Are you telling me that an eight year old white girl found dead on a mesa in the middle of an Indian Reservation had been kept drugged for an undetermined period of time with a substance that most people can't even afford, let alone acquire?"

"That's about right."

"OK." Ben sighed. "What else?"

"As I told you, the large claw-like wound was administered post mortem."

"Yes"

"I did some more tests. I found DNA in that wound along with some dirt and wood traces. I sent the DNA to the Phoenix Lab and tested the wood samples myself which turned out to be bark from a juniper tree. Then the lab called back with preliminary DNA findings. Ben, the DNA is actually from a bear. Do bears roam around on that mesa? Could a bear have found the girl lying there and started to eat her, or something? This doesn't make sense to me."

Silence greeted Linda at the other end. "Ben? Are you there?"

"Yes, I'm here, Linda. Have you got any more surprises? I'm beginning to think Zack could be walking into more than he realizes right now."

"No, that's pretty much it. Oh, the shoes. She had moccasins on her feet...you know, like Indians wear; leather deer-hide moccasins. But the bottoms weren't worn at all, hardly even smudged, as if she had never actually walked in them. And another thing: that locket I found under the body when we moved it; it's gold, real gold, and it has a picture of man and a woman in it. I thought they might be her parents and blew up the picture and posted it on our net trying to get an ID. Nothing has come up yet. And one final thing, I found no prints, absolutely no prints at all. The perpetrator must have used gloves and wiped everything continually. Like I said, this guy knew what he was doing."

"Linda, you're a gem. I'm going to find a way to keep you assigned to us. I've got to run now. I need to call Zack right now and pass this on. If you learn anything else, anything at all...call me right away." Ben hung up.

Linda tingled with pleasure from his praise. But then she thought about spending a lot more time in Tuba City and she shuddered. Then her thoughts turned to the little girl and her eyes watered.

"I'm a mess!" she told herself. "A real mess."

Jimmy Chaparral walked slowly around the old pickup. It had been John Roundtree's work truck and it showed the years of service with dents and scrapes. One wiper was bent, the other gone entirely. Cobwebs adorned the cracked side mirrors. Both tail light lenses were smashed and the rear license plate had been bent under the truck body, its original mounting gone. The tires were worn down to the fabric in several places, the tail pipe hung almost to the ground.

Jimmy pulled open the driver side door. It creaked and snapped as it opened. Inside, the leather seats had cracks and were faded where the sun reached them. A musty smell came from the felt roof liner, which was torn and hung down in places.

But the driver's seat was clean; it did not have the fine layer of dust that the other surfaces did. Jimmy leaned around to look at the ignition. A single key was in it.

When Jimmy had first looked at the truck, he would have bet it couldn't start. But apparently it had. He reached in to move the shift stick, saw it was in neutral. Then he turned the ignition key. The engine roared into life and settled into a well-tuned throbbing hum.

He stood and looked back at the house. Nothing seemed to have changed yet he had a feeling of being watched. Nerves, he told himself. But he hitched the shotgun a little higher on his arm and leaned in and turned off the engine. Then he walked out in front of the truck and studied the drive. There was no sign in front of the pickup that it had passed that way. He walked on out to the road. No, there were no tire impressions, not in the dirt, not on the road shoulder, either. The truck hadn't come this way.

Jimmy walked back to the vehicle, keeping a weather eye on the house, thinking about it. Had John simply tuned the truck at some point, started it up, maybe tried to get it moving unsuccessfully? He looked again at the tire impressions and the flattened grass behind it and walked back from there along the drive. He saw more tire traces, slight indentations in the hard earth. Someone had attempted to conceal them. The drive paralleled the house before it turned toward the brickyard. Jimmy followed it and saw more evidence that the truck had driven this way. The impressions led him out past the brick stacks and toward the overgrown practice walls. In several places the old drive branched off to other brick stacks but the recent indentations continued right down the middle of the property and out to the open country beyond. Jimmy stopped where the brickyard ended and looked out. The old truck had gone on, out there somewhere into the vast flat lands beyond, out to anywhere that John Roundtree wanted to go.

Jimmy turned and studied the house. Roundtree must still be in there, he thought. Otherwise, where would he be? During the day a man walking out in that flat country could be seen for miles. Unless...he wasn't a man at the time. That thought came unbidden to Jimmy; he shook the image away and walked back to the rear of the house where the wind chime hung. No breeze blew now and the ornament hung limp, held there by a rusty hook. Why hadn't he noticed it when he first walked around the house? It was unusual, striking. Each of the chimes was round, three quarters of an inch long with three projecting knobs, all held by a single leather thong through the hollow center. Each tier of three chimes was separated from the next by disks made out of a cardboard-like material covered in felt. The workmanship was unusual.

Jimmy leaned in to study it closely. It came to him where he had seen something like this before but no - it couldn't be. He gasped and leapt back, nearly gagging with sudden understanding. These were not cardboard disks at all; they were small bits of scalp, little pieces of dried skin to which hair clung. And the chimes themselves, he saw now, were the bones of a very small spinal column.

The FBI driver was skilled. He wove the black Buick sedan in and out of the late afternoon Prescott, Arizona traffic effortlessly and efficiently. Ben looked at his watch and was surprised that only twenty minutes had passed since Zack's unsettling call and with it Ben's dawning realization that his own job might well be on the line. It all depended upon the outcome of the impending confrontation with John Roundtree. Ben was comfortable with Jimmy Chaparral handling the situation. Indians confronting Indians on the Reservation was normal, expected and, well, who cared, really? But Zack was a different story.

The sedan picked up speed as it turned onto Iron Springs Road and the inertia from the rapid cornering pressed Ben up against the cushioned door panel and disturbed his thoughts momentarily.

He resumed them. His concern was for the possibility of an incident. Zack, an FBI agent, worse, a white FBI agent, was walking toward a potential showdown with a Navajo man, a Shaman, a witch - that's how the media would paint it, anyway - and any reporter worth his salt would go crazy with excitement at the prospect. But Ben was pretty sure his own boss wouldn't feel uplifted at the thought.

Zack's decision surprised him. Ben knew Zack to be steady and reliable, his decisions always well considered. But now there was potential for a flash fire and Zack didn't appear to see it. The moment Ben hung up the phone he had called the Bagdad Airport just outside Prescott and ordered the Agency's helicopter readied for immediate takeoff. That was followed by the call for a driver to get him there. If his career was going to go up in smoke he planned to be calling the shots when it happened!

The front right tire of the big van slammed into another pothole, and there was the sound of something heavy falling on the metal floor in back.

A holler came from Pete, the cameraman, hanging on for his life in the rear seat. "Hey, slow down up there. Where's the fire?"

"I don't know if there's a fire," Melissa yelled back, "but my gut tells me something big is about to happen in that little Indian village. We need to be in Elk Wells yesterday." She jerked the wheel to avoid a large chunk of loose pavement. "I've felt like this before and I know not to ignore it."

Art never doubted her for her instincts were uncanny. He'd seen her go off in pursuit of obscure story angles that were ignored by everybody else, had seen her race off in what seemed a wrong direction only to end up with the real story in the end, the one that everyone else missed. Art had quickly learned that when everyone turned right and Melissa turned left he should follow Melissa if he wanted to become a top-notch reporter. Which he did.

Art heard Pete grumble behind him and a click as he released himself from the security of the seat belt to recover the fallen piece of equipment in the lurching van. Art didn't know what to expect to find in Elk Wells and he was pretty sure Melissa didn't know either, but if she felt they needed to be there as soon as possible, he was fine with that.

By now a curious crowd of Elk Spring residents, reporters, and the curious were bunched behind Zack and his companions, whispering and laughing nervously and following like a herd of cows headed to the barn, all advancing toward Roundtree's house.

When Zack's cell phone rang he looked at the number and decided to ignore it. They were close now. He would call Ben back later.

By now Jimmy had been alone at the Roundtree's house almost two hours. Zack wondered what could be keeping him there. As they walked along he went over possibilities in his mind, thinking about all the events that had brought them here. Even now he couldn't bring himself to believe that John Roundtree had killed the little girl and left her up there on the mesa, nor did he believe that Roundtree was a witch. Yet somehow since that call that sent him up to the mesa yesterday morning, a series of events had brought him to this time and place, walking along this road toward the setting sun, adrenaline surging through his body, curious and fearful town citizens crowded behind him, just minutes away from a confrontation with this man John Roundtree, a man he knew only by name and reputation. Zack had a feeling that the next few minutes might require every ounce of his training, his experience, and his best instincts.

SEVENTEEN

The office door creaked slowly open and Lenana looked up, prepared to launch into her prescribed announcement for reporters but was instead pleased to see her friend Katie. Her normally jovial countenance was absent though; Lenana realized that Kate had not come for a social call. The office was deserted. Every reporter and most of the townspeople had followed the FBI agent and his friends to the Roundtree place, so Lenana probed.

"Something on your mind, Katie?"

Kate took the empty chair next to Lenana's desk. She sat down and at once her face crumpled, then tears welled over. "I'm so sorry, Lenana," she blurted.

"Sorry for what?"

"You told me to be careful whom I spoke to about...you know...about John Roundtree and Skinwalkers and all that..."

Lenana felt a pang of apprehension but maintained her encouraging smile.

Kate peered at her through wet eyes. "We were just sitting there talking, some of the regular folks there in the café, and this man came in and he sat down with us, and" -a quick sob- "he seemed like he knew everyone and just naturally joined us in our chat. I didn't know who he was but everyone just kind a kept going, you know? Talking about things, and then someone mentioned something about the Skinwalker and this man just kind a nodded like he already knew all about it and then someone else said they were sure it was John Roundtree and the conversation went on and it wasn't until the man got up and left that anybody said, like, who was that?"

Katie paused to wipe away a tear.

Lenana waited, feeling her insides clench.

"Lenana, we're best friends and I don't ever want to do anything to disappoint you or make you unhappy, but now I've gone and done it."

Lenana reached for Katie's hand. "There, Kate. We don't know anything about this person. He's probably just a passing cowhand, just one more curious person."

"Oh, no, that's not who he was." Katie swallowed pitifully. "He was someone else. He called me later on the phone and said he was an investigative reporter and he worked with Melissa Mann, the lady who does the news on Channel Four. Now they want to interview me on TV tonight. They want to ask me questions about John Roundtree and about Skinwalkers." Katie peeked up at Lenana through wet lashes. "They're coming here tonight, right now. They plan to meet me right outside in the street." Katie sniffled. "Oh, Lenana, I just don't know what I should do."

As Lenana patted her friend's hand, she thought, Oh, great, the timing couldn't be worse. John Roundtree is about to become a macabre villain to the public whether he had anything to do with this murder or not.

Aloud, she said, "Don't fret about it, Katie. Believe me, there're no secrets around here any more. Every reporter from Flagstaff to Phoenix knows what's going on. Half of 'em are on their way to John Roundtree's house right now. Go ahead and do the interview, if that's what you want. But only say what you know, not what you think you know." Lenana's look was stern. "And remember who you are," she lectured. "We are of the Navajo, the Diné, 'The People', and our rituals and our beliefs are what make us who we are. Tell them what you know to be true and tell it with dignity and pride. If you do that, you can't be wrong."

"Oh, Lenana, you are exactly right, you always are. I'm so sorry for my carelessness. I knew I could turn to you."

Lenana smiled back at her friend but in her heart she knew that this interview would probably not go well. Her dear but naive friend would be no match for Melissa Mann with all of her leading questions and insinuations. The experienced reporter would undoubtedly lead her to say something she, and the entire community, would regret. All Lenana could do was hope for the sake of her friend that the subject of Katie's interview would be old news by the time Melissa and her team arrived in Elk Wells.

Maybe, she thought hopefully, the interview won't even take place.

Jim Chaparral was standing next to the old pickup truck when his friends arrived. He walked over to them and they gathered there in the middle of the street for an impromptu reunion. The crowd behind them was smaller now; the long walk had taken its toll. Some had drifted away when the Roundtree home, dark and silent, came into view, having decided nothing much was going to happen. Those who remained stood clustered together, talking quietly among themselves.

Jimmy cut right to the chase. "He won't come to the door but I think he's in there."

They all looked at the house; its vacant staring windows appeared sunken and dark in contrast to the walls reflecting the slanting sun.

"I think Blue picked up a scent just now," Libby said. Everyone's tension went up a notch. "He's anxious to go take a look. Maybe we should let him sniff around before we do anything else."

Zack stared at the house, drawn by it. It felt like a living thing. He turned back to the others. "We need to link Bear Man to John Roundtree first. If we can't do that, we've got no business here."

Eagle Feather stroked the dog's head. He asked, without looking up, "How will you know what scents Blue picks up?"

"He knows to focus on the last scent I present to him," Libby explained, "which was Bear Man. Until we formally introduce another scent he'll look for the last one."

Zack made his decision. "Libby, you take Blue around the perimeter of the property. Start over there by the pickup truck, the most likely spot, and take him down the drive and across to the back and on around to the road on the far side. If Bear Man is here, he would have to have crossed that perimeter...unless he flew, of course."

Eagle Feather didn't look up. Zack gave a tight grin anyway and turned to Jim. "Is there a rear door to the house?"

Jim nodded.

"You keep an eye on that door, then. If anybody tries to come out while Blue is working, fire a warning shot in the air to warn us and keep him inside. I'll keep an eye out here at the front."

They started to move but Jimmy stopped them.

"Before we start, I better tell you a couple of things. First, that old pickup truck over there has moved recently, not out here to the road but back the other way to the brickyard and beyond somewhere. Second, when I was at the door I smelled a sweet rotten odor, like something had died. I don't know where it came from, inside or out - could've been just a dead gopher under the house. The last thing and its the worst of all; around back there's a wind chime hanging from a hook. I heard it when I was doing my walk around so I went have a closer look." Jimmy paused for a second, wondering how to say it, then blurted, "I believe it's made from the body parts of a child."

They looked at him in disbelief.

"I know, I know. I didn't realize it at first, but something made me look closer. It's made of bits of bone and what looks like scalp. What I'm saying is, we need to move carefully here."

They all stared at him. Then Zack broke the spell.

"We need to be extra alert. Eagle Feather, stay with Libby when she walks Blue around. Everybody protect yourselves, look out for one another." Zack was thinking particularly about Libby. "If anything happens, just get out of there," he ordered her.

They went to do their assigned tasks. Libby led Blue toward the truck and Eagle Feather walked with her. Jimmy went to the ruined patio out behind the house. Zack watched them go, their shadow caricatures following behind them like dark spirits.

When Blue reached the truck he picked up a scent right away and whined and tugged Libby around the truck. Eagle Feather knelt to look at something on the ground. Blue pulled Libby to the rear of the house where he tried to go off in several directions but Libby tugged him back on route and moved on until she'd circled the house. There was no sign from anyone in the house the entire time.

Everyone returned and they stood quietly in the roadway. No one had to be told that Bear Man's scent was all over the property.

"I found a barefoot imprint in three different places in the back yard," Eagle Feather said. "The same print we followed on the mesa."

"Not a peep from the house," Jimmy said.

Zack sighed. "I guess we'd better take a look inside. We've got all the evidence we need to make a search."

Zack took Libby gently by the arm, speaking in a low voice.

"You take Blue a safe distance away from here. He's a valuable witness and we need to protect him."

He grinned as he watched her walk away. She would have protested had he not said it was the dog he wanted to protect from danger. But Zack was more concerned about Libby.

He turned to the others. "Jimmy, can you get some of those policemen over there to back us up? Then you and another officer will take the back door; Eagle Feather will come with me the front way. We'll try to reason with Roundtree first; we'll give this every chance."

They turned to take up their positions. Tension surrounded them like the charged air before an electric storm.

All of a sudden a large van hurtled toward them out of the shimmering curtain of light that was the setting sun. It skidded to a halt next to them. It had a large satellite dish on top and the Channel Four TV logo painted on its side. Immediately the driver's door flung open and Melissa Mann leapt out and strode toward them.

"What's going on, boys?" she asked, softening her demanding tone with a coquettish smile.

Zack didn't hesitate but motioned to the nearest policeman. His eyes were cold and his voice was hard. "This is a poor time, Miss. I need you to drive your van over by that crowd and stay there. This officer will see that you do."

"There's danger, yes?? Is someone trapped in the house? Can I quote you? What name shall I attribute to it?"

Zack started to turn away and now looked back.

"That's not a quote, that's an order. You're not in Kansas anymore; you're on the Reservation. This police officer can remove you at will, Fifth Estate or not." Zack looked at the policeman. "Please see that this woman and her van follow my instructions precisely and immediately. If they do not, please escort them off the Reservation."

The policeman took Melissa by her elbow and politely steered her back to the open van door, despite her protests.

Art listened to this exchange from the far side of the van where he gathered up his equipment. He paused, aware in that moment of an unexpected opportunity, an opportunity that Melissa herself would never have missed. He snuck a glance from behind the van, saw the small group had their backs to him and couldn't know he was there. Acting on pure impulse, he sprinted across the road and into the thicket on the far side. Once he was hidden from view, he took stock of his situation. He had a mini tape recorder in his pocket and a small digital camera hanging from his neck.

Art watched the van drive slowly away a few minutes later and he knew that Melissa understood what he had done. She drove away at just the right moment to cover his absence. Art felt a swell of pride. Melissa's actions were a statement that she would rely on him to get the story.

Zack glanced at the sun sinking ever closer to the horizon and chafed at the delays. It seemed to take forever to organize for their approach to the house. He called Lenana on his cell phone while he waited. "Where do we stand with a search warrant?" he asked.

"All set," Lenana snapped, business-like. "The Speaker just called. He authorized it and timed it to suit your needs. It's an open warrant."

"Good work, Lenana. Stay close to the phone, we might need you at any time."

Zack rang off, resolute and ready for action. He spoke quietly into his radio. "All set in back?"

"All set," came the whispered reply.

"Okay, we're going to go announce ourselves. Don't enter the house until you hear us go in."

"Ten-four."

Zack followed Eagle Feather along Roundtree's front walk toward the house, their heels sounding dully on the concrete slabs. Their weapons were held low but ready. Zack's eyes flicked across the front of the house, noting details, watching for any movement, any shadow beyond the dirty windowpanes. The sun glowed like embers off the glass and shadows framed the door. Zack's adrenaline surged once more, his nerves signaled his readiness; he felt confident. I'm the one in control now, he thought to himself. I'm coming for him this time, not the other way around.

The front door was wood, solid and thick. Zack responded to Eagle Feather's questioning look with a nod, then Eagle Feather knocked on the door three times loudly.

"John Roundtree, this is Eagle Feather. You know me, born of

Feather People, born to Salt people, of the Bead People and Many Goats Clan. Come to the door and do not leave a tribesman to wait at your entrance way."

He paused; the silence reached out. He tried again.

"John Roundtree, I am here to speak with you on a matter that can not wait. Policemen and a federal agent are here with me. They must question you. But it is I, Eagle Feather, who asks to speak to you now."

Zack had been studying the door. It appeared to be supported on two large hinges and fastened with a modern locking mechanism. He thought they might break it in with a strong blow on the latch side but if there was a slide bar of any size it could be difficult. He listened to Eagle Feather try again and hoped he would be successful this time.

Eagle Feather went on in the same calm measured tones. "John, you and I are Diné. It is customary and respectful to speak of difficult matters first among Navajo before speaking of it to others. You should speak to me now. You should let me into your home so that we can speak together as brothers." He waited a moment. "If you do not do this now, the policemen and the federal agent will enter your home by force. You will feel disrespected and this will cause anger and hostility. That is not the way to deal with these matters."

After another long silence, Zack nodded to Eagle Feather. It was time. He motioned for him to stand back as he traced his fingers along the wood above the keyhole, feeling for any indication of a slide bar. Finding none he backed up several steps and prepared to launch himself at the door. But before he could move Eagle Feather reached forward and turned the doorknob. The door opened easily.

"On the reservation we do not lock our doors," Eagle Feather said.

Ben rechecked his watch. It was well over an hour since he made the hasty decision to fly to the Reservation and take charge of the unfolding events at the house of John Roundtree. The rush hour streets of Prescott had not been a problem for his excellent driver but the situation was different at the Bagdad Airport where he found the crew slow to respond to his needs. He paced impatiently outside the open hanger door and watched them uncover and untether the helicopter and then fuel it. The pilot had to be found and pulled away from his dinner in the airport restaurant. It actually took longer to get airborne than it had to drive through the rush hour traffic to get there.

It suddenly crossed Ben's mind that if he arrived late to take charge of an already out of control situation it would be worse for his career than if he had stayed away altogether, and who knew how the people over in Phoenix might react?

The roar of the whirling blades above him almost drowned out his thoughts. When the helicopter banked abruptly to the right, forcing him to hold on, he wondered again if the pilot's annoyance with him might be causing this flight to be less comfortable than necessary. The aircraft leveled off and Ben went back to his thoughts. He should give the man his due. After all, when had Zack ever let him down? So why was he here, rushing headlong to the scene?

Because the situation was just too volatile, he answered himself, because no matter how it was resolved, he would be needed and he would be expected. The up side? That by the time he arrived Zack might well have handled everything in his typically patient, thoughtful and efficient manner, all wrapped up for Ben to be there and accept the accolades of his superiors. He hoped fervently for that outcome. His time at the agency was growing very short and his retirement package, assuming a nice uneventful conclusion to his career, was more than ample. And then if he topped off his career with the successful conclusion to a difficult and potentially damaging case, it might well mean a substantial bonus.

Ben looked at his watch yet again. How could such a short flight take so long?

EIGHTEEN

Melissa eased the van to the shoulder of the road just beyond the crowd of onlookers and parked it under the watchful eye of the policeman perched on the passenger seat. She had allowed herself to be uncharacteristically submissive, following his instructions meekly, and now she waited with outward calm while the man to climbed out and chatted with a fellow policeman for a few moments before he finally turned and walked back toward the Roundtree house.

She climbed out to mingle with the crowd, to listen to their conversations with one ear while at the same time keeping an eye on the action over at the house. Much of the talk around her was in Navajo and lost upon her but every now and again she picked up an English phrase and zeroed in on it. She left Pete setting up the big camera and tripod in the van for the interview she hoped would still happen. She wondered that no one seemed to recognize her. The van itself should have stirred curiosity; someone in this crowd must occasionally watch Channel Four News! Time to try something else. Melissa shook out her blonde hair and fixed her famous smile on her face and went to stand by the logo on the side of the van and wait. She didn't wait long. A woman approached her almost right away; shy, hesitant, yet purposeful.

"Are you Melissa Mann from Channel Four News?" she asked.

Right on cue. The woman looked to be around forty, round-faced, her brow now furrowed with a mix of anxiety and determination.

"Yes, I am." Melissa lit her brightest bulb of a smile. "I'm surprised you were able to recognize me off camera."

"Oh, no, you are just as beautiful in real life. I saw it was you right away!" the woman gushed.

"What is your name, might I ask?"

"I am Kate Smith. I run a café back in town." The woman rambled on quickly, nervously. "I came over to you because...I'm sorry...but a man named Art said he was from your news station and he called me to ask me to do an interview when you came to town. But I don't see him here anywhere, so I wondered...do you do still want me? I mean, for the interview and all?"

Melissa could see the eagerness in the woman's eyes and thought to herself, Art, you little miracle worker. She looked solemnly back at Kate.

"Well, we could do that, but the person I interview must be just the right sort of person. I'd need to ask you a few questions first, just to see, okay?"

Katie blurted out, "Oh yes, of course."

"Well then, let's get started. How long have you lived here...in this town, here on the Navajo Reservation?"

"All my life, and my parents before me. In fact-"

"Just answer the questions simply and directly," Melissa admonished with a gentle smile. "That's very important in interviews."

"Oh, I see. I'll do better."

"That's fine. Now, who lives in the house that the policemen have surrounded?"

"That's John Roundtree's house."

"And why are they there?"

"They believe that Mr. Roundtree may have had something to do with that little girl who was murdered up on Monument Mesa."

"Oh, up on Monument Mesa," repeated Melissa, inwardly delighted to have her guess confirmed. "And why do the policemen suspect Mr. Roundtree?"

"Everyone on the reservation thinks John had something to do with it. Even the Speaker said-"

"The Speaker?"

"Oh, the Speaker of the Tribal Council. He is one of the most important men on the Reservation. He believes that John Roundtree used his powers to kill that little girl and then leave her there on the mesa. It is the Speaker who insisted that the police go arrest John Roundtree."

"I see," said Melissa thoughtfully. "And the powers you speak of - what kind of powers are they, exactly?"

Katie looked momentarily confused. "We people...we Navajo people...our religion accepts that spirits are all around us, real spirits with real powers. We believe that some people can gain some of these powers and, well, are then able to do things that they otherwise couldn't do. Some people think John Roundtree is one of those people."

"What was it he became?" gently coaxed Melissa. "Is there a name for it?"

"Well, it doesn't translate well, but we call it a Yee Naaldlooshii, a wicked spell master, and he might even have gained the powers of a" - Kate's voice dropped to a whisper at the words- "Skinwalker."

Melissa let her breath out slowly. "A Skinwalker? What is that?" she asked quietly but persuasively.

Kate looked around before replying. "It's never good to speak of such things in the open." She was clearly reluctant.

"Okay, I understand," Melissa said. "I want nothing more than to respect your beliefs and your culture. Let me see...how's this? I think you might be just the person for our interview. We could go into the van and tape it right now. It will only take a few minutes and we can talk in the privacy of the van and everything will be on tape so that you can watch it. If any part of it makes you uncomfortable, well, we can just erase it. What do you think?"

Katie agreed. Melissa took her by the elbow and led her into the van. She hated to take her eye away from the house but she hoped that the usually ponderous police action would run true to form here and develop slowly enough that she would not miss anything. Besides, she had Art in the field to cover it. This woman's interview on tape was critical to the angle she planned to work for her story.

Inside the trailer she applied makeup to a very excited Katie, and surreptitiously texted Art: *Where r u? Can u c?*

The reply came quickly: *Good view waiting yes.*

She typed: *Use ears low vox.*

OK, came the reply.

Melissa turned back to Kate. "Now, my dear, are we ready to become a television star?"

NINETEEN

A sickly sweet decay smell filled Zack's nose as soon as he stepped into the house. Eagle Feather followed and reacted to the odor with a squinched his nose. Zack held his rifle at the ready in front of him. The air in the dark entryway was thick and tomblike, as if it had been left undisturbed for centuries. By the light from the open door he saw that a thin coating of red-brown dust covered the untracked floor.

Eagle Feather noticed it too. "He doesn't use this much," he whispered.

A door blocked their way to the right. They stood facing a solid brick wall - a Roundtree wall? - sparsely decorated with one small mirror and a candle sconce. To the left a hallway extended the entire length of the wall to an archway on the right apparently leading to the interior. The tunnel-like hall and archway beyond were dim, lacking natural light.

There was no sound from inside the house. Zack made a twisting motion with his hand for Eagle Feather to try the door to his right and watched him reach for the knob and slowly twist. It wouldn't give. Eagle Feather shrugged. Locked. Zack turned and moved cautiously the other way down the hall, toward the archway. The floorboards creaked and groaned alarmingly. He waited for Eagle Feather, holding his rifle up and ready, standing flat against the wall.

Then he called out, "John! John Roundtree! I'm a federal agent and I'm here with Eagle Feather to talk to you. We mean you no harm. I have a warrant from the Tribal Council to search your home. I'm coming in. Please show yourself."

They waited, listened. There was no reply. Zack crouched low, his rifle in front of him, and in one fluid motion slipped through the arch, his back against the wall. He was in a room illuminated only by fading daylight filtering in through a single dirty window. Now the sick-sweet smell was overpowering.

Zack was in a living room, a large overstuffed chair next to him and two wood frame chairs across from him on either side of a small lamp table. His eyes adjusted slowly to the semi-darkness and then he could see the shape of a figure in one of the chairs facing toward him, cloaked in deep shadow. A ray of filtered light from the dusky window glinted on a shiny cylindrical object, a gun barrel, he realized, the barrel of a large Colt 45 pistol. It was aimed directly at him.

Art listened from behind his bush. The Indian man with the shotgun called to the house in his own language and Art guessed they were attempting to coax the person inside to come out. He remembered his conversation with the woman in the café, about the Skinwalkers and the powers that the Navajo believed these creatures possessed. Crouched behind the scant protection of this spiny bush in the growing dusk, he admitted to himself that he felt just a bit creepy. Art was a novice in his trade, but already he understood that reality was less important to people than what they believed to be real, and those who believed in creatures that go bump in the night might not always act the way you expect, and the most unpredictable of all were the people who believed they were some kind of supernatural being. Those cases never went well.

His musings were interrupted when the men in the doorway suddenly pushed their way into the house. Art tensed. He stared at the house, waiting for the next sound, expecting any moment to hear the percussive hollow snap of gunfire. Out of the corner of his eye he saw the policemen at the rear of the house edge closer.

Then a sudden voice in his earpiece gave him a start. He realized it was Melissa going live now with her interview. *What a masterpiece!* he thought, filled with admiration at her intuitive timing. Right at the precise moment of a dramatic confrontation between law enforcement and an alleged Navajo Skinwalker Melissa contrived to be on the air live with a Navajo woman telling the world that she believed in such creatures. He shook his head at her genius.

But he must do his part; he must pay attention, stay alert. He kept his vigil at the house and listened to Melissa ask her first question.

Zack crouched back against the wall, frozen. He stared hard at the glint of the gun barrel trained on him, desperate to adjust his eyes to the dark, to see any detail of the unmoving figure behind the gun. Frantic thoughts raced through his mind, all the while knowing he was too late, knowing even as he brought his rifle up that it was useless, a desperate attempt, that the big pistol barrel aimed at him would erupt in flame, would send a bullet slamming into him before he had a chance to fire. He felt Eagle Feather's presence behind him in that split second and heard the shotgun cock but Eagle Feather would be too late. They were both too late. Everything slowed, time crystallized in the face of eternity, Zack's rifle barrel took a lifetime to travel the short upward arc, took long enough for entire dialogues to take place in his mind, time enough for him to sense now that things were not as they appeared, to somehow understand that the pistol aimed at him would not fire, that the shadowy figure holding the gun was no longer able to pull the trigger.

In that moment of understanding Zack released his finger from the trigger and his other hand flew up to halt Eagle Feather. Both men held their respective positions, guns poised, breathing heavily, staring hard at the ambiguous, shadowy figure that threatened them from across the room.

A full minute crawled by. Zack's arm remained up, his rifle trained on the mysterious figure. Then he slowly rose from his crouch and stepped leg-over, crablike along the wall. He breathed slowly, watching intently. The barrel of the Colt remained pointed at the archway behind him. Zack came to the dirt-stained, cracked window where now a globe of suffused light, glowing red-orange from the setting sun burst out in radiance like an open oven door. Its rays cast Zack's rifle barrel on the opposite wall like a cartoon shadow figure. But the window's light failed to reach the enigmatic figure cloaked by darkness, silent, still.

Zack took one cautious step across the floor toward the figure. At once the air thickened, the smell of decay came in a powerful cloud and flooded his nostrils and now he was overcome by a pervasive feeling of helplessness, that same overwhelming sense of hopelessness he had known the night before in the darkness of his camp. Within the thickest shadow in the lap of the silent figure something moved, something writhed and twisted and Zack saw two tiny glowing red eyes, hating, evil, and then the barrel of the pistol swung toward him with impossible speed.

"Would you tell us please; what, exactly, is a Skinwalker?" Art listened through his earpiece to Melissa pose the question all the while keeping his attention trained on the Roundtree house. He smiled to himself listening to the stumbling explanation going live to viewers throughout the tri-state area. He saw in his mind's eye the families around their dinner tables, leaning toward their TV sets, listening as the simply stated yet somehow terrifying description came so authentically from the unpretentious Navajo woman.

It suddenly came to Art that Kate didn't know she was live. She must have been led to believe they were taping this session. She was letting it all flow, groping occasionally for words, not worrying about syntax or proper sentence use; she sounded very relaxed. The result was wonderfully natural and very real. Art smiled again in admiration of Melissa's artful technique.

When he looked back toward the rear of the house he realized he could no longer see the two policemen. He hadn't seen them move but if he couldn't see them it meant they couldn't see him. Apparently they had moved closer to the house when his attention was divided. His own position was too far away, he decided. He couldn't hear or see from here. He needed to be closer, maybe up under that window. He would hear and see best from there if there was any action. The time to demonstrate his abilities, he thought, was right now.

Art rose to his feet and in a crouching run moved shadow-like across the crisp dry lawn and up to the side of the house, directly under the window.

The sun had nearly set. Far below, long shadows reached across the land and devoured its features. Objects were increasingly difficult to identify. The helicopter followed the narrow ribbon of road that ran straight as an arrow toward Elk Wells. And then, there they were, the first buildings of the town, etched dark against the lighter background of the earth, tiny lights glowing. Closer, they saw a single round-topped building. In the roadway nearby an indistinct dark blotch became a crowd of people. Ben saw several tiny pinpoints of light flickering here and there, probably flashlights.

"There - right there," he commanded. "That's the house. Put us right over it."

The pilot instantly changed direction and brought the helicopter to hover low over the building. Ben took a good look. Below him the people in the roadway all faced the house. He made out two shadowy figures near the rear door and another close to the side of the house.

Too late, Ben thought, I'm too late. They're going in.

He shouted to the pilot over the noise of the rotors. "Bring us lower. I need to see the men by the house."

The pilot nodded and brought them down to a hundred feet. Ben reached for the searchlight controls and sent the bright probing beam into the side yard, then moved it slowly toward the building. It illuminated a man crouched next to the house, holding a camera in his hands, bringing it up to the window.

"Reporters." Ben groaned in disgust. "Just what we don't need." He grabbed the radio handset, flipped a lever, and spoke into the microphone. "You! By the house! We are federal agents. Back away from the house. Lie flat on the ground and spread your arms and legs. Do it now!"

In an instant the man leapt to his feet and flung the camera into the air. He dropped straight over backwards onto the ground, both hands above his head.

"That's one hell of a response," the pilot remarked.

"I'm next to the house now, right under the window."

Melissa heard him in her ear, sounding breathless. He must have run pretty hard to get there, she thought.

She kept her encouraging smile for Katie. "You are saying that the people around here believe John Roundtree became a Skinwalker after he lost his wife and child?" she pushed gently.

"Yes," Katie replied. "He hardly ever showed himself after that. And when he did, it looked like he never washed himself and his clothes looked crumpled and he had a wild look in his eyes."

Melissa tried not to let Art's harsh breathing distract her as she went on with the interview. But she began to wonder if Art might be nervous, maybe even frightened. She was framing her next question when they heard the throbbing drone of a helicopter approaching. She was unsure if she was hearing it from outside the van or if it was coming from her earpiece. It grew louder until it seemed to vibrate the van itself. Katie looked around nervously. Then an authoritative voice sounded through an amplified speaker. "We are federal agents".

Had they discovered Art? They seemed to be ordering him away.

Then she heard the percussive but strangely distant sound of gunfire. It sounded like several guns firing at the same time, one a sharp crack, then a boom, and then a deeper boom. In her earpiece she heard the sound of breaking glass. Then she heard a scream, terrifying, loud, and desperate.

Kate too heard the scream issuing out of Melissa's tiny earpiece, tinny and small, but horrifying all the same. In the sudden silence that followed it seemed to echo on and on. The women stared at each other, stunned, frozen in a side-by-side open-mouthed tableau while the camera filmed on.

TWENTY

Zack knew he must act instantly to save his life. The hypnotic red eyes conveyed an intent he couldn't mistake. A primal instinct now directed his movements. It required only a millisecond to move the rifle to aim it directly at the eyes and tug the trigger. His brain gave the order but his muscles wouldn't respond. His finger on the trigger would not move. Then he heard a rattlesnake's loud dry whir and helplessly watched the barrel of the Colt move toward him with increasing speed and point directly at him. Behind him he heard Eagle Feather yell "snake!" and the shotgun roared but at the same moment the big barrel of the Colt belched a long tongue of flame that seemed to reach out to him. Then the spell that held him was gone and he pulled the trigger and the rifle bucked in his hand. At first he thought it was the rifle's recoil that spun him backward off his feet but almost immediately he knew it was the impact of the forty-five-caliber slug punching into his shoulder. He was falling backward in a slow-motion dream. He watched the tiny red eyes launch toward him and he was still falling and then the thick writhing serpent body was passing over him. In the dream his head turned and followed the flight of the huge snake, its grotesque image searing into his brain, the snake's underbody a shimmery white as it twisted and turned above him before smashing into and through the window in a shower of glass. The pale underbody glowed for a moment reflecting a bright light, then was gone. Then there came a scream, terrifying and soul wrenching from somewhere beyond the shattered window. His dream ended when Zack landed hard on his back and his head slammed against the wood floor. He lay stunned, momentarily unable to move, his left shoulder and arm helpless, his right hand still gripping his rifle.

Then Eagle Feather was there, his shotgun smoking, looking out of the shattered window, and then turning back toward the figure in the chair. Zack struggled to rise, to aim his rifle at the menacing figure but Eagle Feather turned to him and told him to stay still, it was okay, it was all over now, done.

Eagle Feather wasn't joking now. He kept repeating Navajo words to himself as he worked. Then other men came into the room, lights came on and Jimmy Chaparral came over to Zack to check on him, encourage him; then he went over to examine the figure in the chair and remove the Colt revolver from his lap.

Zack found he could rise to a sitting position and for the first time he got a good look at John Roundtree, dead in his chair. His torso was blown open by Zack's rifle slug and both barrels of the shotgun. Now he slumped with his head down looking like any middle-aged man dozing in his chair except for the hole in his chest. Zack felt no dread now. There was no more of the cloying fear that the red eyes had brought. He stared curiously at John Roundtree's body. Then a wave of pain swept into his shoulder. At the same time he remembered the snake and felt an overwhelming sense of urgency.

"The snake," he said. "We've got to find that snake."

It took Melissa only a moment to recover. She reached for the camera on its tripod and rotated the lens from Kate's shocked face around to her own. Her fixed smile smoothed into an expression of serious concern.

"We are following the developing story here on the Navajo Indian Reservation as the police action in Elk Wells continues. Reports from our reporter at large indicate that events are unfolding rapidly at the John Roundtree residence where police and FBI agents are believed to have a child murderer surrounded. We are going live to the scene right now."

Melissa switched the feed from the interview camera to a remote and handed it to Pete. She beckoned him to follow her, ordering the still stunned Katie to wait inside the trailer. A helicopter moved low over the road and the crowd dispersed, running in all directions. Pete started to run with the camera toward the Roundtree house with Melissa right behind him. She noticed that the camera was on. Pete had forgotten he was live and was filming the road surface and his own feet as he ran. Even better, Melissa thought. Her confidence was returning. This will introduce the right sense of urgency. She caught up with Pete in front of the house. Darkness surrounded it but light and moving shadows could be seen within. Policemen were holding back curious bystanders.

"Art was at the other side of the house," Melissa said. She tugged at Pete's windbreaker. They walked swiftly along the road beyond the police to the far side of the house. Then they angled stealthily into the side yard. Darkness concealed them. Melissa's penlight eased their way along the far edge of the side yard. A bright pool of light was spilling through the broken window where glass shards twinkled at its edge. Vague cabalistic figures of men moved about inside and they could hear the low murmur of voices.

They inched closer to the house. Then Melissa kicked something, something hard. She looked at her feet. It was a camera, Art's camera. She reached down for it. It was then she saw Art, on his back, unmoving, his mouth agape, face frozen in a look of terror. Melissa gasped. She knelt and shook him by the shoulder and called to him. There was no response. Even as she tried to find a pulse she knew it was useless. Art was dead. But had to try. Damn, she thought, how does this CPR thing go again? She knelt at his side and pushed frantically on his chest, counting aloud, trying to remember the number of compressions and the number of breaths. She looked frantically up to Pete for help. Then she saw that the red camera light was off. Pete had stopped filming.

"Don't stop. Why did you stop?" she demanded.

"Its no good," Pete said. "I tried, but the studio cut away. They won't show this. We'll have to edit the pieces later."

Shadowy figures of men were emerging from the house. One came toward them.

"I think he's dead," Melissa said to him, contritely.

Events unfolded quickly after Ben ordered the reporter away from the house. They could see the man on his back, a cookie cutter figure in the center of the bright searchlight. The men who had been at the rear door were gone, now inside. The men on the roadway in front had surged forward, a simultaneous action as if timed to Ben's amplified command.

"We've got to set this bird down now!" Ben said. It took all of his restraint to keep from reaching for the controls. "Find somewhere to land, quickly."

"It'll have to be the road surface beyond that crowd. I can't risk setting down anywhere I can't see surface features."

"Just do it quickly." With luck, Ben thought, he might be just in time to make a quick assessment before assuming leadership. Judging from the actions of the men below, they believed they had their man. This could work out after all, could actually be the break he needed. The helicopter searchlight probed the road out beyond the scattered crowd. As it move in that direction Ben spoke through the loud speaker.

"Please move away from this area. The helicopter is landing; I repeat, the helicopter is landing." Ben was out the door before the helicopter had completely settled onto the roadway. "Wait here," he ordered the pilot, then turned and ran toward the house.

Melissa recognized the officer looking down at her as Lieutenant Jim Chaparral of the Navajo Nation Police. The man kneeled and reached past her to check for a pulse at the carotid artery, then leaned in and put his cheek close Art's mouth. He gave a negative shake of his head. Standing, he spoke into his shoulder radio. "Lenana, we've got a civilian down, no pulse, no breath, CPR ongoing. We need an EMT at the Roundtree house."

She asked the nature of the injury.

"Unknown," Jimmy said.

Melissa studied the man. Officer Chaparral had reacted professionally but her reporter instincts told her that something other than an injured reporter had brought him out of the house. She had watched his eyes dart here and there around the yard as he spoke. Maybe he didn't know about Art when he first came out. Maybe we diverted him from his original purpose.

He was looking down at her. "That's good work, Miss. Keep that CPR going. Sometimes even when it seems past hope they come around."

Melissa continued the compressions. Lieutenant Chaparral walked to the window and studied the ground beneath it by flashlight. Then he moved slowly across the yard all the way to the thicker growth and shone his light here and there. He walked slowly back to them.

"Lose something?" Melissa asked.

Jim looked at her. "Seems someone was hiding in the brush over there for a while and then ran over here toward the house. Maybe it was your man." He looked at Art. "Was that your plan?"

"There was no plan." Melissa was demure.

Jim ignored her reply. "Well, if that was the plan it got him killed." Then he noticed Art's camera on the ground. "Is that his camera?" he asked. "We'll need it as evidence."

Melissa began to protest, but Jimmy had already scooped it up and slipped it into his pocket.

Two men in rescue jackets with emergency equipment and a collapsible stretcher came running across the yard. The first EMT moved Melissa gently aside and tried a resuscitator. But soon he shook his head. "I'm afraid he's gone," he said. Then he asked, "Anyone here know the cause of death?"

Melissa and Pete looked at each other in surprise. They suddenly realized they had no idea how Art had died.

"You might consider snake bite," Lieutenant Chaparral said. Everyone looked at him in surprise. He looked at the EMTs and nodded his head toward the house. "We could use you inside. We have a gun shot wound needs looking after."

Zack stood unsteady on his feet looking down at the body of John Roundtree. Jimmy Chaparral came back into the room and over to him.

"Look at this," Zack pointed at Roundtree's face. "Look at that thick dark hair. What do you make of that?"

"Some Navajo men have beards," Jimmy ventured, not sounding convinced.

"Like this?" Zack lifted a long thick thatch of it with his index finger. "And how about this?" He pointed out more hair, thick and dark on Roundtree's forearms.

Eagle Feather was back from inspecting the window. "There's no blood on those glass shards that I can find." He shook his head. "You'd think such a large snake smashing through a glass window would get cut."

He saw Zack inspecting the unnatural hair growth on Roundtree's arm. Then he grinned. "Starting to think a bit differently about things yet?"

Zack ignored the jibe and asked Jimmy Chaparral, "Did you find the snake?"

"No, but I can guess where it went. It came down right on top of a reporter who'd been sneaking up to the window. The man's dead, probably got bit. After that the snake must have crawled straight across the yard. Beyond there, it could have gone anywhere."

Zack thought about it. "Let's get Libby and Big Blue and see if Blue can do anything."

Eagle Feather was still inspecting Roundtree. Suddenly he said, "Look at this." He stared at the soles of the dead man's bare feet. They were scraped and raw, layered over with dirt. "Seems he must have done a lot of walking on these."

"His fingernails are long and there's a lot of dirt under them." Zack turned the beefy hair covered hand palm up in the light. "There might be blood on this hand, from the look of it."

Jimmy Chaparral called to a nearby policeman; "I want this house searched from top to bottom. Don't touch anything but call me if you find anything out of the ordinary. And send someone to find the bloodhound and his handler and bring them in here."

They all looked up at the sound of a different voice.

"Zack, they told me you had been shot! Are you alright?" Ben Brewster stood framed by the archway.

Zack felt unexpected relief at seeing Ben. His shoulder radiated with pain despite the medication from the EMT. He found it increasingly difficult to concentrate. Now here was Ben. Zack could transfer all responsibility to him and go get his wound tended.

"Good to see you, Ben. You got here quickly."

"I can order expensive helicopters just as easily as you," Ben said with a teasing smile. "We'll use it to get you to a hospital for medical treatment."

"We'll also need to transport two bodies over to Linda's lab in Prescott. Maybe she can find some answers to some of questions we can't answer." Zack went on to sketch out recent events, including the strange body hair on Roundtree while Ben took notes

After Zack had finished Ben looked up. "Linda and the forensics people are on their way, along with an FBI team. We're taking over this crime scene."

Ben glanced at Jimmy Chaparral. Chaparral nodded.

"We'll secure the premises and grounds. When Linda gives the okay, we'll move the bodies back to the lab." Ben turned to Zack. "You say that Big Blue tied a scent here to the scent he was following on

Monument Mesa?"

Zack nodded.

"And you matched tire tracks you found out on the Ranch Road where the killer had parked his vehicle to the tires on that old pickup truck out there?"

Zack nodded again. "And you have evidence that Roundtree's old truck had left this property recently?"

"Yes, it had gone out the back of the property through the brickyard, more than once. He could easily have gotten to the Ranch Road driving up through the wash back there then over to the main road."

"Have you got anything else to link him to the girl's body?" Ben asked.

"Could be. We're not sure yet. Jimmy found a wind chime hanging outside at the side of the house. He thinks it's made from small human bones and skin. We'll need to get it analyzed."

"Well, then." Ben's face broke into a broad smile. "Congratulations. It seems you got your man."

Zack didn't return the smile. "Look, Ben, there're still a lot of things that don't add up. None of it feels quite right yet."

Ben looked irritated. "For instance?"

"For instance...what's your take on Skinwalkers?" Ben face relaxed into an expression of amusement. "Come on, Zack, you're not really saying you believe that stuff. I know the mystique can grow on you the longer you work on the Reservation. This is a land of ageless rock and ancient peoples. Its very emptiness makes you feel that anything can happen here. Sure, I've heard all about Skinwalkers, and a hundred other superstitions that these Indians have and, yes, it can get to you after a while." Ben put a hand on Zack's arm. "I've seen other agents start to believe these things can happen out here. Soon after that they lost their perspective; some even had to be relieved. It's easy to begin to doubt your own logic and your own common sense. But in the end it's just superstition. The Navajo use it freely as a cop-out. You're a good man, Zack, a good agent. Don't allow yourself to buy into it."

"Ben, I understand what you're saying but superstition or not, that's the way the Navajo will see it once the story gets told. I mean, look at this guy over here, naked, that huge snake in his lap, long coarse hair sprouting all over his body, his feet skinned and scraped up like he'd been running barefoot all over the Reservation. And then those animal tracks where human tracks ought to be. These people will see this crime as the work of a Skinwalker."

Ben looked thoughtfully at Zack. "You're right about that; we're not going to change the views of the Navajo." Then he smiled. "But we can direct the spin of it for the rest of the world."

He went on in low careful tones. "We'll give the press a healthier spin on this whole business. We'll have to be proactive. Zack, you go and get the medical attention you need. Lieutenant Chaparral here can hold down the fort here until our team arrives. I believe I saw a television truck on my way over here; I'll go offer them the scoop of their lives."

Ben chuckled and had turned to go when another thought came to him. "By the way, what happened to that reporter out there?"

"We think he was bitten by the snake after it went through the window."

"My god! How bizarre." Ben sighed. Then he turned and walked resolutely away. It was time to find the press and orchestrate his future.

TWENTY-ONE

"This is your lucky day," the policeman announced to Melissa. She was near her van interviewing passersby. "FBI Special Agent in Charge Ben Brewster is going to give you an exclusive interview, if you want it. Can you be ready to film in five minutes?"

"If we want it? You bet we want it. You bet we'll be ready."

Melissa grabbed Pete by the arm and pulled him into the van. Katie was sitting right where she had left her, confused and shaken, but waiting obediently.

"All of your questions will soon be answered," Melissa said in response to her questioning look. "We're going back on the air in four minutes."

Melissa called the studio. "Yes," she confirmed in the phone. "We have an absolute scoop, an exclusive interview with the FBI agent in charge down here. But only on the condition we go on the air in four minutes." She lowered her voice respectfully. "No, sadly, he didn't make it. The FBI is taking his body for an autopsy, but the policeman said something about snakebite. I know...ironic, right? So you'll make next of kin contacts for me? Thanks." Then Melissa went back to her most business-like voice. "I've got the same interview subject as before, a Kate Smith. I'll interview her here with the FBI guy. We'll play the culture thing back and forth. He should be here in two minutes, then we'll splash some make-up on him and be ready to go."

Right as Melissa hung up there came a knock at the trailer door. Pete helped Ben Brewster up the steps into the interview space.

"Thank you so much for doing this," Melissa oozed. "Let's get some pancake on you. You look quite pale." She began dabbing at his face with a sponge.

Ben saw Kate seated in one of the two folding chairs facing the camera. "Hi, there. Aren't you the lady who owns the little café in town?"

She nodded.

Melissa interrupted briskly. "Mr. Brewster, we-"

"Please call me Ben."

"Ben. First we'll set the scene with broad strokes. I'll ask Katie some questions to establish a local viewpoint and then I'll ask you to put together a brief chronology of events. After that, I'll ask you to talk about what occurred here. Does that work for you?"

Ben smiled. "That's perfect."

"Great. And I see we're ready to go. Pete, all set?" Pete nodded from behind the large camera. "We're live in 4...3...2...1..."

Jimmy Chaparral stood looking at the wind chime where it hung outside the Roundtree house and took a plastic sample bag from his kit. "Where's Lané Shorter?" he asked a nearby policeman.

"I think he's standing guard at the parking area over at the mesa crime scene."

"All this time?"

"I couldn't say."

Jimmy took down the gruesome talisman and looked at it closely. He had no doubt it was made from human bone and cartilage. He carefully enclosed it in a plastic sample bag and gave it back to the policeman. "Put it with the other samples that are going to Prescott. Be sure to write down where, when, how and all that." As the man walked away he spoke into his radio. "Lenana, where's Lané?"

Lenana's reply came within the static. "He took another shift at the crime scene. Do you need him?"

"Lenana, he's my second in command. This is where he should be. Anybody can do guard duty."

"I'm sorry, Jimmy. He assigned himself to it. I'll call him back right away."

"Thanks, Lenana," said Jimmy, signing off, annoyed and a bit puzzled.

Zack found himself with time to kill while he waited for the forensic team to arrive and authorize the removal of the bodies by helicopter, his ride out. His shoulder hurt but the pain was tempered by his knowledge that the bone had escaped and now he was medicated and could stand the pain. He stood near the arch and idly inspected the brick wall that separated the living room from the narrow hallway. It was a signature Roundtree brick wall and the craftsmanship was indeed exceptional. The man had created intricate patterns by aligning the brick designs and the joining was so perfect that it was almost indiscernible in places. Even at the archway, a difficult place for joining, Roundtree had continued the delicate design across the same plane thus creating the illusion that the arch had been cut out of the wall rather than built into it. In the bright lights of the police flood lamps Zack could see details he had not noticed before. He was learning something about the dead man from the meticulous nature of his craftsmanship.

The wall appeared to be a double layer of bricks laid together perfectly, to the casual observer a single tier. But from inside the arch peering along both wall surfaces Zack noticed a slight bulge at the middle where it seemed thicker, just in that one area, a swelling so subtle that when he looked directly at the surface he couldn't see it. What would cause that? Humidity? Not here in Arizona. A mistake by a master bricklayer? That seemed unlikely.

Zack walked slowly along the interior side and studied it closely. At the very center, where he had seen the bulge, there was a design detail different from the others that left adjacent notches about the thickness of a finger. Zack inserted his fore and index fingers into it. They fit perfectly. He pulled but nothing moved. He pulled harder now and to his amazement an entire section of the wall came away smoothly and quietly, as if on ball bearings. A recess in the wall had been exposed, half a foot deep and two feet high. Tiny shelves built into the back held dozens of small vials. On one shelf there was a stack of coins and several bundles of paper currency.

So! This was John Roundtree's safe deposit box.

The busy chatter in the room ceased when the wall opened. Everyone came to stand near him, gaping into it. Jimmy Chaparral found a flashlight and by its light they saw an additional space that extended several more inches to either side. The beam illuminated something dark and furry.

'A rat,' Jimmy said in disgust.

Zack reached for it and using just his fingertips extracted the object. In the light they saw that the object he held in his hand was a large bear paw covered in coarse fur with long protruding claws stitched into a mitt.

They stared at it. It was stained with some black substance.

"That's blood," Eagle Feather said.

"I think we just found the murder weapon," Jimmy said.

TWENTY-TWO

"Good evening. I am Melissa Mann reporting live tonight from the tiny community of Elk Wells on the Navajo Indian Reservation not far from Tuba City where a shoot-out has just taken place between federal agents and a suspect in the white child murder case; the little girl who was found horribly murdered at the very top of Monument Mesa by a party of hunters. With me is FBI Special Agent Ben Brewster, who is in charge of the case.

"Good evening, Ben, and thank you for taking the time to speak with us now."

"My pleasure."

"Would you please tell us who this suspect is and what just happened?"

"Melissa, the man's name is John Roundtree. He was something of a recluse, having suffered the tragic loss of his own wife and child several years ago. Apparently that affected his state of mind. Evidence shows us that he abducted the little girl in question, abused her, murdered her and then dumped her body on the mesa. Tonight, FBI agents assisted by the Navajo Nation Police surrounded Mr. Roundtree's home and called upon him to give himself up. When he did not respond, they forcibly entered. Our agents were fired upon and shots were exchanged. One FBI agent was wounded and Mr. Roundtree was, unfortunately, killed. We have no more information than that currently. Agents and officers are searching the house for evidence. We expect to be able to say more in a short time."

"Agent Brewster, how were you able to link the crime scene on

Monument Mesa to John Roundtree?"

"Well, Melissa, one of our agents backtracked the perpetrator from the crime scene to a local road where Mr. Roundtree's vehicle had been left. The agents used evidence from the roadway to match tire treads to the vehicle and a bloodhound matched the scent from the crime scene to Mr. Roundtree."

"That is indeed impressive detective work, Agent Brewster. Why didn't the agents arrest Mr. Roundtree instead of attacking him in his home?"

"As I mentioned a moment ago, Mr. Roundtree would not respond to the agents' repeated requests for him to surrender. The FBI and the Navajo Nation Police were then forced to enter the home and when they did, they were fired upon. As I said, one of our agents was wounded. Agents and police returned fire and in the exchange Mr. Roundtree was killed.

"How badly hurt was the agent?"

"The agent's wound is not critical."

"And the victim, the little white girl, do we know who she was?"

"She has not been identified. We are following several leads. Once we have identified her we will notify her next of kin, after which we will release her identity to the public."

"Of course. Now you stated that John Roundtree molested this little white girl. Do you suspect that he was a serial pedophile? Is he registered or known in any way?"

"The post mortem exam does suggest that there had been abuse, and although Mr. Roundtree appears to be the likely perpetrator, we cannot be specific about that at this time."

"But you have no other suspects?"

"We have no other active suspects but until our forensics unit is able to establish a DNA link to Mr. Roundtree, the perpetrator of the abuse remains undetermined."

"Thank you, Agent Brewster. I will have some additional questions for you in a moment, so please don't go away." Melissa smiled broadly at him and turned to Kate.

"Our other guest is Ms. Kate Smith, a resident of this community and a full blooded Navajo Indian. She is the proprietor of Katie's Café; a breakfast shop located in the center of Elk Wells. Welcome, Ms. Smith, and thank you for your patience this evening."

"Oh, thank you."

"Kate, what can you tell us about what the people of your community think of Mr. John Roundtree?"

"Oh, everybody suspected him of this murder right from the start. He looks like a wild man and has behaved strangely for many years, ever since his wife died. Everyone knew something like this would happen sooner or later."

"Something like what?"

"Oh, him hurting or killing somebody, that sort of thing."

"Why did people think that?"

"Well, people knew John was studying to become a shaman. His father had been one and so had his father's father. But after his wife and unborn son died people think he became angry and turned to studying witchcraft. They think that he became a Skinwalker."

"And what is a Skinwalker?"

"It's a Navajo witch who has developed the ability to become an animal, like a coyote, or an eagle, or a bear."

"How can such a thing be possible?"

"There are powers beyond those that ordinary people have that can be unlocked by shamans and witches who study how to do that. Only shamans have the knowledge and training to do it. Most people don't know how it is done, but we know that it can happen. My people have always none this."

"And the people believe that John Roundtree had acquired these capabilities?"

"John Roundtree was almost never around during the day. And when he was, his eyes were red and his hair and clothing were all dirty and crumpled. But late at night, people passing by his house would see a strange light inside and some people even saw strange figures pass in and out of the house." Katie caught her breath and waited.

Now Melissa turned to Ben.

"Tell me, Agent Brewster, is it true that the victim, the little white girl, sustained a fatal wound that appears to have come from a wild animal? And that tracks leading away from the victim were also those of an animal, a bear in fact? How was it determined that this wasn't a bear attack, but was actually a murder by a human being?"

Ben laughed lightly and easily at that. "There were attempts to disguise this murder, to portray the killer as an animal in order to throw law enforcement off the track. Once the body had been examined more carefully in the lab, other possible causes of death were found. In fact, the large claw-like wound that you refer to does not seem to have caused her death. As to the tracks near the scene, it soon became apparent that they were attempts to confuse the investigation. Normal human footprints were eventually found. Forensic evidence makes it quite clear that the little girl's death was perpetrated by a human, not an animal, or"--Ben smiled teasingly--"a mythical being."

"Do you believe that Mr. Roundtree acted alone?"

"Yes, I do." Ben's reply was solemn and spoken with conviction. "Mr. Roundtree fits the profile. He suffered the tragic loss of loved ones, which left him angry and bitter. Then he displayed significant routine and behavioral changes, he lived alone, and he rejected all normal social networks. I have no doubt that he is our man."

Melissa turned back to Katie. "Do you believe that this killer was a disturbed human or do you think he was an evil shaman with extraordinary powers?"

Katie looked away from Melissa. "All I know is we will all rest easier knowing that John Roundtree no longer walks among us."

Melissa faced the camera for a gradual close-up. "There you have it, up to the minute. We will continue to follow this story closely. But for now, this is Melissa Mann for Channel Four News, live from Elk Wells in the Navajo Indian Reservation in Arizona, saying Good Night and Good Dreams."

Eagle Feather reached a hand into the wall recess and brought out one of the small bottles from the rear shelf. He took it into the light and looked at the label. It was written in the Navajo language. He looked inside the bottle and sniffed.

"John was a practicing shaman. This secret place appears to hold the tools of his trade," he said.

"It doesn't take witchcraft to slice open a little girl's abdomen with something like this." Zack held up the bear claw.

Jimmy Chaparral had been examining John Roundtree's body. "You know that smell we all noticed before we entered the house; the sick-sweet smell, like something had died? It's coming from Roundtree and it's strong. He must have been dead a while."

Jimmy looked at Zack and Eagle Feather. "That means you didn't kill him. He was dead already."

Zack and Eagle Feather looked up in surprise. "Now that you mention it, I did notice that smell," Zack said. "We were too involved to think about it. But ...who shot me?"

Zack looked at Eagle Feather, who shrugged. "You don't want my answer, white man."

Jimmy answered. "Try this on. That big snake stays curled up in John Roundtree's lap after it kills him. Maybe it was coiled around his arm. Roundtree's finger is already on the trigger of the Colt, frozen by rigor mortis. Then Zack comes in and walks across from the arch over there"--Jimmy showed them with a sweep of his arm--"left to right in front of Roundtree and the snake. Mr. Snake turns to keep his eye on Zack, coiling to strike. His coils tighten up on Roundtree's rigid arm pulling back on the trigger finger. So by the time Zack gets over there the arm has been pulled far enough that the finger pulls the trigger and the gun goes off...Bang!" Jimmy pantomimed the kick of the big Colt and grinned at Zack. He did an impression of John Wayne. "It was the snake that shot you, Pilgrim."

"That's pretty darn good," Zack breathed. "So according to your theory John Roundtree damn near killed me by accident."

"No such thing as accidents." Eagle Feather was shaking his head. "There's a purpose to everything."

"Let's see if I can keep it going." Jimmy said, ignoring Eagle Feather. "Mr. Snake, startled by the roar and the flash and the vibration of the gun right next to him immediately launches himself away from danger in the only direction he can go, straight toward Zack. It's a very big, very powerful snake; its life preserving instincts are on full alert, and the momentum of its strike carries it all the way to the window which is already cracked and which breaks easily from Mr. Snake's weight. Mr. Snake falls through the window and lands right on top of Mr. Reporter, who is crouching there trying to get a peek inside. Mr. Snake bites Mr. Reporter in self-defense and escapes across the lawn." Jimmy looked pleased with himself. "As for John Roundtree, I found two punctures that look like fang marks in his neck. A snake that large must pack a lot of venom and could easily have killed him hours before we got here."

"I've got to admit, your theory makes a lot of sense," Zack said reluctantly. "But it still leaves quite a few questions. First off, why was the snake in his lap to begin with? Was it a pet or was he trying to extract venom for a potion? He didn't have the tools for that anywhere near him. And even so, why did he have that big revolver in his hand? Was he trying to shoot the snake? But if the snake wasn't already in his lap, how'd it get there? And only one chamber of the Colt was empty, so the only bullet he fired is now in my shoulder."

Eagle Feather picked up where Zack left off. "Even if the snake did somehow get into his lap before he could shoot it and then it bit him, why did he just sit there holding the gun with the snake in his lap until he died, instead of jumping up from the chair, a normal reaction for a snake-bit man?

"Suicide by snake...or pistol? If one didn't work, the other would." That was Jimmy's solution.

Zack gave it up, his shoulder pain interfering with his thinking. "We've still got too many questions and not enough answers. Once Agent Whittaker has examined the body and some of the other evidence from this house we'll have more to work with. Maybe then something will point us to a place that we just can't see right now."

"If you think you have too many questions now, you're not going to want to hear what I have to say." Libby came toward them from the rear door, her face etched with concerned.

Before she could say more Ben Brewster swept back into the room, looking very pleased. He spoke loudly for all in the room to hear as he walked toward them.

"Zack, Jimmy, Eagle Feather, Libby - all of you. A job well done, well done indeed. You've solved the case and we have our perpetrator. Now it's simply a matter of sorting out the details. You've all done great work. As I pointed out to the Channel Four anchorwoman just moments ago, the murderer has been identified, located, and captured in less than thirty-six hours. That is truly excellent police work in anybody's book."

Zack tried to get Ben's attention, speaking quietly just for him. "Ben, I'm not comfortable with declaring this case closed just yet. There are too many questions, too many loose ends."

Ben smiled magnanimously at him and spread his arms wide. "All of those questions will be resolved in time, you'll see." He looked hard at

Zack. "You do believe that John Roundtree is our man, don't you?"

"Well...certainly all the evidence we have points to him... but ..."

"Yes, it does, it most certainly does. And it does so for a reason. The reason is that he's our man. You are very thorough, Zack, and very careful and I value you highly for those qualities. But you need to learn to accept a pat on the shoulder every now and then." Ben grinned and patted him hard to demonstrate. Zack winced in pain, but Ben didn't notice.

Ben now turned to Libby who waited impatiently to get a word in. "And don't you think we don't appreciate your talents as well, young lady, and those of your amazing Big Blue." Ben gave her a huge smile. "Where would we be if old Blue hadn't tracked the culprit to his lair, eh?"

"Thank you, sir," Libby said quickly. "But I'm afraid we have a lot more of the kind of questions Zack was talking about."

Everyone looked at Libby.

"Blue just found another child's body out in the brick yard," she said. "In fact, from Blue's behavior I'd say there might be a whole lot more bodies."

PART TWO: THE OTHER

TWENTY-THREE

Supervisory Special Agent Zack Tolliver sat in the worn but comfortable lawn chair and stretched his legs out their full length, his lukewarm coffee forgotten, luxuriating in the healing rays of the warm morning sun. Zack didn't usually have a weekend all to himself and he intended to make the most of this one. He could always find inner peace when he was home on his ranch, just south of Page, Arizona, far enough away from his responsibilities in Tuba City and the reservation to feel a sense of freedom yet close enough to respond quickly if there was an emergency.

This morning he positioned his chair in the south yard just beyond the front porch of his modest three-bedroom ranch house. He faced away from the red barn with its big double doors toward the roping corral so he could look out over the stone-lined gravel drive, one of his many continuing projects. Even now a lone shovel poked its handle up from the ditch, waiting for his gloved hands to grasp it. Out there, beyond the shovel, a row of sentry cottonwood trees marched on over the rise on their way to the intersection with the Cameron Road, almost quarter mile away.

But Zack wasn't thinking about the driveway project or the cottonwoods or even the reservation right now, not even about the Navajo people who so completely changed his life over the past ten years. His thoughts were fully on the pleasure he felt just to sit still and feel the warm sun and maybe even doze a little. His shoulder didn't ache so much these days although he still felt tightness around the wound where scar tissue formed over the hole the forty-five caliber slug made the night they entered John Roundtree's place.

Zack's thoughts turned to his fellow passengers in the helicopter that night, both dead men, one the young reporter who'd been in the wrong place at the wrong time and the other John Roundtree himself, dead from snake bite and dead again from shotgun and rifle bullets and who knew what else, really? Ben had sent Zack off in the copter that night despite his protests, electing to stay himself and finish up the investigation with Jimmy Chaparral. The team spent the whole next day digging up bodies of little girls where Big Blue had sniffed them out at the back of the property, the final count an unlucky thirteen. All had been fair skinned, all very young, the oldest maybe fourteen. Zack's same old nagging thoughts returned and he wondered why he couldn't get his head around the idea that John Roundtree was a serial killer. He must have begun killing the girls within a year of the loss of his wife and stillborn son. Linda Whittaker at the lab had confirmed that all of the girls were sexually abused over a long period of time. Figuring thirteen victims, Roundtree would have kept each girl right there in his home an average of six months before killing her, burying her, and looking for the next one.

Zack caught himself. That very morning he had promised himself not to think about John Roundtree for once but enjoy the sun and a cup of fresh coffee and stop revisiting memories of that night in the dark interior of Roundtree's house; the cloyingly sweet smell of death, or those red eyes...especially those red eyes. And he wouldn't think about the torch-like flame reaching toward him from the big gun's barrel or the writhing snake flying over him.

He shook his head as if to physically clear away those thoughts. He opened his eyes to reach for his coffee mug and saw a car approaching down the drive. He studied it lazily and recognized it as Libby Whitestone's old woody station wagon. He sighed seeing his blissful morning of solitude slip away, but on the other hand the prospect of seeing Libby was well worth the loss.

Zack and Libby had grown close in the months that followed the Roundtree case. Her tracker dog Big Blue was the reason they solved the case as quickly as they had and became even more important in the days that followed. He had located the burial sites of all the little girl bodies one by one, sniffing out the paths used by their killer around the property. It meant that Libby and Zack, awkward and needing assistance with his right arm in a sling, had been thrown together daily in a partnership that grew even closer. They had found that they complimented one another in the way they thought and in the way they went about things. Each felt a growing professional respect for the other that blossomed into new feelings and soon brought them together in a different way. Wonderful feelings, Zack admitted to himself, but ones that touched on old emotions he had stuffed away out of sight, old ghosts now forced into the light by new decisions.

He was saved from further self-analysis when Libby's old station wagon with its deteriorating wood trim, a luxury vehicle in its day but now all about utility, came to a skidding gravelly stop near Zack's chair. The heavy door creaked open and Libby slipped out from behind the over-sized steering wheel. She stood a moment, stretching her long sinewy body with cat-like unawareness, and then grinned and jerked open the rear door. Libby's grin grew into a laugh when the big bloodhound barreled out and slammed into Zack's chair, bowling him over onto the lawn. Blue slobbered Zack's face with big wet dog kisses as he tried ineffectually to fend him off.

"I suppose I should warn you before I release Blue but one would think you would remember and be prepared, " Libby said.

Zack grinned back. "It's a good thing for you my shoulder is healing well, if I'm to be mauled every time you come visit me."

Zack rubbed Blue behind his long floppy ears while the dog rolled his eyes in pleasure. "How about a coffee? I brewed a large pot thinking I'd spend my day not doing much else."

"Sounds perfect." Libby walked toward the house. "You two stay and play. I'll get my own cup and bring out the pot."

She climbed the creaky steps to the porch and slapped in through the screen door with the familiarity of one who knew the house well.

Zack set his lawn chair upright and sat back in it rubbing Blue's ears with the other hand. The dog settled contentedly next him, sitting tall enough to rest his big head on Zack's lap in the low chair. Zack began to drift off once more in his reveries but then Libby was back, putting her own steaming mug down to fill his empty one from the pot. She pulled the other lawn chair over next to him and lounged into it.

"A penny for those thoughts."

It took Zack a minute. "Libby..." He was reluctant to share his disturbing thoughts but decided to go ahead. "Libby, I hate to keep going back over all this but I can't seem to let it go. Tell me, looking back on all that happened, what's your take on the whole John Roundtree thing?"

"I don't know what you mean."

"I mean, it's been over six months since that night and since then I've gone on to other cases. We haven't talked about it much, you and I, beyond the details we discussed when we were digging up Roundtree's brickyard. And now as far as everyone else is concerned, it's all over, done, case solved, move on. Ben gets the recognition and honors he deserved, he retires and thinks only about golf and umbrella cocktails. And even Jimmy Chaparral and his Navajo Police seem content with the outcome. Eagle Feather was with me every step of the way, he saw everything I saw and should have felt everything I felt, and here he is back guiding hunters like nothing ever happened, not another word about it. So why can't I get it out of my head and move on like everybody else?"

Libby smiled. "I can think of two reasons, and I'm ready to bet on one of them."

"OK, then, let's have 'em."

"Well, the first reason is your shoulder wound. An injury like yours that came as part of the investigation makes the case highly personal and intimate. It's something you don't forget so easily, something you can't let go. Every time it aches or twinges it brings you back to the events that were happening when you received it."

"That makes a lot of sense," Zack conceded. "Is that the one you're betting on?"

"Actually, no. Knowing you, and I do, I'm betting on the second one, which is that you don't really believe deep down inside that the

Roundtree case was solved. You keep thinking there's more to it. Am I right?"

Zack stared over the corral fence to the cactus-peppered hill beyond and turned it over in his head. Finally he turned his head and looked at Libby.

"I do believe you are correct, Dr. Whitestone, and maybe on both counts. The stiffness in my shoulder is a constant reminder and I do think about the case pretty much every day and every day I try to make all of the puzzle pieces fit neatly together so that I can get on to thinking about other things, but the pieces never quite fit."

He sighed. Libby encouraged him. "Well, give me an example. Sometimes just hearing yourself talk about it can give you a new perspective."

"Worth a try," Zack agreed. "But I'm afraid that what I say may seem silly; it's all really a bunch of small details that may add up to nothing."

"If those small details keep nagging you I'd guess you probably don't really believe that. They must mean something. Your subconscious is contradicting your conscious conclusions. You need to resolve that contradiction to put your mind at rest."

"OK, Madame Psychologist, here we go. First detail: that white SUV that passed us on the MacPherson Ranch road. It tried to run me over and as it passed I felt this wave of incredible malevolence issuing from it. You remember how I talked about that after the incident? You may also remember that I dispatched a very expensive helicopter to backtrack that truck along the Ranch road hoping to find where it'd gone. They found nothing. So where did it go? There's no other way off of that road. And how could John Roundtree have been driving that truck? By then, according to Linda, he'd long been dead in his chair in his house. So who was in that truck, why did he try to run over me?"

"Coincidence?"

"See what I mean? Small details; puzzle pieces that I can't even confirm. Here's another one: the soles of John Roundtree's feet. When we examined them they were bloody and scraped just like you might expect with someone who'd been running around barefoot all over the reservation. Perfect, case solved, right? But the prints we saw on the mesa didn't show blood or cuts or scrapes - not once. Just the opposite; those prints showed no sign of foot distress at all. No limp, no weakness, no cuts, no blood. The man we tracked had perfectly conditioned feet for running barefoot. That's not something you can change at will even if you are a witch."

"Hmmm. I see what you mean. But what about the blood you found around the bear tracks? Didn't Linda later identify that sample as Roundtree's blood, not the victim's? Doesn't that pretty much finalize it?"

"I thought so, at first. Yet we never did learn why he was bleeding up there. And tell me this: did you ever have Blue actually come in and sniff John Roundtree's body that night in his house to directly tie him to the scent Blue had been following on the mesa?"

"Well, no. In fact, I was told not to bring him into the house. I had to leave him outside with a policeman when I came to tell you about finding those other bodies."

"So we never positively connected the man whose scent we followed from the scene to John Roundtree specifically, only to a scent that was on his property. You aren't helping me get past this."

"Maybe not, 'though when Blue picked up that same scent all around the truck and the property there just didn't seem to be any other conclusion that was reasonable. Who else could it have been? He lived alone."

"Yeah, he lived all alone."

"Anything else?"

"Oh, yeah. I've got lots more where that came from." Zack smiled wearily. "Try this one on. How did John Roundtree acquire all of the

Rohypnol that he used on those girls, not to speak of the dose he injected into my horse Diablo and tried to inject into me? No one ever saw him driving anywhere. That drug is restricted in the United States, which means he couldn't have mail-ordered it. The nearest place he could have gotten it is Mexico and even if he somehow managed to get it from down there, it has a relatively short shelf life and he'd have to resupply several times a year. For that he'd need good connections down there and, not the least of it, he'd need money. Lots of money."

"Hmmm."

"Which brings into question that old truck of his. Notice those tires? Not in very good shape, fabric showing and all. I wouldn't drive that truck down the road to the gas station, let alone to Mexico. Or for that matter, to wherever he had to go to find all of those little girls. And there's another thing. Why can't we learn the identity of those dead girls? How can that many little blonde white female children go missing and nobody's out looking for them?"

"Well! Anything else?"

"Yes, Madame Doctor Whitestone, quite a bit more, but I think that's enough for now. Maybe it does help to talk about it but right now I'm growing frustrated all over again. I just want to relax and enjoy the day with you and Blue. Tell you what. Let's throw some bread, cheese, and wine in a picnic basket and go for a ride. What do you say?"

"I say that's a spectacular idea. You go saddle up the horses, I'll go put a picnic basket together."

The leisurely ride up the familiar old sheep trail to the dry grass top of the plateau was just what the doctor ordered, serene and restful, the only sounds the scuff and clomp of the horse hooves on the hard packed trail and the occasional call of a western Jay up in a pinion pine.

They left the horses to graze and found a spot under their favorite tree where they spread a thick blanket and put out some cheese, a loaf of bread and the red wine that Libby had selected. Tinkling their glasses together they agreed that life couldn't get much better. Big

Blue's heavy tail thumped down on the blanket in agreement.

"How are the boys?" Zack asked, steering to a fresh topic.

"Oh, a pain, as always!" laughed Libby. "George is never around, always off at a class or teaching a seminar at the junior college. And when he's home, he's always too busy with that damn computer to do any household chores. And, well, you know Lenny! He's always underfoot, always having a dramatic moment."

"Well, in a few years they'll both be married and off on their own."

"Lenny, maybe. But I'm not betting on George. He's too much of an old lady." Libby laughed again. "He'll be in school for the rest of his life, never able to afford a place of his own, married to his books and his computer, and still living with me, I'm afraid." Libby looked at Zack, teasing. "That kind of describes you, doesn't it, except that your marriage is to your job, not to books?"

"And not the old lady part, for sure. But no, I'm not so married to my job that I don't appreciate life away from it. This"--Zack waved his arm in a wide sweep--"refreshes me and allows me to go on with my work without going insane."

"Yet you never married?"

"I'm only forty," Zack retorted. "Give me a break."

"I'm only forty-seven and I've got two mostly grown boys, a farm full of animals and a full time job as a dog trainer and occasional man tracker. Give you a break?"

"That's my point, I think. Besides, my hours are random, my job is dangerous some of the time and I have to travel way too much to be able to keep any woman happy."

Libby smiled fondly at Zack. "I will say, selfishly, that I'm glad it worked out this way. I really enjoy our time together. And believe me, as much as I loved my husband, now that he's gone, I'm in no hurry to tie myself down again. All in all, maybe I owe John Roundtree a debt of gratitude for bringing us together this way."

"Cheers to that." Zack raised his glass. "And here's to John Roundtree staying firmly in whatever vase he currently occupies. I need the ghosts of this case to go away."

TWENTY-FOUR

Less than twenty-four hours later Zack had a call from FBI forensics expert Linda Whittaker in Tuba City. She got right to the point.

"Zack, I need to talk to someone about the inconsistencies that I've been finding in the John Roundtree autopsy data. And the bodies of some of the girls."

"Shoot."

"What? Oh...well, it's very detailed and more than I can get into over the telephone right now. I hoped you could drop by my lab here in Tuba City and give me an hour or so."

"Uh, sure, I could do that. Let's see...I'll be coming down that way Thursday. I could be there around noon, we could do lunch. Does that work for you?"

"I'll make it work. But I'll supply the lunch; I think we'll need to eat in."

"It's a plan. I'll see you then." Zack rang off, surprised. Why call him? Why not discuss it with Ben's replacement right there in the same building? Zack's curiosity increased as the meeting time approached.

The FBI liaison office in Tuba City was a third party lease in a building just south of the Navajo Interactive Museum. The city, more of a town really, fell under Navajo Nation jurisdiction and could not officially host U.S. federal offices. But when the lack of immediacy of federal response exacerbated several difficult situations, with delays caused by the excessive distances FBI agents were called upon to travel, the Navajo National Council agreed that it would be helpful to allow the FBI to maintain a quiet presence on the reservation.

Zack left his truck by the sidewalk and pulled open the glass door that read Navajo Nation FBI Liaison Office. He flashed his badge. The young receptionist smiled at him and pressed a button to deactivate the weapons alert system that guarded the inner hallway. Zack's heels echoed down the pleasantly cool corridor to the far end. He knocked on a door labeled 'Forensic A'. Linda answered his knock immediately looking very much at home in her white lab coat.

"Thanks for coming, Zack. How's that shoulder?"

Zack rolled his shoulder forward and back. "Good as new."

"That's great. Come on in. I've got some sandwich makings and some ice tea ready to go. We can talk as we eat."

Zack followed Linda across the spacious laboratory to a table by the window where shiny metal instruments and chemical bottles had been pushed aside to make room for an assortment of cheeses and meats in unopened packages, a loaf of bread with slices tumbling out, a stack of paper plates and an open mayonnaise jar from which a plastic knife protruded. Two tall lab stools had been pushed up to the table. Zack watched Linda pull out a stool and found himself thinking about Jimmy Chaparral, his friend in the Navajo Nation Police who somehow had become the object of Linda's affections during the Roundtree case. Although Jimmy consistently resisted her advances he hadn't totally rejected them and in fact seemed fascinated by her, rather like a mouse with a snake, Zack thought. Zack himself found Linda quite appealing, particularly here in her lab where she seemed most at ease.

Linda took a scalpel out of the pile of tools on the table and sliced open a meat package with professional ease. They prepared their sandwiches.

"Congratulations on your promotion to Supervisory Special Agent," she said.

"It's only a temporary assignment, just until Special Agent in Charge Forrester gets his feet under him. An assignment to the reservation isn't quite like being assigned to a district anywhere else, there's a whole lot more to learn in addition to just figuring out the lay of the land. You have to be brought along gradually, you have to be accepted by the population you need to work with."

"I never understood why you didn't step up to his position. It just makes sense. You wouldn't need to start at the beginning like anyone else. And you are already accepted by the Navajo."

Here it comes again, Zack thought to himself. He was a little tired of explaining his decision.

"I know that it seems logical but it would mean a huge change for me. I'd have to stop doing the things I enjoy and start doing a lot of the things I don't. I said yes to the role of Supervisory Agent just to bring Luke Forrester in gradually and to cover that ground until he is ready to go on his own. After that, I fully expect to get back to my old routine."

Zack looked at Linda with an eyebrow raised. "Is that why you brought me down here today?"

"Oh, no. But it is why I wanted to talk to you before I speak officially to Agent Forrester. I need to bounce some things off you first, to get a sense of where I should go with them...politically, if you know what I mean."

"Well, no, I don't really. But maybe I will after you tell me what those things are."

Linda took Zack by the arm and tugged him over to her desk where her laptop sat open. "As you know, I've done all my testing and all of the data from the Roundtree case is finally entered into the FBI data base. There was so much of it from the thirteen little bodies, not to speak of Roundtree himself that I had to prioritize my starting point and begin with the most obvious and necessary findings before sorting through more speculative and tangential areas. On top of that there was pressure from now-retired Special Agent in Charge Ben Brewster, who was very anxious for me to finalize my findings as quickly as possible. But now that all of the priority work is done and the furor surrounding the case has died down, I've had a chance to look through all of the data carefully and with a much wider focus. And I've uncovered some interesting elements that don't necessarily support our earlier conclusions. Here, let me show you what I mean."

Linda typed some code into the computer and a stream of letters and figures filled the page. "Right there." Linda pointed to a line part way down the page. "Almost all the girls from whom we were able to collect skin samples showed traces of a mixture of sodium carbonate decahydrate with about 17% sodium bicarbonate and minute quantities of household salt and sodium sulfate."

Linda turned her face up toward Zack with a look of triumph.

Zack shook his head. "Linda, you've got to break that down for me."

"Well, it's basically salt. Salt found in dry lake beds in arid climates, like those in the Atacama Desert in Chile or along the shores of the Baja in Mexico, although the samples from these girls are of a purity that suggests it might be a refined natron powder, but it's all pretty much the same thing: salt."

"Why is it there?"

"Ah, that is indeed the question. Today natron has a number of industrial uses, most of which involve the preservation of organic materials. It's been used to make soap and even mouthwash." Linda turned to look at Zack. "But in ancient times, it was used for embalming."

Zack was momentarily shaken. "Embalming?"

"Yes. The ancient Egyptians collected salt from lakebeds, added a simple ingredient or two, and covered over the bodies they intended to embalm with this natron mixture. It draws out the moisture and behaves as a drying agent and it even increases the PH of the skin, making it resistant to bacteria. It was a perfect tool for their purposes."

Zack's mind raced, trying to understand the implications of an embalming agent in the skin samples of those little girls. "Why the hell would Roundtree want to preserve those children after he buried them?"

"Why indeed? And you will remember that we had found significant amounts of Rohypnol in the indicator form of plasma flunitrazepam concentrations in all the girls who were not too decayed to test accurately. Some samples had degraded to 7- aminoflunitrazepam but when considered along with the evidence from the less decayed samples and from the little mesa girl, not to speak of the concentrations from the cacti spines, there can be no doubt that he was indeed using Rohypnol consistently as a tool. And we found significant residual amounts in yet another place. Would you like to guess where?"

Zack's head was spinning. "Uh, yes...no. Okay, where?"

Linda gave him another triumphant look. "In John Roundtree himself."

"In Roundtree? How could you have found it in Roundtree? What are you saying?"

Linda spoke slowly and deliberately. "I'm saying that John Roundtree appears to have administered the drug Rohypnol to himself prior to playing with his snake. We are now certain that snakebite was the actual cause of his death, even though you and your Indian buddy did your best to blow him in half after the fact."

"Why would he do that? I mean, self-administer the Rohypnol?"

"Why indeed? One might speculate that he expected to die, with the law closing in and all, and knowing the tranquilizing effect of the drug and its power to block memory chose to end it all in the easiest possible way. But there would have been significant risk with that plan. He could have fallen asleep after taking the drug or simply have forgotten what he had planned to do and let the snake slip harmlessly off his lap. In that case, you would've arrived to find a very sleepy and confused John Roundtree and taken him into custody him easily. I don't think he had that in mind."

Zack's brain leapt ahead. "Linda, did you discover the way in which the drug was administered to Roundtree? Where it entered his system?"

"Ahhh, very good. Yes, in fact, I did. There was a tiny pinprick of a spot just at the hairline on the back of his neck. That's where it was administered. In terms of how, my guess is it was with a-"

"Pigmy Cactus spine."

Linda smiled and nodded her head.

"He could've poked it into himself," Zack suggested.

"He could 've poked it into a vein in his arm. That would've been a lot easier and just as fast acting."

"True."

"And…"

"More?"

"While we were poking around in John Roundtree's fluids we also found more than trace amounts of synthetic HGH, which might well account for all that extra body hair he was growing."

Zack pulled a chair up and sat, thinking. Finally he asked, "Have you found anything else I should know about?"

Linda smiled again, quietly. Zack was learning not to like that smile. He watched as she tapped her laptop keys again and a picture suddenly filled the screen. At first, Zack couldn't make it out. The picture was blurry and dark around the outer edges with a bit more detail toward the center. It was a pattern of small circles surrounded by dark lines and in the middle something like a reversed smiley face, or maybe a mouth tipped by a little splotch of a nose, all dark and brownish. But what caught his attention immediately were the glowing red points above the cartoon-like mouth. Instantly that feeling returned; the feeling that he had almost forgotten, a feeling of dread and fear that even here in the safety of the lab threatened to overcome him. He knew now what he was seeing. Those tiny red points were eyes and this was a close-up picture of the huge snake that had attacked him in the Roundtree house.

"Where did that come from?"

"I see you recognize it." Linda watched his reaction closely. "This was the very last picture from the camera that belonged to that young reporter, the one who died from snake bite outside the Roundtree house. Great shot, isn't it? He captured the snake coming right at him. It's a little blurry but it shows amazing detail under the circumstances. A reporter to the end, eh?"

"So the eyes were really that red," Zack breathed.

Linda looked curiously at him. "You saw them? Those eyes, I mean? They looked like that?"

"Oh, yes."

"They don't seem quite natural," Linda remarked. "I don't think I've ever seen a snake with such red eyes before, so very shiny and bright. Must be the effect of the searchlight on them."

"Must be," Zack replied slowly.

But Linda wasn't done. "But look at that mouth. It's closed and that little face actually seems to have an expression. Smug, I'd call it. I've never seen a thoughtful rattlesnake. This one almost seems to have a plan."

"Yes," Zack agreed, "A closed mouth, yet milliseconds from biting the photographer. Snakes always strike open mouthed with their fangs protruding."

"I thought that photo might interest you." Linda glowed with satisfaction.

Zack was exhausted by it all. He sat quietly for a long time sorting it out, putting everything in some kind of logical order. Then, almost reluctantly, he asked, "Anything else?"

"That's all." Linda smiled. "But perhaps now you understand why I hesitated to take these findings to our new supervisor right away."

Zack's eyes held Linda's. "You know what all this means. You've put it together. You know it's very unlikely that Roundtree self-administered that Rohypnol. That means there is almost no doubt that we have a second killer. He escaped in that white SUV that almost hit me on the Ranch road. He drugged John Roundtree, then put the Colt in his hand and the rattlesnake in his lap and caused it to bite him. He's out there somewhere right now and he's extremely dangerous. This means that we have to start all over, that we have to re-evaluate every bit of evidence that we have and rethink everything that happened in the John Roundtree case. We have to think in terms of two perpetrators, not just one."

"And Forrester? And the press? It seemed like that Melissa Mann woman would never stop headlining this case on Channel Four News. I can only imagine what she'll do with these developments."

"That simply can't happen." Zack paused, feeling conflicted. He looked at Linda with regret. "Linda, I hate to ask this. But I feel we have no choice. We have an advantage...a very slight one but still an advantage. Our advantage is that this killer doesn't think that we're on to him. He probably wondered if I suspected him, but after all this time he must now be thinking I believe Roundtree committed the crimes all by himself. He must be feeling secure. We need to hold on to that edge.

Linda, I need to ask you not take this to Forrester. In fact, don't take it to anybody at all. And I won't breathe a word, not yet. We need to pretend that this meeting never took place. But I want you to check over all of your data one more time. Look for any other indicators, any other proof that another killer was involved. Is all of your DNA evidence in?"

"Yes. I've got no mystery DNA. All of it is from our known subjects."

"Have you checked the two cacti spines that we have, the one we found in Diablo and the one from my stirrup? He must have blown them through a primitive reed dart gun of some sort and he might have left some saliva residue on them."

"I gave them both a preliminary check and found nothing," Linda replied. "But I'll send them out for a more thorough test this time. I should have the response in less than a week if I prioritize it."

Zack put a hand on her shoulder. "No, no, don't do that. Don't prioritize anything to do with this case. As far as everyone else is concerned, the case is closed. Let's not cause anyone to believe we think otherwise."

Linda understood, and nodded her agreement. "I'll get right to work."

"Thank you, Linda. Don't worry, we'll be able to act openly with this soon enough." Zack picked up his hat and looked at her. "Linda?"

"Yes?"

"Thank you. Thank you for talking to me first." He broke into a grin. "And thanks for the lunch."

Zack headed out the door and down the corridor and then out into the bright Arizona sunshine, into a sunny world that seemed a little grimmer somehow for all the dark thoughts spinning around in his head. He checked his phone, which he had silenced during his meeting with Linda and found several messages. One was from Special Agent in Charge Forrester himself. Zack turned right around and re-entered the FBI office building. This time at the long corridor he turned hard left into a shorter foyer where there was only one door. He knocked. He heard a muffled command to enter and stepped inside.

This was Zack's first time in his supervisor's office since Ben had occupied it. Then, Zack had enjoyed frequent and causal drop-ins with his mentor and friend. He looked around curiously. Where Ben had the walls lined with shelves crammed with books on Navajo lore and culture, FBI protocols and procedures, forensic science, and other work-related tomes, now there were only white walls, hung with the collectables of a traveler; African shields and spears, a pith helmet, various animal skins, and maps of exotic locations around the world. The large desk, which in Ben's day had been completely covered by a mass of paper and notebooks, now showed an empty shiny hardwood surface with only a neat little message tray, a pad of sticky notes, and a small laptop, all of which seemed even smaller on the large desk surface. Zack stood for a moment, taking it all in.

Special Agent in Charge Luke Forrester, brown haired, round faced and pleasant, looked up from the letter he was drafting and observed Zack's expression. He smiled.

"Not what you are used to, I expect."

"No, sir, not at all."

"Well, this"--Forrester gave a sweep of his hand to indicate out beyond his office to the city and the surrounding reservation--"is not exactly what I'm used to either. But life has a way of changing all our well laid plans and expectations, haven't you found?"

"In fact, sir, I've found that to be particularly true of late."

"Have a seat, Zack," Forrester said. There was the one stuffed chair facing the desk. Zack slipped into it.

"Let me first say how pleased I am to be working with you. I had heard about you and your excellent work once I learned I was coming here. And of course your friend Ben speaks most highly of you. I must say, the prospect of partnering with you promises to be the best part of the equation for me."

"You are very kind, sir."

"Not at all. But enough of that. I noticed your truck outside just now and thought that this might be a good time to lay some groundwork for our future relationship. I hope I can immediately dispel any anxieties you might feel about working with me. I intend to look to you for your advice in all matters involving Navajo protocol and culture. In return, I expect you to attend any and all meetings with the administrative arm of the Navajo Nation, at least until I can get my cultural legs under me. It will mean more time in the saddle for you, I know, but it will also ensure that I don't somehow undo all the work that you and Ben have done to this point in furthering the relationship of the FBI with the Navajo, which I understand is now very strong. Fair enough?"

"Very fair, sir," Zack replied, with a sense of relief.

"I will expect you to follow normal FBI protocols, of course, particularly in terms of communicating with your superior before undertaking any active field operations, including ordering helicopters for vehicle surveillance" -a knowing smile crossed his face as he said this- "or making jurisdiction contacts beyond this office. In other words, I expect that your supervisor will be kept informed at all times. Simple enough, I should think, eh?"

"Yes, sir."

"Zack, I recognize that you and I are partners now, just the two of us out here in the back of beyond. It is my belief that for this office to be successful our partnership must be built upon the trust that comes from a personal relationship. I understand that you benefited from that sort of relationship with Ben and that it had been built over many years. You and I don't have the luxury of that kind of time but we can do our best regardless. I have read the reports and I am aware that you ended up with the lion's share of fieldwork from this office, a natural situation with Ben approaching his retirement year. But that will no longer be the case as I intend to be a presence on the reservation and to respond to calls regularly."

Forrester waved at his walls. "As you can see from my interests, I am not one to be bound to an office by choice." He smiled at Zack.

Zack waited.

"So. Two things. First, my wife and I would like you to join us for dinner tonight. I know that you are not married but please feel free to bring a special friend if you would like."

Zack nodded his appreciation.

"Second, you've had a difficult few months lately with the Roundtree case and your wound and all. So I hope that you will regard my first assignment for you as a bit of a holiday. I need to send you to Palm Springs, California to meet with Supervisory Special Agent Ray Donner, who is the regional supervisor over there. He has an interesting case on his hands, one he seems to think bears certain similarities to the Roundtree case and he would like to consult with you. All accommodations and expenses will be on us. Oh, and take a friend if you'd like." Forrester smiled again. "Enjoy the ambiance, which I understand is quite nice. Feel free to mix some pleasure with your business. Can you leave tomorrow?"

Zack looked up, shocked. "Tomorrow? Uh...Yes, yes sir. Thank you, sir."

But Zack felt a pang of anxiety. More than anything right now he needed to process all he had just learned this morning from Linda, to put things in some sort of order and create a plan of action. Forrester's request was very bad timing. It was frustrating but there was nothing he could do about it.

"I'll give you all the information you need for this junket at our dinner tonight," Forrester said. "Here's my card; it's our new home address. About six?"

He stood up behind his desk and reached across for Zack's hand. His grip was firm.

When Zack re-entered the hot Arizona sunshine his head was spinning even more than before. His plans were entirely uprooted but there was nothing to do but relax and enjoy it. He called Libby immediately.

"What do you say to dinner tonight?" he asked. "And a trip to Palm Springs tomorrow?"

Dinner with Special Agent in Charge Luke Forrester and his coiffed and dimpled young wife Louisa was very pleasant, if awkward. Zack and Luke fell all over one another trying to put each other at ease, and Libby and Louisa spent the evening hopelessly searching for common ground. Louisa was a proper Academy wife. Back East she spent all her time making a proper home for her new husband and scheduling their busy social life within the whirl of Washington politics. Luke emerged at the top of his graduating class at the Academy and was given a series of important assignments at the nation's capital. This allowed the Forresters to remain among their friends and supporters. Luke's superior language skills meant frequent assignments to the embassies, cushy work which increased their social standing. But the Agency is not known for being sentimental. When the need arose for a linguistically talented, culturally aware and politically sensitive Supervisory Agent to serve as liaison to the Navajo Nation in Arizona, the most qualified agent available was Luke Forrester and he was immediately assigned.

And so Louisa Ambrose Forrester found herself unceremoniously expelled from the well-manicured hedges and quietly expensive houses of Silver Spring, Maryland; banished thousands of miles away to an Indian reservation in Arizona and a small rented home in a dust-covered town where lizards and snakes rested in the shade of ragged creosote bushes in her dust filled back yard. She could not have been more out of her element, or more miserable.

Yet Louisa knew that the move spelled opportunity for Luke. Indeed, the assignment had come with a promotion, although the posting itself was not seen as entirely desirable in FBI circles. Louisa was determined to do her best to promote her husband's career in any way within her power and if that meant living on a tumbleweed-lined street where half naked Navajo children played and packs of wild dogs roamed, then so be it.

But tonight it was clear that she shared very little in common with this country-grown girlfriend of Luke's new assistant, a woman who managed a ranch single-handed and trained bloodhounds and galloped around on horses. But Louisa was determined to be a successful hostess, even out here, and she gave it her best effort.

The following day when Zack's truck turned onto Interstate 17 south of Flagstaff, Libby remembered the awkwardness of the evening and giggled.

"I'm afraid I'm destined never know the difference between a Wedgwood teacup and a Korinware mug," she confessed to Zack. "But I tried hard to appear interested."

Zack smiled. "Your efforts were noted and appreciated. But I'm afraid Louisa is going to find it hard to adjust to this place." His grin became mischievous. "Your latent social talents may be called into play several more times, I'm afraid. She latched on to you like a drowning person clutching at a life raft. I suspect she's going to need your support at future soirées."

"I guess I don't mind, if you don't. But may I point out that watching you and Luke dance around each other last night was a bit like watching an elephant quadrille." She laughed and added, "He does seems a nice sort, though."

"More to the point, he seems willing to give me the space I need to do my job. And he seems willing to learn."

Zack became more serious. "But I'm afraid his learning curve may need to be a short one. I had a meeting with Linda, the forensics agent at her lab yesterday. She wanted to show me some additional evidence that didn't fit quite so neatly into the Roundtree case."

He was silent until he had passed a slow moving truck. He continued. "She didn't put any of my concerns to rest."

"Do you want to talk about it?"

"I do, but not now. I haven't had time to square away this new information for myself yet. But I can tell you that all the instincts that led me to think that we were not yet done with the John Roundtree case may be right on the money."

"So there is a second person," Libby said quietly.

Zack looked at her and nodded. Then after a few more moments he turned on the radio. They listened without speaking.

"I always liked Hank Williams," Libby said as the strains of *Your Cheatin' Heart* poured mournfully out of the speakers.

TWENTY-FIVE

The drive to Palm Springs took them the entire day and it was dark and cool outside and starry and clear above them when they stepped wearily out of the truck. The grounds of the hotel were well lit and they could see the luxurious green lawn molded to frame a large pink stucco two story building. The hotel was trimmed in immaculate white with an arched exterior corridor leading to a royal palm-shaded swimming pool. In the twinkly fantasy lights the hotel presented an image taken right out of a travel brochure.

Libby stared in wonder. "Didn't I understand you to say this was a business trip?"

"I did, and it is. But that doesn't mean we can't enjoy ourselves."

After checking in to their room Libby took a glass of wine out onto the balcony and Zack called the number Luke had given him. A brusque male voice answered, and then turned cordial when Zack introduced himself.

"I'm glad you decided to come, Agent Tolliver. I think what I have to share will interest you. And by the same token, I'm pretty sure you can help me."

"Well, that all sounds good," Zack replied. "Shall I come right over to the office?"

"Oh, no, no. No need right now. Relax and enjoy your evening. Tell you what. Let's get together for some breakfast tomorrow morning. There's a pancake place on East Palm Canyon Drive called Elmer's, just down the road from your hotel. You're at the Desert Sun, right? Say eight?"

"I'll see you then."

The next morning Zack left Libby sleeping blissfully on more than her share of the luxurious king bed and navigated his truck along the as yet empty streets of Palm Springs. The pancake house was not difficult to find. Agent Donner's directions had been simple and precise and it was the only parking lot with any cars at this hour.

Entering, he saw that the diners chatting and enjoying their breakfasts were obvious law enforcement types. Immediately he felt a hand on his arm.

"Agent Tolliver? Welcome to Palm Springs."

Supervisory Special Agent Ray Donner was a man of medium height, wiry and strong looking, with tanned and chiseled features. His alert brown eyes held a twinkle. With his polo shirt and slacks he might easily have been mistaken for a vacationing golfer.

"Call me Zack," Zack said. "He nodded toward the other customers. "It seems all of Palm Springs law enforcement is here with us."

Donner laughed. "This is a favorite gathering place for cops. Large servings, good food, but most of all a place where we can talk shop without interference." He tugged Zack's arm toward a table. "We've got our spot right over here. Why don't you look over the menu and get your order in and then I'll tell you why I dragged you off the reservation."

Zack put in his breakfast order and enjoyed a few needed swallows of coffee, then sat back in his chair.

Agent Donner began. "We don't get a lot of serious crime here, Zack. The local police deal mostly with aggravated assault and burglary, that kind of thing. Maybe a dozen forcible rapes a year, which go hand in hand with the vacation mode and the drinking and but we've only had a handful of murder or manslaughter cases in the last several years. That's too many, of course, but for a resort town like this that's not bad. Here at the agency I deal mostly with drug trafficking and terror prevention. I'll give the local police a hand with a case now and again if they need me but usually I'm already on the case because it's drug related, whether trafficking, dealing, forgery or whatever."

Donner paused to breathe, then grinned. "So why am I here, you're asking yourself? I think the best way to tell you that is to tell the story as it came to me and let you see for yourself."

Zack nodded and settled back with his coffee.

"Let me give you the lay of the land first. As you came along East Palm Canyon Drive this morning, you must have noticed this town snuggles up to the mountains. They're tall, abrupt and steep. You should go ride the tramcar over west of town while you're here. You'll gain almost six thousand feet in elevation from base to top, traveling from twenty-six hundred feet at the Valley Station to over eighty-five hundred feet at the top. People like to ride it 'cause it's cool up there, cooler than the desert floor by thirty degrees sometimes. In winter, there can be snow up there even when it's hot and dry down here. That can be a dangerous situation. These are serious mountains within easy reach of sometimes not so serious people who come out here for a good time and a chance to get laid. It's not uncommon for us to lose a tourist now and again who decides he's Jim Whittaker. San Jacinto Peak up there is over ten thousand feet in elevation; professional climbers often use it in winter for mountaineering practice.

What I'm saying is these mountains are a formidable barrier. Now if you catch Route 74 from Palm Desert east of here you can drive right across these mountains to I-15 south or you can stay on Route 79 and take back roads pretty much all the way down to the Mexican border. Not many tourists drive very far down Route 74 before deciding to turn back but if you stick it out all the way to Route 79 you're gonna spend a lot of time waving to yourself because you won't be seeing anyone else along that road, it's that isolated.

That's why I'm here and why the FBI terrorist and drug arm is here. It's no problem at all for drug mules to slip across the border down around Tecate and from there travel pretty much unobserved up through these mountains. Once here they lose themselves among the tourists and then head over to Los Angeles or out east to Phoenix or wherever they want to go with their product."

Donner paused when Zack's order arrived; a plate overflowing with pancakes topped with blueberries and whipped cream. He waited while Zack prepared himself for some serious eating.

"You go ahead while I yack."

Donner noticed Zack's look of anticipation and smiled. "They feed you real good here, but unfortunately I've already had all my wife allows this morning."

Zack dug in and Donner continued. "So that's the situation. The FBI maintains vigilance over these mountains, all along Route 74 and along Route 78 from where it begins at the Salton Sea, and we even go up into some large canyons around here, called the Indian Canyons. They have foot trails leading out of them that eventually connect with roads in the mountains and traffickers will sometimes haul drugs in that way, too.

And there's another issue. Over thirty thousand acres of land in the mountains and even right here within the city limits are part of the reservation of the Agua Caliente band of Cahuilla Indians. As you know from working out there on the Navajo reservation, we can't just go charging onto the Indian land or send our copters hovering over their canyons and other inaccessible places without their say so and their cooperation. There's a lot of red tape and bureaucracy just to gain access. And the Indians up in the mountains aren't very likely to turn to law enforcement just because a stranger passes through their property. They'll deal with it themselves and we just won't know about it. Anyhow, drugs are pretty natural to the Indians; it's all wrapped up in their culture. Smoking a little hash or chewing a peyote button now and then isn't such a big deal. Their shamans have been doing it in rituals and ceremonies forever."

Agent Donner picked up his water glass and took a swallow. He peered over the rim at Zack. "You starting to get the picture? Some of those canyons that run up into the mountains here are long, steep and deep, and all of that terrain is extremely rugged. Then there's the climate. At mid-day in summer or early fall, temperatures of 105 or 106 degrees are pretty common and we've had it go over 120 degrees. Not too many people care to step out of their air conditioned homes and cars when it's that hot. You need water up there, too, a lot of it. On top of that, there's a whole section of those mountains that's closed off to hikers to protect the mountain sheep. So you begin to see that these mountains are not widely traveled.

That's why I was so surprised when the local police chief mentioned to me over coffee one morning that they were dealing with an accidental death way up in a canyon outside of La Quinta near a place called Bear Creek Oasis, and why I was most especially surprised when he mentioned that the victim was a little girl, maybe twelve years old, apparently up there all by herself. By herself! No one had turned her in as missing, no one seemed to be concerned or looking for her. She was found up there by a couple of UC students, in an area that is part of the college desert research preserve. The students were up there to check on soil samples or something like that. The chief said the girl had apparently fallen and broken her neck, that there were abrasions and contusions all over her body to bear that out."

Donner watched Zack closely.

"I hiked up there later to take a look around. It's really rugged terrain and a lot of work just to get up to the Bear Creek Oasis by that trail, but beyond there, where there isn't a trail, it's just ridiculous. What the hell was she doing up there? The part of the canyon where her body was found is extremely narrow and the walls there are what I call vertical. The rocks in the canyon walls are hard and cutting sharp, like volcanic rock, you know? You slice a finger just touching it. And the stuff it's embedded in is all crumbly. I tried to climb up the wall a bit to see if I could find where she fell but had to give it up because big chunks of the stuff kept breaking off in my hands."

At Donner's pause Zack asked the obvious question. "Why did the chief involve you? An accidental hiking death doesn't seem like it would fall within your purview."

"That's exactly what I asked the chief," Donner replied. "Our meeting was casual, we have breakfast together occasionally just to catch up on things, to keep the old communication lines open, you know? But it became clear before long that this girl's death was the real reason we were meeting. Those two UC students who found the little girl had a SAT phone with them and called their professor over at the university and he called the police. So the cops were there within a few hours, looking around, but they didn't see anything worth noting and they simply packed the girl's body out and took it over to the city morgue. When the chief learned about her he went down to take a look, just because it was that unusual to find a little girl up there all by herself like that. He saw right away that she had the wrong clothing on for a hike in the mountains, just some little frock kind of thing with slippers on her feet - slippers, for Christ's sake! It didn't set right with him and he asked forensics to do some tests, you know, blood and fluid groups, X- rays, that stuff. It was after he got the results that he set up our meeting."

Warning bells started going off in Zack's head. "Tell me, what was the little girl's ethnicity?"

Donner grinned. "So you're catching on. She was a blonde Caucasian with very white skin."

Zack sat there, the turmoil inside him growing. "Go on."

"So I asked the chief why he thought he needed to inform me about all of this. Then he told me what his forensics people had found." Donner ticked off the points on his finger. "Her neck had been broken, right enough, but not by the fall. They found finger and thumb sized contusions on her neck suggesting that it had been deliberately broken before she fell. In fact, his forensics people believed all those scrapes and bruises that we attributed to a fall had actually occurred post-mortem, as if to deliberately try to conceal the cause of death. And, she had been sexually abused repeatedly over a significant period of time. Twelve years old! And here's the even weirder part. While examining a tissue sample they found evidence of salt. She had been salted. Salted! Like a side of beef."

Zack leaned forward in excitement. "Did they find any drugs in her?"

"He didn't mention any."

"What about footprints at the scene?"

"Chief said they didn't see any, not human, anyway."

"What do you mean?"

"Well, the crime scene is just up canyon from the Bear Creek Oasis, like I said, which is a water hole, at least some of the time. So there were animal prints coming and going, as you would expect."

"Any large animals?"

"No. Uh...wait. Now that you mention it, there were some mountain lion tracks moving up the canyon a little ways away from the body. The cops were saying the girl couldn't have been there too long or she would have been some animal's lunch already. In fact, they were kind of concerned about a mountain lion hanging around, which was one of the reasons they decided to take the body with them right then."

Zack tried to stay calm. "I need to get up there and look around," he told Donner.

Donner smiled quietly. "Hit a nerve, eh? I thought it might. I read about your case over in Navajo Land. Pretty bizarre, what with the way it ended and all. We've been talking about it here. So when we found this little girl, you came right to mind. But now it's your turn. D'ya think there might be a connection? You got your man in that case, didn't you?"

"Well, yes, or at least we thought so. John Roundtree sure seemed to be the guilty party, all the evidence pointing right at him, so we closed the case. But I learned of some new evidence just a couple of days ago that strongly suggests that he wasn't working alone."

"A partner - for a serial killer? That's unusual."

"Yes, it is. Which is why we never thought about it that way before. But now, with this new evidence, and looking back at the way things went, it does seem possible."

"So he could be here, right now..."

"He could be, and if it is him, it looks like he hasn't slowed down a bit." Zack looked across at Donner. "Maybe I can help, at least to resolve the question of whether this is related or maybe even is the same guy." He did his own ticking off on a finger. "I'd need to talk to the police chief's forensic team. If I find what I'm thinking I might find, the FBI needs to take over this case. Sounds like your friend the chief won't mind. Then I'll need to bring out my own forensic specialist, the one who worked my case to work along with your people. And I'll need to visit the scene with Big Blue, the scent dog I used at home; I can have him sent right away. The dog will tell us beyond a doubt whether this is connected and if it's the same guy. First, though, I need to get up to the scene right away, today if possible while there's still a chance to find some evidence. How long ago did they find her?"

"Two days ago now. But this is the desert, remember. Anything that was there two days ago is still going to be there now."

"Not if our man came back to erase it."

"He'd do that? That's pretty bold."

"This guy? He's that bold."

Donner stood up and took out his cell phone while continuing to talk to Zack. "You go on back to your room and grab some hiking shoes and a hat. I'll meet you at your hotel in twenty minutes. I'm calling the chief right now to claim jurisdiction and get the girl moved to my lab. He's expecting my call, one way or the other. I'll have my people debrief the police forensics team while you and I are up on the mountain. Then you can meet with my forensics chief this afternoon. Go ahead and have your dog sent up. When he gets here, we'll take him straight up. Is all this quick enough for you?"

TWENTY-SIX

Libby was on the balcony sipping a cup of hotel courtesy coffee and soaking up the warm morning sun along with the view when Zack returned. He came to stand next to her at the railing.

He looked at her cup. "That stuff is usually pretty terrible. Would you like me to find you some real coffee?"

"This is actually quite good." Libby smiled up at him. "It's serving its purpose, to awaken and focus me. How was your breakfast meeting?"

"Surprising...or maybe not so much, depending upon how you look at it. Agent Donner will come by here in ten minutes and then we're going to hike up into the mountains to visit a crime scene. I hope I'm wrong, but his description of the circumstances surrounding the death of a little blonde girl up there fits the John Roundtree murders. Maybe he did have a partner, and maybe that partner has moved his activities into this area."

Libby took a sharp breath.

"We don't really know anything yet," Zack hastened to add, "but we need to make sure one way or the other. If there is a connection, I'll need to stay on and work with Agent Donner. If not, we'll enjoy a day or two here, then go home and forget about it."

"How will you be sure?"

"Well, my dear, that's where you come in. I'll go examine the crime scene this morning and this afternoon I'll meet with the forensics people who examined the body. But without fingerprints or DNA we can't be positive of a link between the two crimes. At least, not without Big Blue."

"Blue?"

"Yes. We need to see if Blue can connect the scent from the Roundtree case to a scent here at this crime scene. If he can, we'll know for sure it's our man."

"But Blue would need a scent sample. He won't remember that one scent from so long ago, and even if he did, we couldn't be sure. We don't have anything to use for him to smell to establish that scent."

"Actually, we do. It's the only solid evidence Barefoot Man left behind. Those Pigmy Cactus spines, the ones he used to drug Diablo and to try to drug me. They'll have his scent because he handled them. We bagged the spines right away so the scent shouldn't be contaminated, even after Linda worked with them."

Libby thought for a moment, sipping her coffee. "Yes, that should work. I'll call Lenny and have him prepare Blue for travel. Who can bring him out here?"

"That shouldn't be a problem. I'm planning to ask Eagle Feather to come out. I've got a feeling I'm going to need a good tracker. He can pick up Blue and the two cacti spines and bring them along. With any luck he could be here by tomorrow morning."

Zack was pulling his cell phone out to make the call when a knock sounded at the door of the suite.

He chuckled and looked appreciatively at Libby and the way what she wasn't wearing beneath her sheer nightie was illuminated by the sun's rays.

"You might want to throw on a robe. It wouldn't do to distract Agent Donner too much during this investigation."

A short time later all arrangements had been made and Zack was in Agent Donner's black pickup truck with an ATV on the trailer behind it speeding down the Redlands Freeway toward La Quinta. The trailhead for Bear Creek Oasis was located at the southern most end of the town of La Quinta in the barren desert across the street from a row of expensive suburban houses. The point of demarcation between town and wilderness and between modern and primeval was abrupt. Where the water stopped, so did the town.

Donner parallel parked his rig on the wide shoulder of the barrier road.

"The land beyond this point is protected," he explained, "otherwise these homes would march right on up the valley floor to the base of those mountains over there."

Zack stood and looked around while Donner prepared to unload the ATV. It was approaching midday by now and the heat was already oppressive, beyond even what he was used to in Arizona. The flat sandy terrain stretched out in front of him, featureless except for a solitary mound-like hill a half-mile away. Far beyond that blue knife-edge ridges rose precipitously to join up at the mountain summit.

"You mentioned the Indian reservations when we spoke this morning. Is there one near here?"

"Actually, yes."

Donner looked up from the four-by-six ramp he was unlatching. "Fact is, we are very near what could be called the spiritual center of the Agua Caliente Bands of the area."

Zack helped Donner slide out the heavy wood ramp.

"Over there" -Donner paused to wipe away some sweat and gestured to the east- "beyond that saddle is the ancient shoreline of what used to a huge lake. The Salton Sea is all that's left of it now. But marshes and some remnants of the woodlands that were part of the ancient shoreline are still there. That land is sacred to the local band of Indians because the ancient shore was important to the activities of their forefathers. Up there" -he gestured back toward the mountains" -other groups control the land, the University of Southern California for one. There's a large Federal Preserve up there but the Agua

Caliente still consider it their spiritual homeland. They keep a close eye on it."

The conversation ended when Donner turned the key on the ATV and it roared into life. He backed it carefully down the ramp and onto the road surface. Zack saw that it was loaded with several gallons of water.

Agent Donner leaned close to Zack's ear. "We'll be taking the ATV up the dry wash. That way we can save some time and energy and we can bring a large water supply as close as possible to the place where we will start walking."

Zack squeezed on behind Donner and they bumped quickly up and over the curb and across the sidewalk to the trailhead. Donner throttled past the signs that warned of flash floods, mountain lions and rattle snakes and gunned it up a wide sandy trail. Almost immediately an oasis of palm trees that seemed right out of *Beau Geste* came into view.

"The state keeps a picnic ground over there," Donner shouted over the noisy engine. "It's a real oasis with a natural spring. But we'll be turning off before then."

True to his word, the ATV soon turned onto a smaller track that passed between the foot of the mound-hill and a large concrete spillway.

Donner leaned back and angling his head toward Zack and shouted. "When the rains come they come hard and fast in a flood down from these mountains. Without this dam here, those expensive houses below would all wash away."

They came to a well-defined sandy wash about a half-mile wide created by the flood bed, a natural road that led toward the base of the mountains. The dry wash was wide and hard-packed and Donner cranked up the speed. Dust billowed behind them as they roared along. After a time the high banks of the dry wash crept closer together and the ride became considerably rougher. The flood course was eddied and rutted by erosion and Donner needed all of his concentration to maneuver along the narrowing path between high sand islands capped with cholla and cactus and the large rocks that had been swept into the middle of the dry bed by the unimaginable force of the floodwaters. They came to a stop when the towering banks of the wash were no more than a hundred feet apart and the flood course so choked with boulders and deadfall that not even their nimble little vehicle could find passage. Donner coasted over to the cliff face and turned off the engine.

"It's Shank's Mare from here," he said, leaping off. "There's a decent trail on top of that bank. Fill up a water bottle. It's at least three miles to the oasis, all steep and all dry."

The trail where it began was surprisingly wide and well groomed, even lined with border rocks in some places.

Zack saw a lot of footprints. "Who comes up here?"

"Tourists, and the college kids to get to their preserve, and most anybody who enjoys a hike will start up here. It's very scenic with great views that come along quickly and then there's the promise of water once you finally get to the oasis, something most of the trails in this area don't offer. But it gets steep real quick and most day hikers get discouraged and turn back before Bear Springs."

"So our suspect must have known this - that there could possibly be a fair amount of foot traffic going up here." Zack looked at the maze of barren mountain ridges and canyons that surrounded them. "Couldn't he have picked a more isolated spot than this?"

"That thought came to me, too."

They climbed in silence for a while, each caught up in his thoughts. The trail wound precipitously onward and upward until the terrain became so steep that switchbacks were required. On the return from each traverse they found increasingly dramatic views where the canyon floor fell away.

During a rest stop Donner saw Zack look down and he guessed what he was thinking.

"Some people do try to walk up the floor of that canyon down there, thinking it must be shorter, but they are never prepared for how rough and steep it is and for the thick brush that gets piled up by flash floods. It's almost impenetrable and there are large boulders they've got to climb over, not to speak of the rattlesnakes. This way is quicker and easier even if it is steep and long."

Looking out from their vantage point several hundred feet up above the canyon floor Zack saw the main canyon split off into two separate canyons. The sun was frying pan hot and both men sweated freely through their shirts. Donner pointed out the canyon that forked to the left.

"That branch over there twists over to the east and then dies out after a long while, but you don't know that when you're down in it. This branch" -he pointed toward the right fork- "is where we want to go. If you look way up there where the canyon bends you can just see a green patch. That's Bear Creek Oasis."

"That's a long way yet."

"Sure is. This is where most of the greenhorns turn back."

Conner slapped the lid back on his water bottle and grinned encouragingly and started on up the trail. After another half hour of steady climbing the trail dropped down along the inner wall of the canyon and began a gradual descent. It steepened and Zack saw that they were headed directly to the canyon floor. When the green patch they had seen from above came into view next it was close enough so that he could distinguish the individual palm trees that provided its color.

There was a lot of coyote brush and cholla choking the canyon floor now and the trail led them up over boulders and around large tree limbs scattered about by the flood torrents. Entering the oasis, though, Zack saw that the ground here was clear of debris, protected by a dam-like rock protrusion upstream that divided the flow and sent the flood waters to either side, thus creating a safe refuge below it. Here in the shade of the oasis it was cool. Muddy swamp water provided life to the flora growing in this protected circle, like an irrigated field in a desert.

Plastic water bottles were scattered about, evidence that some tourists had indeed made it this far.

"The water here can be a life saver and it's probably good to drink right where it bubbles up." Donner stirred it with a stick. "But animal urine and feces makes it risky so I stick to my water bottle unless I'm desperate and have brought along some iodine." He grimaced. "I don't particularly care for Montezuma's Revenge."

"How far from here?"

"Not too far. It's tough sledding, though. We have to climb over that rock ledge up there and then pick our way through more debris in the dry bed. There's a trace of a trail made by the UC kids but it's not the highway we've enjoyed so far."

Donner was right. The last half-mile to the crime scene was more strenuous than any part of the hike up to the oasis had been and just as long, or at least it seemed that way to Zack. But then he saw a bit of bright yellow tape through the brush ahead. When they arrived, Donner looked around and grunted in satisfaction.

"It looks undisturbed. Not many people come up here. In fact, it was sheer luck that those students came when they did, when you think about it. Their inspection teams only come in here every couple of months. That little body could have been nothing but bones by then."

"Luck?" Zack echoed thoughtfully. "I wonder."

There wasn't much to see with the body gone. They looked at the bare patch inside the circle of yellow tape where it had been. Clumps of tough grass and some beavertail cacti were the nearest vegetation. Zack could make out a slight depression in the dirt just inside the yellow tape where the body must have lain. But he wasn't interested in that. He walked slowly around the perimeter and inspected the ground closely.

"Done some tracking back in Navajo Land, have you?" Donner watched him curiously.

"Had to learn," Zack explained. "Out there on the Rez, the perpetrator is always gone before you get there and it's up to you to find out where he went." While he was speaking Zack's eyes continued to dart about. He searched in gradually widening circles, finding several animal tracks, as Donner had forecast; lots of lizard skids, some small pad prints of something in the weasel family possibly, a raccoon, and where a fox had approached.

Zack found what he was looking for a full fifty feet beyond the tape. It was the clear pugmark of a large mountain lion, pressed firmly into the sandy soil. He knelt to examine the track closely. Ordinarily he would have thought that the print had been made only moments before, but in these incredibly dry conditions Zack knew it must have been there for at least two days, when the policemen first found it. A big boot print nearby confirmed this. He looked for another print. The cat had walked on a bed of debris for a while where it left no prints but then a few yards on he found more; a right rear, then a left front, and then a right front. The prints were headed up canyon away from the scene. Zack took his time and studied each print closely, the scorching sun on his shoulders unnoticed.

Finally Zack let his breath out slowly. He was satisfied. He could see now that the weight of the animal was distributed evenly across each of the prints and that there was no natural depression at the forefoot from weight shifts foot to foot that should have appeared in the tracks of a quadruped walking naturally.

Just like that bear, Zack thought to himself. He stood up and called Donner over.

"I've found the cat tracks you were telling me about," he said after Donner got there. "They lead on up the canyon. I'm going to follow them but I want you to come along with me to see what I find when I find what I think I'll find."

"What do you think you'll find?"

"I won't tell you because you won't believe me. If I find it, you'll see it."

Donner was puzzled but curious and followed when Zack led off.

They found no prints immediately beyond those Zack had just examined and then they were on rocky terrain but beyond that they found more prints in softer ground. They were pressed in deep, the detail perfect, and they confirmed Zack's previous thoughts about their evenness and unnatural perfection. The creature that made these tracks had walked carefully with its weight falling evenly above each print, a gait unnatural for such a lithe sinewy creature as a mountain lion. It was a gait similar to Bear Man. Zack felt his excitement grow in anticipation. And then, just a few yards further on, there it was. A bare human footprint following immediately after the last mountain lion print.

Zack turned to look at Donner and pointed to the print. Donner, startled, pushed past him to take a closer look. Zack almost laughed at the chain of emotions chasing one another across Donner's face like the lighted windows of a train at night. First came incredulity and disbelief, then suspicion, and finally confusion, all appearing one after the other on his countenance.

"This can't be!" Donner blurted.

Zack remembered his own feelings on Monument Mesa, the disbelief followed by the rising feeling of confusion and helplessness in the face of evidence of something that should not exist but could not be explained away with logic or science. It felt nice to have company.

Zack mercifully broke the silence of the moment. "This is our perpetrator. We have his footprint. Now we need is to call for a technician to come up here to get a cast of this print and any others we find. We need to do it right now, because as soon as we leave he'll come right back down here and erase them."

"You think he's here, now, after four days? Waiting? Watching us? Why would he do that? And if that's true, why hasn't he already erased them?"

Zack thought he knew the answer. "Because of me," he said slowly. "He's been expecting me. He knew I would be called in because of the Roundtree case and he knew that I would come and he's been waiting, maybe not up here, maybe down in Palm Springs, waiting to see if I'd come. This is a message to me, this print, left out here in the open. He knew I'd be the one to find it. He needs to watch me find it, to watch me understand."

"You think it's personal."

"This tells me it's personal. Only once before has he deviated from his practice of burying the girls' bodies where they wouldn't be found. That was when he left the body in plain sight up on Monument Mesa. There it might have had something to do with Roundtree or he might just have become bored. Or maybe, just maybe, he had already decided on me; maybe he knew I would be called in and wanted to engage me in his game. I don't know. But whatever it was then it wasn't an accident; it was deliberate bravado. This" -Zack nodded at the prints- "is to send me a message and a challenge. He could've just let things go and buried this girl somewhere and no one would have realized he was here. But he didn't. He knew I'd be called in and that I'd look for this print. He's been waiting for me and he's out here now. He watched me look for the print and find it and right now he's watching me understand his message."

Donner looked all around at the canyon walls and at the thick brush of the dry bed, consternation on his face.

Zack pushed his point home. "That's why we need to call for assistance and get that plaster kit up here right now. We have to stay here and guard the prints until your people arrive."

Donner placed the call while Zack walked back along the tracks, wishing for the hundredth time that he'd had the presence of mind to make a plaster cast of the tracks on Monument Mesa back in Arizona. He had no doubt in his mind they would have matched these. They had the same look, the same stride; the prints of a man accustomed to traveling barefoot in the most difficult terrain, such as the terrain they were in now. He walked back to the first barefoot print and sat on a shaded rock to think. Might he find blood splatter among the tracks further up this canyon? Probably not, he decided. Donner hadn't mentioned any open wounds on the victim, only scrapes and abrasions. Apparently the girl's body had been found before scavengers had time to do their damage.

Donner put away his cell phone and looked at Zack.

"Okay, I've listened to you and gone out on a limb here despite not knowing what's going on. Now it's time for you to fill me in. Are you certain that this is your Navajo Land killer?"

"Yes, I just can't prove it yet."

"And how the hell did he pull that little trick with the cat prints. Was there ever really a mountain lion here?"

"I can't answer either question for sure yet. But I don't believe there was a lion here. I think he made these tracks in some way, the same way he made those bear prints on Monument Mesa. All we can do right now is gather all of the evidence we have from this scene and then compare it to the evidence we have back in Tuba City. And we need to backtrack this guy, to follow these prints back to wherever they started. Do you have any really good trackers on your team?"

"No."

"I've got one of the best. He's already on his way out here."

Donner looked exasperated. "You were expecting this."

Zack grinned sheepishly and shrugged his shoulders. "I could've told you what I thought I might find but what would you have thought? That I was a nut case, probably."

"Look, this is a lot of information for me to process all at once. First, you're telling me you think this guy is right here in these hills, maybe even watching us right now?"

"I'd say he is definitely watching us right now. And I'd guess he's real close by. So keep your eyes and ears open. We don't want him getting closer than a hundred feet; that would be too close."

As if to illustrate his point Zack took his gun from its holster, checked the load, and set it on his lap.

"A hundred feet? Why would he try to come that close? How can this guy be a threat to two armed FBI agents?"

"He's a deadly threat," Zack said quietly. "His weapons are not conventional. The sooner your guys get here, the sooner we can feel safe." He smiled briefly at Donner. "In the meantime, let me tell you a few things about the John Roundtree case you probably didn't hear through official channels."

Zack took a sip of water, settled back on his rock and began at the beginning, leaving nothing out.

TWENTY-SEVEN

"Can't talk now! You do not want to be near me until I've showered," Zack called as he walked straight to the bathroom of the suite.

Libby waved a lazy hand in response and took a sip from her drink. She was enjoying the balcony that was cleverly oriented to promote sun in the early morning and provide cool shade during the hot afternoons. It was mid-afternoon now. Zack was hot and exhausted and fantasized about his own cool drink. But he had barely freshened up when a call came to tell him that Donner's forensic people were waiting for him at the FBI lab.

Zack debated whether to tell Libby what they had found up in Bear Spring canyon, then decided not to spoil her pleasant interlude quite yet. She smiled absently at him as he rushed by on his way out again and then fell happily back into the pages of her book.

The forensics lab was located in the basement of the Palm Springs FBI building, a square, fort-like edifice on Tahquitz Way nestled among attractively landscaped two to three story buildings which were mostly occupied by small retail stores and offices. Zack showed his credentials at the reception desk and was immediately ushered to an elevator and escorted to a lower floor and a corridor where a balding man in a white coat took him in hand.

"I'm Special Agent George Flood. Welcome to the Palm Springs branch of the Bureau, where career opportunity and vacation ambience meet," he grinned.

George was short and leaning toward stoutness with crinkly blue eyes that nearly disappeared now in appreciation of his own humor.

Zack shook the offered hand. "I think I've already sampled some of your vacation ambience up in your mountains."

"So I heard, so I heard. You managed to shake Ray up this morning. As soon as he got back down he called and asked me to step up this meeting. He doesn't rattle that easily, generally."

George steered Zack through the lab's thick glass door into a room filled with tables and testing equipment. At the far end of the room they paused at a sealed door with an embedded temperature gauge. Zack guessed it must be a refrigerated room.

"You're going to need these," George said.

Zack took the sanitary paper coat and gloves offered him and followed Flood inside. Vertical rows of slab drawers lined one entire wall. Four autopsy tables, each with its own equipment tray, electric outlet, and long fluorescent lamp marched down the center of the room like grotesque pool tables. All were empty except the second table, which held a body; the pale white corpse of a young girl partially draped by a body liner. She seemed very much out of place on the shiny wide surface.

George led Zack to the table. "I'm told you have some questions about our little girl."

"A few."

"Ask yours and then I'll ask mine."

"Good deal. First, I'm told you found salt in her skin tissue."

"Nahcolite, to be exact. Sodium carbonate decahydrate and about 18 to 19 percent sodium bicarbonate with traces of halite and some sodium sulfate."

"How do you think it came to be on her?"

"Well, at first glance it might easily have come from rolling around in any one of several dry lake beds in the area where salt deposits were left when the salt water lake dried. We're collecting salt samples from them to compare, to see if we can match the exact composition. That shouldn't take too long."

"Assuming it's local salt," Zack probed.

George raised a bushy red eyebrow at that. "Exactly. As to the tumbling around theory, there's one problem. She would have had to tumble around starkers because she's very evenly coated. We took skin samples from ten different areas of her body and all had residue in exactly the same proportion."

"Almost as if she had been deliberately coated," Zack finished.

Again George looked at him strangely. "Exactly."

"Of course you did toxin blood screens?"

"Of course. Around here it's second nature to test a corpse for drugs. In this case, once we found the contusions indicating that her neck had been deliberately snapped, we went the whole nine yards. And with a little girl like this" -George nodded down at her- "our guys go all out to find the bad guy."

"And?"

"Not much unusual. If I were her family doctor at her annual physical I'd advise her to step up the proteins a little bit and maybe cut back on the simple carbs but that's pretty much true for any preteen kid. We found no actual drugs or toxins at all except, and this is a big exception, some trace elements of plasma flunitrazepam concentrations of about twenty unit grams per liter, enough to suggest to us that she could possibly have been receiving regular doses of Rohypnol, maybe as a nighttime hypnotic. The evidence of vaginal penetration and the contusions we found suggest that she had been repeatedly molested over a period of six to eight months prior to her death. The perpetrator may have used the Rohypnol to keep her passive and forgetful."

Zack nodded and then said, "One more question and then it's your turn. Did you find any unusual marks on her body, like pin pricks or insect bites or that kind of thing?"

George's eyes narrowed. "Not that I noticed."

"May I?" George nodded.

Zack reached for the body and gently lifted the little girl's shoulders to turn her head slightly. He looked closely at her hairline and grunted in satisfaction. He pointed it out for George. "Just here, right at the hairline. See that little red mark? If you take a sample and test the tissue there, I think you'll find it's where the Rohypnol was administered."

"How did you know to look there?"

"It's in the same location on all our girls."

"So maybe there is a connection," George said. "We'll get right on that."

"Ok, I'm done. Now it's your turn," Zack said.

George looked down at the small body. "Our examination suggests that the girl was killed well before she received those scrapes and cuts. There was little to no bleeding from them yet the marks are consistent with tissue damage caused by falling from a great height onto a hard rough surface, like for instance from a canyon wall to the canyon floor where she was found. Did you find any post mortem injuries on your Arizona girl?"

"Yes," Zack affirmed. "Her large post-mortem wound was from a slash, not from an impact, but beyond that the parallel is exact."

"Meant to give the impression that death had come from the post-mortem wounds?"

"Exactly."

"Another thing. Beyond the obvious abuse, this girl appears to have been well cared for; that is, fed substantially if not very nutritiously, given plenty of sleep, and so on. This doesn't square well with the serial abuser/rapist who chains kids in the cellar and feeds them from a dog dish kind of thing. In fact, there are no ligature marks on her wrists or ankles, no signs of constraint at all. Did you find that as well?"

"When we first found Mesa Girl, we were not thinking serial kidnapping or rape so we weren't looking specifically for any marks of that sort. But had they been there, we would have noticed them. Our forensics person was very thorough. So the answer to your question is no, there were no indications that she was ever physically restrained."

"And yet the healed labial abrasions and partially healed vaginal injuries suggests molestation over a period of months if not years..."

"Yes, it was the same with all of our girls. Our evidence suggests that Roundtree molested the girls regularly for a period of time before he apparently grew tired of them and finally disposed of them. We guessed the length of time each had been kept by the extent of the decomposition of the girl's body, suggesting how long she had been buried, and then confirmed the result by dividing the number of years following the death of Roundtree's wife and child by the total number of girls. It came to about four to six months each."

"Do you think that's what we'll find here?"

"Do you mean serial killings over a long period of time like that? Well, if Roundtree had a partner, and if this is the guy, which I hope to prove one way or the other, then I'd say no. It seems more likely that once we chased him out of Arizona he came here and he's just now setting up shop all over again."

"But why begin with such an audacious act that he immediately puts law enforcement into an uproar? Seems to me he'd want to start quietly so that his new location stays a secret..."

"That makes sense. But I'm not sure this guy fits any of our normal profiles. And there are other complications. Let's catch this guy first and then we can ask him."

"One final question. How do you deal with ...this?" George stared down at the tiny victim.

"I don't know if I am dealing with it yet." Zack picked up his cell phone and punched in some numbers. "There's someone in Tuba City I want you to talk to." He spoke into the phone. "Hello, Linda? Zack.

I've got Agent George Flood here with me. He's the forensics chief at the Palm Springs branch. I'd like the two of you to share some technical notes about the Roundtree case. You might well be working together very soon."

Later after Zack had wearily carded his way back into the hotel suite he found a note from Libby. He followed her written instructions and found her sun bathing at the pool with a drink resting on the table near her. She looked over the top of her sunglasses at his approach.

"I figured I'd better get in the vacation part of this visit before Blue arrives."

Zack slid wearily into an empty lounge chair next to her. "You figured right. This is probably your last chance to relax." He sighed. "I could use a little of this myself," he said, turning his face toward the sun.

"When does Blue arrive?"

"I called Eagle Feather; he's bringing Blue right away. They could be here by morning."

"And then?"

"And then we go right up to the canyon crime site. Eagle Feather will have the Pigmy Cactus spines and we'll see if we can set Blue on the scent from those. That will answer our first big question, whether we're dealing with the same man. If not, we turn the whole shebang back to Donner and we go home. But if it is him, you and Eagle Feather and an FBI posse will follow the trail as far as Blue can take you."

"And you?"

"I'll start doing some local research from here." Zack closed his eyes. "Agent Donner wants to go with you tomorrow to be sure you'll be well protected. But I'm thinking your best protection will be the fact that I'm not up there with you. I think Bear Man will want to keep an eye on me down here."

"You're starting to take this a little personally, aren't you?"

"I didn't intend to - I'm just reading the signs."

Libby changed the subject. "How is your new boss Agent Forrester with all of this?"

"He's taking it in stride. I think he figured there was a good chance I might end up assisting with this case when he sent me out here. I've no doubt he'll pull me back if he needs me at home."

A loud knock echoed in Zack's sleeping brain. He sat up abruptly. It was full dark; he could barely make out the form of Libby next to him. He looked at his watch. Five-thirty. He sat there, fog brained. Then another knock sounded. So it wasn't a dream. He willed himself out of the warm bed and onto the cold floor and shuffled over to the door and pulled it open.

A sudden weight pushed him backward. It was Big Blue, standing on his hind legs with two big paws planted on Zack's chest, slathering his face with a thick wet tongue. The big dog dropped to the floor and lumbered across the living room to the open bedroom door. Zack watched him leap up on the bed and shower a very startled and squealing Libby with his large wet kisses.

Zack turned back and saw Eagle Feather grinning at him in the doorway.

"You've grown soft in the last few months," was his comment as he took in the luxurious suite. But it showed in his eyes that he was happy to see Zack. "Does this hotel permit dogs and Indians?"

"As it happens, you're on an Indian reservation right now," Zack replied with a laugh. "Seems to me the question is, do they allow white men?"

Zack started to explain how the Aqua Caliente Tribal Indian

Reservation had been parceled by the government in a hopscotch manner throughout the community, deliberately alternating public and reservation land with an eye to promoting development, but Eagle Feather waved him off.

"Too much information, white man. Blue and I've been traveling since dinner last night. And he's the one got to do most of the sleeping."

"Well, I'm glad to see you both." Zack went to find another key card on the desk while Eagle Feather peered into the bedroom and waved to Libby.

"Here's the key to your room just down the hall. Go freshen up and Libby and I'll get dressed and meet you in the little café on the first floor in about half an hour."

Zack laughed, looking at Blue stretched out comfortably on Zack's of the bed. "I guess you'll need to leave Blue with us," he said.

When Zack and Libby arrived at the café, Eagle Feather was already enjoying a coffee and a pastry. They joined him at the table and immediately dispatched the waitress for a full pot of coffee.

"The phone message you left me was a bit vague," Eagle Feather said. "I gather you need me for a little high quality tracking. I guess that means they don't have anybody here with the level of talent you require. So what's up?"

Zack smiled. "You and I haven't talked much about the Roundtree case since the night I was shot. You may remember that I was sent off to the hospital and Ben took over the investigation. I was kind of out of the loop. All of the evidence pointed right at John Roundtree so Ben closed the case and stamped "solved" on it. But there were too many loose ends, too many things that didn't add up for me. I moved on to other cases but I kept going back to it in my head."

Eagle Feather looked at Zack over his coffee cup. "You just couldn't accept the notion of a Skinwalker, or the idea that Roundtree might have had special powers. Think that might be part of it?"

"Maybe," Zack conceded. "But there was evidence that didn't quite fit, like the drugs that Roundtree shouldn't have been able to obtain or even know about and some time sequences that didn't quite go together. And then I got a call from Linda Whittaker, the forensics agent, who couldn't make her data quite fit either. When we compared notes, it seemed pretty clear that Roundtree must have had an accomplice."

That got Eagle Feather's attention. "I never really felt it was John Roundtree up there on that mesa," he said slowly. "But I decided that when someone becomes a Skinwalker they probably change completely."

"Seems we both have our blind sides," Zack remarked.

"So you believe it was this partner who was up on Monument Mesa..."

"I do."

"And you think he's here now?"

Zack nodded. "We're going to try to prove it today with Blue. That's why I had you stop by to pick up the Pigmy Cactus spines. If Blue can pick up a scent from those and identify it with a scent up in this canyon we'll have our answer for sure. Then you and Libby and Blue can track him, just like we did on the mesa."

Zack took another sip of his coffee and when he spoke again it was in a whisper. "They were the same prints, the same barefoot prints that appeared out of the bear prints. But it wasn't a bear this time, it was a mountain lion."

There was an intake of breath from Libby.

"Barefoot human prints out of mountain lion tracks," Eagle Feather repeated.

"Yes."

The table was silent. Eagle Feather poured himself another coffee.

"What else do you know?" he asked. "Was there another little dead girl? I assume there's a reason you're here."

Again Zack nodded.

"A blonde white girl?"

Another nod.

"Made to look like a mountain lion kill?"

"Not this time," Zack said. "It was made to look like a fall."

Eagle Feather thought about it. "It's a message. What do you think he wants?"

"He wants me," Zack replied. "And maybe you, too. I didn't think of that before, but he would have to know I would send for you. He's a step ahead every time. He gets in your head. He wants to play, and apparently he considers us worthy opponents."

Eagle Feather's eyes glistened with excitement.

Zack went on. "Maybe today we'll learn which one of us he wants. I won't be going up there with you; I need to follow some leads down here in the valley. If he turns up with you then it isn't me he's after."

"If he wants me, I don't want to keep him waiting, "Eagle Feather said. "When do we go up?"

Zack stood, stretched, and reached for the check. "Right now."

TWENTY-EIGHT

Libby, Eagle Feather and Blue all piled into Zack's truck for the drive to La Quinta and the Bear Creek Oasis trailhead. Donner's big white SUV and the ATV trailer would lead the way. As they stood near the trucks in the hotel parking lot that morning, coffee in hand, they had learned that the plan had changed yet again. Donner would guide them to the crime scene as before but he would leave them there with a second agent to assist the Arizona team with the tracking. Donner had decided to run the operation from his Palm Springs office. He would dispatch a helicopter to fly over them at regular intervals - Zack thinking how nice it must be to have such a fat budget - to maintain visual as well as radio contact and to offer an option in case of emergency. When the trackers reached the end of the trail, wherever that might be, the helicopter would extract them.

Zack too planned to leave the team at the trailhead and not participate in Operation Barefoot Tracker, as it was dubbed, but he expected to check in with Donner from time to time and be ready to assist if needed.

At the trailhead Zack helped the team prepare for departure and watched Donner roar off up the trail on the ATV with the water supply. After the dust had settled the second agent, who introduced himself as Tubby Tibbs, led out on foot, with the Arizona team right behind.

Zack watched them go. He knew it would be several hours before there could be any news. He went to sit in his truck in the early morning coolness to study a map of the area. He was parked on the shoulder right behind the empty trailer. The road here was wide and seldom traveled, as it looped back on itself and served only the trailhead and four or five homes across the street. Zack was deeply absorbed in his map when something made him glance in his mirror. Another vehicle was approaching, moving very slowly. It crept toward him and crunched to a stop just two car lengths behind. It sat there, unmoving, its engine running. No one got out. Unaccountably, Zack's pulse began to race and he experienced shortness of breath, as if the air had suddenly thickened. The vehicle behind him was a truck, a black truck with a big upturned mouth of a grill and two vertical headlight eyes. Its windshield was impenetrable. He felt panic grow in him. He sat there, his map forgotten, his eyes locked on the rearview mirror, unable to look away but not able to see anything through the truck's dark tinted windshield, somehow knowing what would come next and then seeing and feeling the two penetrating red eyes reach out through the darkness and enter his rear view mirror and sear into his very being. He observed his own fear like a witness of an accident, detached yet involved, helplessness holding him. He saw his fear about to overwhelm him and nullify him and he suddenly felt great anger and the intensity of that emotion freed him and his gun leapt into his hand. He thrust himself out the door, found his feet and ran hard toward the dark truck. As if it had read his mind, the vehicle slammed into reverse and with rear tires spinning and smoking it exploded into a sliding K turn in the wide roadway, rocking precariously side to side, then accelerated powerfully away. Zack straddled the middle of the road, his chest heaving, his pistol at his side in a wrenching grip, fighting the efficacy of those two red eyes, feeling their loathing.

Shaken though he was, Zack's training served him and his eye went automatically to the license plate. It was a California tag. He memorized the number. But he knew even as he walked back to his truck that the plate numbers would lead nowhere.

"That settles one question," Zack said aloud to himself, his confidence returning with the sound and feel of his own voice. "I'm the one he's after."

Back in the truck cab it was just as cool and pleasant as it had been before and Zack resumed studying the map, annoyed with himself that his hands shook but ignoring them to focus hard on his purpose.

Zack was looking for the closest Indian reservation. Earlier research on his computer had revealed five Indian reservations existing in the Palm Springs area, each of which belonged to smaller bands of the Aqua Caliente tribe. Most of the bands were headquartered in city centers with their tribal offices in great tall buildings and casinos. But one band had caught his eye, the Torres-Martinez Indian Tribe. This tribe's reservation was parceled out close to the ancient sea-bed that Donner had described and its headquarters, according to the tribe website, was located in Thermal, a small town just north of the present Salton Sea, no more than ten miles from La Quinta. The town claimed fewer than five thousand full time residents, he had learned, but the population more than doubled with migrant labor during the harvest season from May to July and then tripled during the winter snowbird season. Zack guessed that a stranger could slip in and out of Thermal and never be noticed. He decided to begin his investigation there.

Stretching the map out to another panel Zack saw that Thermal was on the desert floor almost due east of his present position. As the crow flies it lay directly across a narrow but precipitous mountain ridge and through a green patch on the map, something called Lake Cahuilla County Park, then across the Salton Sea basin along Fifty-eighth Street to the Thermal Airport. The town of Thermal was just east of the airport.

Staring at the map, Zack saw how easy it could be to put a little girl's body into a large SUV like the one he had just seen and drive it to a hidden area in the park and unload it unseen in some deep arroyo. From there the body could be packed up into the remote canyon where it had been found. It would be easy for Bear Man, anyway, with his great strength.

Zack's eye flew back to the airport. How very simple to fly to Thermal from Tuba City. In fact, Zack thought, his mind racing and his excitement growing, how convenient to fly from Thermal down into Mexico for his drugs or whatever else he needed.

Zack willed himself to slow down. First things first. He must investigate every link in the chain one by one. He pulled out his iPhone and looked up a number and placed a call. When a voice answered he said, "I am FBI Special Agent Zack Tolliver. I hope to learn something about the Torres-Martinez Tribe in relation to a case I'm working. I'm in La Quinta right now. Would you be willing to meet with me and answer some questions? Possibly in the next hour or so? I could drive directly there."

Zack entered the address he was given, started up his truck and drove off.

The town of Thermal might be an easy finger stroke away on the map but by car it was much more than that. A tall mountain ridge separated the La Quinta desert basin and the trailhead from the lakebed of an ancient predecessor of the Salton Sea that was the table-top-flat cholla dotted furnace-hot desert upon which Thermal resided. Zack would have to drive the full length of the ridge north and then around its prow and then south again the same distance on the far side. It took him forty-five minutes. He found the east side of the ridge even hotter.

On the Coachella side of the ridge the contrast between ancient and modern was notable. An ancient uprising fin of batholithic granite, stark and mysterious, loomed to his right and emerald fairways with expensively dressed golfers maneuvering little white golf carts on them intersected one another like a string of enormous green sausages on his left. Zack drove along Madison Street passing between famous golfing names like TPC, Greg Norman, and Arnold Palmer. He understood now why the population of Thermal trebled in the winter; it was here that golf fanatics come to die.

At the intersection with Fifty-eighth Avenue Zack pulled onto the shoulder and climbed out of his truck. He squinted west toward the granite escarpment. He now stood directly opposite the Bear Creek Oasis trailhead and only the rugged height of the great rock fin preventing him from seeing the mound-hill that marked it. Looking around, Zack saw that he was once again at an abrupt divide between man and nature. On the north side of Fifty-eighth Avenue as it ran east and west was a mirage of water-infused green lawns and luxury homes, yet just south of the pavement was the yellow sand and cholla of the unclaimed desert. The heat was an oppressive blanket. Zack studied the profile of the rugged ridgeline noting even from this distance that erosion had carved it deeply in places to form wide dry washes and arroyos. It seemed certain to him that the terrain must yield passage deep into the mountains and ultimately to the distant canyon where the small body had been left.

Zack climbed back into his truck and turned east toward Thermal. As he drove he reviewed the directions in his mind. He recalled his surprise when he learned that the Torres-Martinez Tribal Chairperson was a woman He was accustomed to the male dominated Navajo political hierarchy, which had only recently begun to experience change.

In Thermal, Zack found Palm Street and following his directions came to Center Street where he found the small house that the Tribal Chairperson had described. Her office must be her home, Zack realized with surprise. He admired the landscaping and the variety of desert plants bordering the concrete walkway on his way to the front door. A broad faced sturdy woman with a generous smile and two very alert brown eyes answered his ring immediately and ushered him courteously into her home's cool interior. She showed him to a sitting room that appeared to function as her office with walls lined with bookshelves and a roll-top desk overflowing with papers. Zack's chair was comfortable, and the ice tea she handed him was refreshingly cold. A smell of fresh baked cookies hung in the air. Zack knew instinctively that he would like this woman.

She sat in the chair opposite him and smiled. "How can I assist an FBI agent who has come all the way here from Arizona?"

"Madam Chairperson-" Zack began.

"No," she interrupted. "Please call me Ida. I would like to begin as if we were old friends rediscovering each other after a long journey."

Zack considered this opening and decided he liked it. "Ida, then. Thank you for seeing me so willingly and with such little notice."

She smiled again.

"I have come to the Palm Springs area, as you might have guessed, for a specific reason. That reason has led me to you because of my need to understand the culture of the Aqua Caliente Indian Tribe and more specifically your Torres-Martinez band. Will you indulge me and answer a few questions about your tribe?"

"Of course. That is the most pleasurable part of what I do. But I do have conditions."

Zack raised an eyebrow at that.

"My conditions are that you in turn teach me something about the Navajo from your long association with them."

Zack was surprised. "How did you know of my connection with the Navajo?"

"Agent Tolliver-"

"Zack, please," he insisted in his turn.

"Zack, I never accept an interview with strangers without knowing something about them. The internet is a wonderful thing."

Zack made a gesture of submission. "I'm impressed. Let me begin, then, since it is I who trespass upon your time." He thought about how to shape his question. "Let me ask first if you have any mystical traditions involving shamanism, specifically witchcraft and more specifically shape shifting."

It was Ida's turn to be surprised. Her brown eyes widened and she paused for a moment before responding. "We do have our medicine men or shamans, as you describe. They have historically worshipped and celebrated ancient gods, among whom is Taqwus, a trickster god who has the ability to take the form of an anthropomorphic animal in order to play tricks or to disobey normal rules and conventional behavior - is that what you mean?"

"That's exactly what I mean. Is this creature significant to the Agua Caliente people today?"

"I wouldn't say so, really. My people are very practical and quite modern. We own resorts and casinos, which are the backbone of our financial solvency. Every officially identifiable tribal member has an interest in these properties." Ida's eyes crinkled teasingly. "Our tendency today is to be businesspeople rather than romantics or mystics."

Zack tried another tack. "To come to the point, I'm tracking a suspect who has successfully preyed upon Navajo cultural fears and beliefs as a means to conceal his activities. Those activities involve the abuse and serial murder of young girls."

Zack expected shock from Ida at this disclosure but her expression didn't change.

Zack went on. "My question centers on whether the possibility exists that my suspect could utilize similar cultural taboos among the Aqua Caliente tribes."

Ida studied Zack's face. "Am I to infer that your suspect has moved his activities here?"

"I believe so, although we have no direct evidence to support that belief just yet. I'm here because the Palm Springs police found the body of a young white girl in a canyon above Bear Creek Oasis six days ago. Evidence at the crime scene suggests that this may well be the same perpetrator. On the Navajo reservation fear of Skinwalkers prevented the Navajo people from inquiring too closely into his activities. My question centers on whether you think any tribal taboos here might cause a similar fear and thus afford him cover?"

Id laughed at this. "Not tribal taboos, so much as tribal snafus," she quipped. At Zack's questioning look she elaborated. "You see there's great confusion surrounding the question of proprietorship of lands around here; which are tribal and which are public. The problems began with the 1877 Directive from the Department of the Interior ordering that the reservation be sectioned into square mile alternating blocks all along the valley in a transparent effort to encourage the development of a railroad. With Indian land now in alternate lots with public land, things became confusing. But when in 1959 the Secretary of the Interior created what people later called the 'Golden Checkerboard' to equalize the allotted Indian lands and at the same time designate them to be overseen by appointed guardians and conservators, things got even worse. The Indian lands could now be legally sold and the so-called guardians, recognizing the escalating value of land that even then was growing into the resort it was to become, did not waste time in 'helping' many of the Indian owners to do just that. This obscured the tribal boundaries even more. Although that failed program was halted in 1968 and a ninety-nine year lease was put in place to protect the Indian lands that remained, the damage had been done. It's now very difficult to distinguish public land from private, or private land from Indian, or Indian land from other Indian land. Administratively, it creates a huge bureaucratic mess with miles of red tape. Law enforcement is in a constant struggle to figure out who has authority where."

Ida paused to sip her tea. Then she got to the point. "If I were your man, I'd be thinking that I could dump bodies anywhere up in those mountains on property leased to tribal members because no one will ever take ownership. But you said the body was found above Bear Creek Oasis? That's not reservation land up there, not quite. The Oasis and the canyon above it fall just inside the University Preserve owned by CSU and therefore is under the jurisdiction of the local public police, and in turn I would imagine, your agency."

She looked thoughtfully at Zack. "But had he intended to leave the body on reservation land he would have been making another mistake. Historically, since the 1885 Major Crimes Act, all serious crimes committed on federally recognized Indian reservations fell under the jurisdiction of U.S. agencies, and those agencies in turn tended to give them very low priority. That meant that you could literally get away with murder on the reservation because the feds would ignore it and the maximum sentence that any reservation judicial system could impose was restricted by law to one year."

Ida grimaced at Zack. "Imagine. Only one year for a capital crime. That might be what your man was counting on. But that did change recently. The Tribal Law and Order Act of July 29, 2010 now allows tribal courts to impose a maximum sentence of three years, which is a bit more of an inconvenience to a criminal. Hand in hand with that legislation came a prod from the Justice Department, called the Indian Country Law Enforcement Initiative, which essentially says to the Feds, the job you've all been doing for the Indians up to now is inadequate so make serious crime on the reservations a top priority. In other words, law enforcement on both sides of the reservation boundaries is lining up to get more involved these days."

Ida smiled again at Zack. "But you must have known all of this."

"I was generally aware of the initiative," he affirmed, writing down some notes. He cleared his throat. "Another question. Could our man live somewhere around here and carry on unnoticed? I suspect that he is not Caucasian in appearance nor originally from this area. Yet he appears to come and go as he pleases."

"Nothing could be simpler," Ida replied. "We have a huge influx in our population here at least twice a year, first for the harvest and then for the golf season. Strangers are the rule rather than the exception. And no one really knows who lives down in the Duroville Trailer Park among the migrant workers." She shrugged helplessly. "He could hide out in that place forever."

"I'm thinking our man might be concealing himself among the golf resort snowbirds," Zack said. He described the expensive looking black SUV from his encounter that morning in La Quinta.

"That sounds like an Escalade," remarked Ida. "They're plentiful around here."

"How about the Thermal Airport?" Zack asked. "Who flies in and out of there?"

"You mean the Jacqueline Cochran Regional Airport," she teased. "Lots of private jets. Some days during high season it looks like the airport in Medellin, Colombia, there are so many jets parked there."

"Is there any private industry?"

"We have agricultural import and export companies. They regularly fly farm equipment, fertilizers, produce containers and that sort of thing in and out. There's an airpark for small businesses being developed at the airport. But by far the greatest traffic is from private jet travel during the golf season."

"Do large cargo planes ever fly in there?"

"During the war the airport served as a transport facility for the desert warfare training camp established by the United States Army. Patton's tanks trained here, in fact, so, yes; the runways are capable of supporting large propeller craft but I think they lack the length for the larger jet transports. FedEx type planes fly in and out with farm and resort supplies. Nothing larger, I don't think."

"Ida, you've been extremely helpful to me. I've tried to be frank with you in the interest of keeping you informed on behalf of your tribe. I do have just one or two more questions."

"Please."

Zack was opening his mouth to speak when his phone rang. He looked apologetically at Ida. "I have to take this," he said. "It's my team up on the mountain."

Ida rose from her chair. "I'll just go and replenish our teas."

Zack quickly put his phone to his ear. Libby's voice came loud and clear.

"Zack, we're at the scene. What a wild place it is up here. Beautiful, though, in a hot desolate kind of way. But here's the news. As far as Blue is concerned, these tracks, cat and man, were made by the same person who handled the Pigmy Cactus tines. This has to be our man, Zack. It makes my skin crawl to think that he escaped us in Arizona and is doing the same horrible things out here."

"Libby, that's great news. That we've identified him, I mean. The other good news is he didn't follow you; he stayed down here with me. He actually pulled up behind my truck while I was still parked at the trailhead. What's next for you?"

Libby exhaled audibly, thinking about Zack's encounter. "That's not good news to me, Zack. You be very careful."

"I will, I promise. He ran as soon as he knew I spotted him. Part of his game, I guess." Zack was trying to sound upbeat.

Libby was silent, absorbing the news. Finally she said, "We're about ready to begin tracking. I don't know this terrain and there're many rocky outcrops where a person can disappear from sight so I'm keeping Blue on the long lead. We have the helicopter pilot on radio and he'll do his first flyover to orient us in a couple of minutes. And - what? - Oh, here, Agent Donner wants to talk to you." Libby quickly whispered, "Be careful."

Then Zack heard Donner's crisp voice. "Hi, Zack. Seems it was indeed your man who was up here to spoil my day. We're about ready to send your team off with the dog. Tubby will stay with them to help out. He knows the area better than most. What are you up to?"

"I think I can guess where they'll go. I'm over on the east side of the mountain ridge." Zack when on to briefly explain his new theory.

Donner seemed cheered by Zack's progress. "I'll call you when I get back to the office," he said. "I've got some other work in my stack, but we can go ahead and plan the next few steps."

"Sounds good," Zack agreed, and rang off. Ida was just returning from the kitchen with more tea and a plate of cookies. "I've just had confirmation that our man is indeed here," Zack informed her. "The scent dog identified him."

"Then I am relying on you to catch him and safeguard my community," Ida declared. "How else can I assist you?"

"Maybe you could put yourself in this man's shoes," Zack suggested. "Back in Arizona he had a partner - or possibly a victim, we're not sure which - a man who lived a solitary existence on the reservation. The man's home was set away from other houses and backed up to open land, perfect for coming and going at night without being observed. The locals were convinced that the man was a Skinwalker so no one ever went near the place. Apparently our suspect took advantage of this man and his solitary lifestyle to come and go at will. He seems to have enlisted the man's help in confining, molesting, and eventually burying a score of young girls in the back yard of his home over many years without anyone being the wiser.

If you were this man, where would you go to find the same

situation, say, within easy reach of the airport and maybe near that mountain ridge that separates this valley from La Quinta?"

Ida thought for a long time before answering. "Now I see the reason for your taboo question," she remarked.

Thinking aloud, she attempted a scenario. "So I need isolation, probably some willing assistance, a vehicle that won't draw attention wherever I go and an area of ground for disposing of bodies, again without drawing attention. The Escalade you described wouldn't work at the trailer park, that's certain. Nor is there any room there for burying bodies without being noticed. The Escalade works fine at the golf resorts but they probably wouldn't appreciate someone digging up their greens to bury little girls. The ranches and farms around here are isolated, true enough, but the ranchers working these farms know who works for them, even during the harvest season, which is weeks away from now anyway. So...that pretty much leaves us with the mountains. And here's my best guess. Try Cahuilla Lake State Park. It's back west the way you came in and it's up against the mountains. The park has a fancy golf course but it also maintains a museum with some Indian artifacts and it's actually in an area once inhabited by the ancestors of the Aqua Caliente Indians when Lake Cahuilla, the original Salton Sea, lapped up against those mountains. The reservation leases over are among the oldest still inhabited and some of those people cling to their original home sites and traditional ways. I can think of a couple of properties right up against the mountains. It's isolated there. Yet the Escalade would fit right in because of the golf resort and some very nice homes in the area. And finally, digging is easy in that sandy soil."

Ida looked up apologetically. "Unfortunately, I've lost touch with the original families there because they've pulled away from the rest of our tribe."

Zack was impressed. "I'm glad you haven't taken up a life of crime," he remarked.

Ida laughed merrily at that.

"Now comes my final question, maybe the strangest one of all."

"Go ahead."

"Does anyone around here harvest salt, or supply salt, or deal in salt in any way?"

"That's not such a strange question," Ida replied. "All around us here is one giant salt water lake bed. When the Colorado River delta backed up and the earthworks here were breached, salt water back-flowed in from the Gulf of California. Later on the earth dam was permanently breached and the lake shrank and salt deposits were left all over the valley floor. My tribe has long harvested it. Various business enterprises attempting to market salt have come and gone over the years. Today most of the old lakebed is either built up or dug up. But, come to think of it, a company did come in maybe ten years ago. They salt fish and preserve meats in the old way for fishermen and hunters as sort of a natural side market to a small import/export business. Just a little outfit, with a cute name...let me see" -Ida slipped on a pair of reading glasses and reached for the yellow pages under the phone- "here it is. Pemtemweha Industries. Cute. Pemtemweha was an ancient deity of the Cahuilla people that protected animals and went about in the form of a deer, which I believe is one of the animals this company preserves and ships. Preserves? Protects? With salt? Very cute."

Zack smiled at the pun. "Where are they located?"

"They're among the companies that recently moved into the new airpark. They were among the first, as I recall. Right there at the airport."

"Are there any other salt harvesters? Independent native harvesters, for instance?"

"None that I'm aware of."

Zack rose and put his tea glass on a table. "You've been extraordinarily helpful, Ida. I'm afraid I have not kept my part of the bargain, but you haven't asked me anything about the Navajo People. Would you accept my rain check, perhaps accompanied by a drink some time?" Zack presented his card.

"Count on it," replied Ida as she showed him out. "And I'll be checking in to follow the progress of your investigation."

TWENTY-NINE

Zack's cell phone rang again as he climbed into his truck and his stomach clenched immediately. He was more worried about Libby's safety than he realized. But it wasn't Libby calling; it was Linda.

"Well, hello, Linda."

"Sorry to disturb your golf game and cocktails out there, Zack. However, we learned something from the tests we ran on the little girls' bodies that I thought you ought to know right away."

"I suppose I'll have to put down my margarita and listen."

"I think we had all assumed up 'til now that the victims were local… you know…four corners to eastern California kind of thing, right?"

"That's how I've been thinking."

"Well, we may need to broaden our horizons."

"What do you mean?"

"I'm talking about minerals. We took dirt samples from clothing, shoes and from under fingernails or anywhere else we could find them and sent it all to a geo-forensics expert to try to determine a place of origin. He ran all of it and I've just been sifting through the data. To understate it, the results are interesting."

Linda paused dramatically.

"And?"

"None of the minerals in our samples are found in the American Southwest. In fact, scrapings from the shoe tread of one of the victims contained volcanic ash mixed with fine sand of a particle size and composition that could only have come from the Hawaiian Islands. And we don't believe she was just vacationing there because the layering within the sneaker tread is consistent top to bottom."

"What do you mean by consistent?"

"As the child runs around and plays, soil is compressed into her sneaker tread and then the next day as she runs around more soil is compressed on top of the previous soil until no more can fit into the tread. The outer layers may fall out with the flexing of the shoe and sometimes mom might throw the sneakers in the washing machine but often the inner layer of soil remains. So what you get is a chronological geo-topical history of the places that child has been from the early days of the shoe to the more recent wearing."

Linda paused. "Generally, you can find quite a variety of soils and places. But not in this girl's shoe. It's all the same soil mix in every layer of her tread, indicating that she most likely lived in the Hawaiian Islands for as long as she wore those shoes. We found no other soil traces of any kind to suggest that the girl ever walked on any other soil, not even the good old Arizona dirt where her body was found."

"Whoa, wait a minute. Are you telling me that this girl came all the way here from Hawaii and never touched the ground, like in a wheel chair or something?"

"I'm simply saying that the shoes she had on when she was buried spent little or no time on our local soil, or any soil other than this volcanic sand mix found only in Hawaii. Of course she could've walked on hard surface areas - concrete or tile, for instance - without gathering additional soil evidence. Or she could've worn other shoes here and then been buried in the sneakers. But beyond that I can't say.

And that's not all. The soil samples we took from the shoes of the other victims suggest locations in other countries ranging all the way from Sweden and Germany to Bolivia. Again, our most important finding is what we did not find; soil from Arizona or Nevada or southern California or for that matter any place we can identify in the western United States. What are the odds of that? All of these girls are apparently imports."

Zack fell back in the seat of his truck. The ignition keys dangled from his hand as he tried to digest what Linda was telling him.

"Are you thinking this guy snatched these girls from airports?"

"Again, Zack, its not for me to say. I'm simply passing along the results of the tests."

"No chance of errors, I suppose? Sample mix-ups, that sort of thing?" Zack heard Linda chuckle.

"My first question exactly. But no, there's not a chance. These guys are professionals and they do this work every single day. The systems they use just don't allow mix-ups."

Zack decided he would think some more about it later.

"When are you coming out here?"

"I've got a flight booked that departs at one pm Mountain Standard Time from Flagstaff. One of the forensic guys out there is meeting me at the Palm Springs Airport. I'll pack along all of our test results so that we can do a comparative analysis with your latest victim out there."

Zack flicked off his phone and tossed it into the empty seat next to him and thought about things as he started up his truck. What was he dealing with here? Was this man hanging around the international terminal at Los Angeles Airport, waiting there for an unaccompanied minor blonde girl to come along so he could snatch her? Or was there some other explanation? And where did John Roundtree fit into all of this?

Zack realized he needed more information. Might as well go on to the next step, he thought, and punched the name Pemtemweha, Inc. into his truck's GPS unit. An address popped up on the screen and a sultry female voice issued directions sending him along Airport Boulevard toward the airport and then south on Higgins Street. Before long he was in front of a long low building that looked rather like a large hen house, built like an egg carton with identical rows of doors and windows.

Zack walked along the front of the building until he found a door with a sign that read Pemtemweha Industries, Inc. It was locked. He knocked loudly. No answer, no sound. Zack walked around behind the building and found himself on a concrete apron smeared black by airplane tires. The apron connected directly to a parking area for several small planes. Beyond that was the runway.

Zack walked along the rear of the building passing several loading docks until he saw one labeled Pemtemweha Industries in tiny letters under a large white No Trespassing sign. The metal door was padlocked but tiny bits of something all over the loading dock sparkled in the sun like sequins on a dress. Zack scooped some up for a closer look. They were crystals of salt. He put them in a zip-lock bag for future analysis and deciding there was nothing else to be done and walked on.

A pickup truck nosed around the far end of the building and backed up to a loading dock and a man climbed out. Zack saw by his shirt that he worked for a local golf resort. As Zack approached the man looked up.

"Hi, there. Can I help you?"

"Well, maybe. I was looking for the man in charge of the meat shipping company back there with the funny name. I want to see about preserving and shipping some meat from a deer I shot yesterday. No one seems to be around."

The man grinned. "I recommend that you give him a call instead. His hours are irregular to say the least. He's a one-man operation, as far as I know, and he comes out here only by appointment."

"You don't happen to have his number, do you? I'd like to catch him while that deer meat is still fresh."

"I do in fact," the man said. "We get inquiries from people dropping by here from time to time so we keep the number handy. Come on in."

Zack followed the man up the steps to the dock and waited for him to unlock the garage door. They entered a large storage space and walked past a row of golf carts to a small glass cubicle. The man pulled a card from a stack on the desk, wrote down a number, and handed it to Zack.

"That's his cell number and that's my card. You'll be asked to leave a message and a number but it's the only way to reach the guy. I had to do it the time one of his deliveries got dumped in front of my door. He got back to me just a few hours later."

"What did you say his name was?"

"Mr. Black? Or was it Mr. Brown? Some simple name like a color. I can never remember."

"His shipment was large enough to block your whole door? What was it?"

"About ten wooden rectangular crates maybe three feet tall, about the same width, six or seven feet long, all lashed together on a couple of flats. That's all I can tell you. No way I could move them without a fork lift."

"The shipment must have come in by plane."

"Oh, sure, that's why we're all here, to ship by air. Usually the guy is right there when a shipment arrives, even if it's two in the morning, except for that one time I mentioned. When I called him he was right pissed that the shipper hadn't notified him and was real apologetic about blocking my door. He seemed grateful that I had called him right away."

"What does he look like, in case I run into him?"

"Well, funny you should ask because I'm not so sure I can describe him even though our shops have been next to each other for years. He always has the shades on, you know, and a hooded sweatshirt thing going. Beard. Dark complexion. But beyond that, I really can't tell you.

He never hangs around, always on the run like he's stacked up more work for himself than he can handle. Every time I see him he's in a big rush."

Zack thanked the man for his help and walked out. When he returned to his truck he made another attempt to peer through the dust covered window of the Pemtemweha Industry office but soon gave it up.

He climbed into his truck and drove west on Airport Boulevard toward the golf resorts, trying to make sense of it all in his mind. He decided he would place a call to Mr. Brown or Mr. Black when he got back to the Palm Springs FBI office. There he could record the call and maybe even get a trace if the answering service the business used was configured to call the man's cell automatically.

Right now, though, he wanted to drive to Lake Cahuilla County Park to take a closer look at a dry wash area carved into the mountains behind it and see how far it led. Ida's suggestion that the tribal land around the park might be where their man was hiding supported Zack's own thoughts. He kept track of the elapsed time during the drive and at the Quarry Lane entrance to the park noted that it had taken him not quite ten minutes. If the man was operating from here, he could be at the airport to meet a shipment in fifteen minutes or less, even at the most congested traffic times. Zack felt his confidence grow.

He followed signs to the park headquarters, which was a trailer in the middle of a parking lot and went in. At a reception desk in the cool interior he found a bored docent very ready to chat. She supplied a map of the park and offered suggestions for sightseeing and dining and answered his questions.

Yes, that was a public trailer park he passed on his way in, used mostly by vacationers and golfers. The park had trailers to rent but most people trucked in their own and rented a space and utilities. Yes, a few people did live there year round but most were seasonal. The same people tended to come each year and they all pretty much knew each other. Yes, there were a couple of private residences within the Park boundaries, grandfathered properties. The owners had received cash advances on their homes with the understanding that they would transfer over to the park when they left them, for whatever reason. The Park commission would then raze them and put in some nice landscaping and picnic areas. Where were those properties? Well, two of the families lived right here on Quarry Lane behind this building. Nice people. Always willing to help out if needed. Both couples were older. The other folks lived up Cahuilla Park Road a bit further, just opposite the lake up there. They were tribal folk on a ninety-nine year lease. That property would transfer to the park when the lease terminated. Only one family lived there now, as she remembered, an older man, a widower with a couple of grown-up sons and daughters. It was an an old family that had been there forever. The place was a bit of an eyesore, really, with old vehicles left around and several unoccupied houses that were kind of run down. Those people kept to themselves and didn't cause any harm.

Trails? Yes, there's a trail back over those hills. It's the Cahuilla Lake Trail and it leads to the preserve lands over near La Quinta. You drive down to the end of Tom Fazio Lane and leave your car and follow the cart path around the last couple of greens of the golf course. The trail leads out from there and heads up over the rise. It's well marked and relatively easy, but take lots of water.

Zack thanked her and accepted several more brochures. He climbed back into his truck and drove slowly up Quarry Lane to its intersection with Cahuilla Park Road. He had already dismissed the trailer park as unlikely. And the homes directly behind the park headquarters seemed too public. No, Zack pinned his hopes on the property opposite the lake on reservation land.

He turned left and drove slowly up Cahuilla Park Road. The lake on his right drew closer until it forced the road to bend left. Then it straightened out and there in front of him in a horseshoe fold of steeply rising foothills were several large cottonwood trees with buildings scattered among them. Zack drove by slowly. He saw two large buildings and several small cottages connected by a rutted roadway. The place reminded him of a retreat or a camp. A couple of the buildings sat deep among the trees near the cliffs. Zack kept moving, not wishing to draw attention to himself and followed the road toward the northern tip of the lake. Then, unexpectedly, the road ended.

Zack swore under his breath. His GPS unit showed the road looping all the way around the lake. He saw now that the compound was well suited as a hideout for the child murderer. Any vehicle that came up this road would be suspect and could be studied closely during its inevitable return. Only a lost tourist would come up here - or someone deliberately searching for him.

Zack would have to drive back past the compound. His truck was known and he would certainly be recognized if the man was there now. Zack regretted the exposure but there was nothing for it, so he might as well take a good look. This time as he drove by he took his time and studied the grounds. He looked for the Escalade, knowing it wouldn't be in plain sight yet illogically feeling better for not seeing it. Could be I just got lucky, he thought hopefully.

Zack accelerated. It was time to return to Palm Springs. He'd freshen up and have a bit of lunch and then drive over to the FBI office to connect with Donner and make that call to Pemtemweha.

Zack was changing his shirt in the hotel room when Libby called.

"What have you got?" Zack held the cell with his shoulder while he slipped his arm into the sleeve.

"Just a long thirsty trail. This terrain out here is unbelievably difficult. But the scent is strong; Blue is just pulling me along."

"Any change to the prints?"

"None. Still barefoot, with the usual strong and consistent stride, although sometimes it seems as if the man goes out of his way to take us through clumps of cholla or into cactus patches. We've been continually scrambling in and out of gullies. Everyone is all scratched up and tired out."

"Where are you?"

"I've got absolutely no idea. Here, let me put Eagle Feather on..." Just before she surrendered the phone Libby whispered, "Zack, be careful."

"...Zack?" It was Eagle Feather's gruff voice. "Hello, Eagle Feather. Where are you now?"

"The tracks seem to be gradually swinging to the southeast. We've been on the ridge tops most of the way since climbing out of Bear Creek canyon, skirting some sizable canyons."

"Is he playing with you?"

"Maybe. It's like he knew we'd be coming along, and as Libby said, he wants to entertain us."

"Any blood, any changes to the prints, any trail going in the direction of the crime scene?"

"Nope. Same as up on Monument Mesa, just bare human prints leading away. But we've seen no blood this time. The footprints look just like the ones we followed on the mesa, trotting along like he's strolling down a sidewalk. No hurry, just striding along."

"Keep your eye out for him. He made his presence known to me right after you left but I haven't seen him since. He could still double back up there to play some tricks. He knows exactly where you are, don't forget."

"Thanks for the advice, white man. But if he wanted to harm us he could do it at any time. He could hide himself so we'd pass within two feet of him and never know he was there. It's that rugged up here"

"Understood. I'm thinking you'll end up at a place called Lake Cahuilla County Park. You'll know you're there when you look down a large wash and see the fairway of a golf course."

"That'll be weird."

"If I'm right, he's operating from a place near there. He'll know you're coming along his trail so he'll have figured a way to make his scent go away so Blue can't follow, maybe by driving off in his car like he did the last time. But he might still be watching his back trail for you. Look for a black Escalade. There's a million of them around here but watch for it anyway, just as a precaution."

"And do what...?"

"Just be alert."

"As you wish, white man. And how about doing something for us, since you've been lying around in the lap of luxury all morning."

"Sure, what's that?"

"How about meeting us with some nice cold drinks? We'll sure be ready for that."

"You got it."

THIRTY

Zack drove to the FBI building and found Donner in his office. When he saw Zack he immediately pushed his work aside.

"It would appear that Special Agent in Charge Luke Forrester reopened the John Roundtree case over at Tuba City, apparently on the basis of our new evidence," Donner said.

"Glad to hear it. You got to admire the guy. He's reopened a very sensitive case just on the basis of the similarity of the victims and a dog's nose. But it's beginning to seem like part of a much larger operation."

Zack went on to tell Donner about his conversation with Linda.

"What are your thoughts?" Donner inquired. "Do you think he hangs about the airport and lures girls somehow to his truck, then drives them all the way back here? Then what? And what about the girls in Arizona?"

"Yes, I know. It just doesn't fit. Our perp is so very efficient in every other way, so well planned, so patient. He just wouldn't take that kind of a risk. He doesn't rely on chance. And he certainly wouldn't expose himself to discovery in a place with security as tight as an airport in the random hope that an unescorted little blonde girl happens by." Zack gave in to a wave of discouragement. "No, there's got to be something else going on. My gut tells me it's linked in some way to that salt company in Thermal. I want to call that number and record the call. Can we set that up?"

"Sure."

Donner flipped some switches on his phone console and pointed to a handset on the coffee table. "Use that. I'll monitor from here. Give me a moment to set up for the trace."

While he waited Zack pulled out his notebook and checked the number. At Donner's nod he reached for the phone and punched it in. It began ringing. Both men leaned forward. After several rings a professional voice came on the line.

"You have reached Pemtemweha Industries, Incorporated. No one is here right now to take your-"

The taped message was abruptly interrupted and they heard only a tunnel of echoing emptiness. Zack waited for a moment, then shrugged and reached down to terminate the call. Suddenly a voice, course and distorted, spoke out of the reverberating hollowness.

"Agent Tolliver, I presume? I've been expecting your call."

Zack, startled, looked at Donner, who stared back at him wide-eyed.

"Yes, this is Zack Tolliver, but you have the advantage of me."

"I have always had the advantage of you." There was no humor in the voice. "But we digress. Is there something you wish to preserve and to ship? Some venison, perhaps? Isn't that what you told my neighbor this morning?"

"You've been busy on your back trail, I see."

"Yes, it's been necessary. You have become quite the nuisance, Agent Tolliver - or shall I call you Zack?"

"Agent Tolliver will do."

"Well, Agent Tolliver, perhaps I could suggest something to preserve and ship, something even more succulent than venison. Quite tasty looking, in fact. If I squeeze my trigger finger just a tiny bit more, I can have this morsel ready to salt and crate. Of course, we'd have to separate it from the dog and the Indian. And who is the other man? He looks quite like an FBI agent to me. Am I right?"

"Are you hoping to negotiate?" Zack tried to sound calm despite his suddenly racing pulse.

"Negotiate? Me? I don't think I'm the one who needs to negotiate here. I'm simply offering you a possible reason to do business with my firm. I don't think you actually have any venison to ship."

"Where are you now?" Zack tried to sound soothing. "I could come talk to you."

"Agent Tolliver, as delightful as this brief conversation has been, I have much to do and I know you do as well. I must hang up now. But we'll talk again soon."

The connection went dead. Zack put the handset back with trembling hands.

Donner breathed out slowly and looked at his computer. "Nothing," he said. "He knew just how long to stay on."

But Zack had already picked up his cell phone. Libby answered right away.

"Libby, don't say anything and don't be obvious but get behind some cover right now. There's a sniper near you."

Zack waited for her to obey, listening to her movements through the phone. He wiped a small trickle of sweat from his brow.

"Zack, what's going on?" Libby asked breathlessly a few moments later.

"We just made contact with the man you are tracking and he claims to have you in his rifle sights. Where is that helicopter right now?"

"It passed just a few minutes ago, just after I called you."

"Call it back. Tell the pilot to do a low level search immediately. Get the others under cover until it's done."

Zack could hear Libby passing along his instructions. Zack wiped another trickle of sweat from the tip of his nose. The air conditioning in this building wasn't very efficient, he thought. He waited. Then Libby was back on the line.

"Do you really think he's out here?"

"I don't know for sure. But we have to assume he is. Call me back after the helicopter has thoroughly searched the area, before you move out of your protection. And keep your head down."

After hanging up, Zack looked at Donner. They stared at each other for a long moment.

Donner spoke in disbelief. "He actually answered the phone."

"That may have been his first real mistake," Zack said, slowly and thoughtfully. "We had nothing but strong suspicions before now but this confirms my whole line of investigation from this morning."

"I don't think it will help much. We didn't get the trace and I'm quite certain he used a voice synthesizer."

"Regardless, it's our first hard evidence that he is really out there. He wants to play harder now."

"What's next?"

"First and foremost is to have that helicopter stay above our team and provide protection for them the rest of the way. The killer may not be up there at all - it could be a bluff - but let's not leave them exposed again. Second, we get a search warrant for Pemtemweha Industries Inc. and we take a look inside."

"Maybe we should check on Escalade rentals?"

"Long shot, but why not? And let's get to some property files and see who lives along Lake Cahuilla Drive out there beyond the park headquarters. And while you're at it, you might consider calling in some assistance. I think his gloves just came off."

The Palm Springs FBI building was a beehive of activity by that afternoon. Off duty agents were called back and new agents from other jurisdictions were brought in to assist in the operation. The soft clicking of computer keys was everywhere and coffee and donuts passed through office portals in a steady stream. Donner moved an extra desk into his office for Zack and the two of them went over an action plan while they waited for the search warrant for Pemtemweha Industries to be approved and for their tracking team to emerge from the wilderness.

"If we search that shipping company before the tracking team is down and it turns out our man is actually up there, he'll know about it." Donner was thinking out loud. "He seems to have good connections. Who's to say he won't learn what we're up to and decide to go ahead and shoot one of our people just to teach us a lesson?"

"Agreed. We need to time the search to coincide with their safe return."

"Furthermore," Donner went on, "our search of his company might precipitate an attempt to escape. We should to be on guard against that. We'll be right there at the Thermal Airport. We can control all departures from there."

"He'll have anticipated that, I'm sure, but we should do it anyway."

"We need to set up a command center close to Thermal." Donner was studying a map. "We need one or two vehicles right along here" - his finger came down on Calle Tecate at the Bear Creek Oasis trailhead- "to keep him from escaping through La Quinta."

Still studying the map Donner pointed to another place. "We've got a safe house here, right at the end of Interlachen Drive. It's a nice big house with a little casita, it's private, it provides good access to all the places we need to go, it's maybe ten minutes to the airport from there, five minutes to the park, and there's a big empty field right across the road where our bird can put down. We'll make that our command post."

Donner picked up his telephone to work out the details, leaving

Zack to think back over the events of the day.

Zack felt pressured. Everything had begun to move quickly, maybe too quickly. It felt like everything was starting to move out of control and it gave him an uneasy feeling. It all seemed too ordered, too prescribed, like they were rushing to follow a script that had already been written.

Zack shared his uneasiness with Donner after he hung up the phone.

"So I ask myself, what was it that got me involved in this thing in the first place?" He answered his own question. "It was that little girl's body dumped up on Monument Mesa. Why was it left up there? Why not simply bury her like he did all the others year after year in Roundtree's brickyard? And why am I here right now? Because another girl's body was left for us to find. What does that tell me?"

"Well, what does that tell you?"

"It wasn't an accident. Look at the sequence of events. Out on the Reservation, we find the body, we track the perp, we search Roundtree's house, we find the other little girls, we close the case, or...so we think. But Bear Man or whatever we call him is never revealed, never even suspected. But there I am with my suspicions; these puzzle pieces that just don't fit. I'm the only one unable to let it go. The forensic evidence to support my suspicions doesn't come along until later. The man himself planted these suspicions in my brain. Do you see what I mean? He revealed himself to me alone. No one else saw those eyes and his appearance at my camp that night or in the truck behind me at the trailhead. Looking back at it, he was drawing me in. This guy took huge risks, hanging around when he could have been gone. He plays with me all along the mesa while I track him, showing me he can do what he wants when he wants, even going so far as to drive past us as we walked back along the Ranch road.

There are two things going on here. One, he wants to play, or he wants to test himself, or maybe he wants to test me. It isn't enough for him just to commit multiple murders and get away with it. It's like he's become bored with it all. Did he really miss me with that drugged

Cactus spine we found in my stirrup? Or did he want the game to go on; did he want me to see that he could have killed me if he wanted. Was he trying to make it personal with me?

But the other thing going on here, the important thing is that he was done with what he was doing in Arizona. He had already decided to give up that area of his operation with the girls and the burials. What made him decide that? Had Roundtree become too much trouble, maybe grown a conscience? Or had they simply run out of room to bury any more girls? We'll probably never know the answer to that one but I think I do know the reason he dumped the girl on the Monument Mesa. That was his final play there. He had tidied everything else up and was all set to move out but he had to leave his signature."

Zack drew a breath. Donner stared at him in amazement. Then Zack gave him a tight grin.

"What that tells me is he's done here, too. That's why he dumped this girl where she would be found. That's why he left the footprints. That's why he allowed us to find the puzzle pieces that connected him to Pemtemweha. That's why he answered the phone, why he allowed us to get this close to him. He's writing his signature again, Donner. We're going to find another Roundtree. And we're going to find more girls. A lot more girls."

THIRTY-ONE

"Where, Zack? Where will we find them?" Donner actually sounded discouraged for the very first time. "There are more places to bury bodies around here than you can possibly imagine, places where they will never be found. Even you admit that this man's tracks and scent will probably have disappeared before our team is down from the mountain."

"I agree it's a needle in a haystack. But if I'm right in my way of thinking we won't need to search, he'll lead us. We just need to follow the clues and take whatever he leaves us, step by step."

An agent appeared at the open office door as they sat staring at each other.

"Sir, we've been going over the mortgages on those properties off of Lake Cahuilla Park Road. Some members of the Torres-Martinez band of Cahuilla Indians originally owned the property you described. It was a small splinter group that later moved out. It's one of the original ninety-nine year leases and only one family, the Gonzalez family, occupies it now. The most recent lease update shows one Andre Gonzalez, deceased, as the original lease designee, succeeded by a son Chet Gonzalez who lives there now. He lists his occupation as carpenter but mostly does odd jobs. We checked him out; he's been involved in some petty crime, mostly poaching and trespassing, that sort of thing. Apparently he can't let go of the old ways, acting like all the lands around there still belong to the tribe. No violence, no resistance, nothing like that; he just helps himself to wild game. A bit of a boozer, too. He's been in the tank more than once. One parent still living; his mother, no age on file, best guess must be up in her nineties. He's a widower with three children; two sons and a daughter. The boys moved out after high school and both now work in the local casinos. The girl married, has two children, and lives in Los Angeles. The old man apparently still lives on the property by himself with his mum, if she's still alive. He rents out some houses in the compound from time to time to make ends meet. All the houses are kind of falling into decay, according to the Park officials who can't wait for the family to move on and leave the property so that they can bulldoze it."

"What happened to Chet's wife?" Zack asked.

The agent looked at his notes. "Deceased several years ago. Auto accident, it says here."

Donner waved his thanks and the agent left. He turned to Zack. "Think your man might have wormed his way in there?"

"Very possibly."

"Let's take a look," Donner decided. "We can set up a search, coordinate it simultaneously with a search of that salt business - what's its name? - at the airport. It's another long shot, I know, but what else have we got? And we'd better go through the tribe for this one; it could be sensitive. Can't be out there digging up their ancient ancestors by mistake."

"Let me take that on," Zack said quickly. "I just spent some time with the Tribal Chairperson. She wants this guy caught as much as we do."

Zack was right to assume that Ida would cooperate. She immediately faxed over a signed form permitting a search of the Gonzalez lease. To cover all contingencies, Donner applied for two federal warrants; one for each search location.

Zack's phone rang. It was Luke Forrester.

"Zack, good work out there. Seems we've got something a lot larger than anybody thought. I'm calling just to be sure you know you have my full support. I've reopened the case here and we'll re-evaluate all of our evidence from the John Roundtree case working with Lieutenant Chaparral of the Navajo Nation police. Agent Whittaker is on her way out to you now. She'll remain with you until the forensics stage of the investigation is complete. I promise not to recall the two of you unless I really need you. Is there anything else I can do?"

"No, sir, not that I can think of right now. Thank you for your support."

"That's my job. But while I have you, a reporter from Channel Four News, a Melissa Mann, has been down here and also out on the Reservation asking questions. She seems to know a lot about the case and apparently has also learned of the Palm Springs connection. She's probably on her way out there now. We can't afford a negative publicity splash at this time, particularly for our Palm Springs office. That region depends upon the tourist trade. Just giving you a heads up."

"Thank you, sir. I'll tell Donner to watch out for her."

"Very well. And Zack...?"

"Sir?"

"Regular reports, please. Don't leave me hanging here."

"Yes, Sir."

Forrester hung up. Immediately Zack's phone rang again. It was Libby. She had to shout over the noise of helicopter blades thumping in the background.

"Zack? We're on our way again. We've got the helicopter so low over us that we can't even think and it's blowing away the tracks before we can get to them, but at least we're safe. Thanks to Blue and Eagle Feather we can still make progress...can you hear me?"

"Yes."

"The footprints seem to be headed down to a dry wash below us. I can see the Salton Sea all shimmery on the horizon. It's really beautiful. Agent Tibbs tells me that we're approaching the Lake Cahuilla Park area; we can see the lake down there every once in a while. He thinks we'll be down in half an hour if we keep going in this direction."

"Okay, Libby, we'll move out now to be ready to meet you. Keep us posted...and stay watchful."

Libby promised, and rang off.

Donner had been listening from his desk. He seemed excited and ready for action.

"Time to move," he said. "The warrants will catch up to us along the way. We'll set up shop in the safe house first and then be ready to scoop up the search team as soon as they come down."

Donner reached under his arm to check his pistol and looked over at Zack. "How are you armed?"

Zack reflexively felt for his own firearm. "The Sig Saur 228 I was originally issued."

"That weapon will certainly do."

"I don't use it much out there on the reservation but I clean it regularly. It's pretty dusty out there."

"Our firearms get dusty here, too. We've all been re-issued the Glocks here in Palm Springs per the latest home office directive but I still carry my original 23 because I prefer it. If I have to shoot, I want stopping power. But this guy inferred that he had a rifle so we'll be bringing along a couple of short action HTR's in case we need to engage at longer range. Why don't you go grab an overnight bag at your hotel and meet us at the safe house? Need directions?"

Zack shook his head. He remembered the safe house area from his drive to the park that morning. He headed out the door, waving.

After a brief stop at the hotel Zack was once again rolling along the Redlands Freeway toward La Quinta, but now he was thinking about Libby. In the hotel room he'd been caught off guard by a sudden anxiety for her, possibly brought on by a lingering scent and her nightgown draped carelessly over the bedroom chair. He felt a wave of regret for putting her at risk.

He chided himself now as he turned onto the Washington Street exit ramp. There was nothing he could do about Libby and he must maintain a disciplined focus to ensure his own safety.

It took him twenty-five minutes to arrive in the Lake Cahuilla Park area. He turned right on Fifty-Eighth Street and drove toward the park. Just as the lake was coming into view he made a right turn into a gated entrance. The FBI safe house was on his left just as Donner had described it. It was an impressive house. Zack rang the bell at the big front door and a young agent showed him inside and down into the living room where Donner and another agent sat on a couch going over maps they had spread out over a coffee table. Two more agents were connecting a cable feed to a router and setting up folding tables to accommodate the bank of laptop computers piled on the floor. Donner looked up as Zack entered and grinned mischievously.

"Go take a dip in the pool out back while you're waiting," he said. "It's pretty nice."

Zack grinned. "I forgot my trunks."

Donner laughed. "I was half serious, you know. We've got an observation team out there with a great view of the mountain ridge where the tracking team should come down. With our optics we can see a gnat on a cactus up there. The boys are hanging around the pool trying to look like they belong and the telescope is camouflaged inside a cabana." Donner chuckled again, pleased with himself, and turned back to the map.

Zack went out through the sliding door to take a look. From the patio, the mountains loomed close with their ridges sharply outlined in the clear air, crisp in the play of light and shadow. They looked like they were just across the street. Two agents lounged in the pool on air mattresses listening to music. Zack grinned when he saw that the iPods they wore were in reality a communication system. Under the cabana at the far end of the sparkling blue pool two more agents dressed in flowery Hawaiian shirts huddled together at a bar and monitored the ridge line through a telescope.

Zack was impressed. Donner had committed huge resources and a sizable team of agents just to capture a single man. For the very first time he felt confident about their chances for success. He exhaled a long breath that he didn't realize he had been holding. Now if only Libby were safely down from the mountain.

He wandered back into the house, feeling a little bit like fifth wheel. He was on Donner's turf now; Donner's team knew the territory, they would plan the campaign. He walked over to the coffee table where Donner was folding up a map.

"No swim, eh? And no foo-foo umbrella drink at our cabana?" Donner chuckled. "You've got to love our theatrics."

"Very impressive."

Donner patted the sofa next to him. "Sit down. Let me give you the sequence for Operation Blondie."

Zack winced at the name.

"As soon as the call comes in from our tracking team, we'll go pick 'em up. They'll most likely emerge here." Donner pointed to an area on the map near the golf course. "After we've got 'em all safe in your truck I'll send a search team to the Gonzalez lease to execute that warrant and at the same time send a second team to the airport. The second team's mission will be to seal up this whole northeast quadrant here quickly and quietly," -Donner's finger circled an area that encompassed the buildings and runways- "nobody in, nobody out."

He turned and brought up a satellite view on his laptop. "We've warned the tower that a no-fly restriction will be imposed. You know from your earlier visit to the place that it's pretty easy to box up. I've even got a couple of four wheel drive chase vehicles ready to go in case our man decides to bolt across this runway over here and drive across the desert to get to that road over there." The computer cursor traced the routes that Donner described. "As soon as we drop your civilians here at the safe house, we'll head out to the airport to supervise that search. If our man is there or if he's over at the Gonzalez lease, either way, he'll be trapped."

"That may be too firm a conclusion to apply to our man," Zack commented. "But it does seem pretty tight. I sure hope you're right. At the very least, we'll know shortly whether our hunches were correct."

Donner's cell phone rang. Zack continued to study the map, half listening to Donner's abrupt reply. He looked up when Donner reached for the remote and turned on the large flat screen TV that hung on the living room wall. The familiar blonde perkiness of Melissa Mann filled the screen. She held a sheaf of notes in the bright sunshine somewhere with palm trees and a light color stucco building in the background. Donner turned up the volume.

"...and no one will speak to me from the Palm Springs FBI office behind me. I have it on good authority, however, that another little girl's body has been found up there in the hot inhospitable mountains that rise above this town" -the camera panned to the mountains- "and that her death has been linked to the serial killings of all those little blonde girls found buried in Elk Wells, Arizona, in the back yard of John Roundtree; a shocking crime reported exclusively to you by this reporter six months ago. That case was declared closed by the FBI following the death of Mr. Roundtree who, at the time, was thought to be the only individual involved. Now we have learned that the FBI has reason to suspect that there was indeed a second perpetrator involved in the case, a vicious criminal who remains at large within this community of unsuspecting tourists..."

"Damn." Donner clicked off the TV. "How did she get all that?" He gave a pained look at Zack. "Well, there's our first complication."

Zack's own phone rang. It was Libby.

"Where are you?" he asked.

"Bear Man just walked off the edge of a cliff and disappeared. His tracks, scent, everything - all gone."

Then Eagle Feather was on the phone. "You've got to love his stuff."

"I wish I could say I'm surprised," Zack said. "Where are you now?"

Libby had taken the phone back. "We're walking around the base of a wall made out of a high spine of rock that sort of loops back on itself to form a fort-like enclosure. It's maybe fifty, sixty feet high here on the outside and forty feet or so on the inside. I'm no geologist, Zack, but it probably was made from magma in an ancient volcano that has since partially eroded away. Whatever, it forms an enclosure twenty feet wide. We followed Bear Man's scent along the top of the rock wall to where it got so narrow we thought we might lose Blue off the edge. Then right at the end, right at the highest point the scent just disappeared. This place has a very old feel to it, Zack. There're pictographs here and other etchings on the rock in places. I'll bet there's some spiritual significance to this place for the local tribes. We walked Blue all around, inside and out, but he couldn't regain the scent. I've got a feeling we won't find it again."

"How close are you to Cahuilla State Park?"

"From the top of the wall here we can see down this wash to a golf course. Tubby here says it's the Lake Cahuilla course. We can be there in twenty minutes."

"Everybody's Okay?"

"Everybody's good, just hot and thirsty. Got those drinks Eagle Feather asked for?"

"Don't worry...we've got 'em. If Blue can't recapture the scent, come on out. We'll meet you at the end of that fairway. But stay alert. You're not home yet." Zack hung up.

"They lost him," he told Donner. "But they're close enough to be able to see the golf course."

"Alright then," said Donner. "Let's move."

He spoke into his headpiece and agents began moving about

gathering up equipment. Vehicles started up.

Donner looked at Zack. "How'd they lose him?"

"His prints and scent simply disappeared. He does that a lot."

Donner and Zack waited for the men and vehicles to depart for the two separate missions. They enjoyed a glass of cold lemonade and relaxed on the couch in the cool comfort of the living room.

"I've got a good feeling about this," Donner said. "We know he's around and he's most likely in one of the two places that are about to be sealed off."

Zack liked Donner, but he wasn't ready to express his doubts nor share with him the experiences he'd had with the man they sought; the total helplessness, those hypnotic red eyes, the sweet sickly smell of death.

"This man has always managed to be a step or two ahead of me right from the start," he said. "Looking back, it's as if he anticipated the way events would unfold and the decisions I would make. And when I think about the amazing, the almost superhuman things he did somehow..." Zack lost himself in reflection for a while.

Then he said, "I'm certain he's finished with Palm Springs. He's cleaned up and he's ready to move on and he has plans for me to somehow be part of it. But then I wonder if maybe, just maybe, we're ahead of him this time. How could he possibly guess I would find his little shipping company? Or locate the Gonzalez compound? Both were huge intuitive leaps. I don't think even he could have anticipated that."

"Well then, here's to our success." Donner wasn't going to allow Zack's doubts to dampen his spirits. He raised his lemonade glass to him.

"Now let's go rescue three tired people and a dog from the ninth hole."

They left the coolness of the house and walked into the desert heat and climbed into their vehicles, loaded and ready to go. Donner led them down Fifty-Eighth Avenue and south along Jefferson to Remington and then down Tom Fazio Lane where the pavement circled to an end. Then he drove on across the grass shoulder to a service road on the golf course. It ran out along two fairways and two greens that glistened from a fresh sprinkling, the thirsty yellow desert contrasting sharply on the opposite side. When the road looped around the farthest emerald circle Donner drove off the gravel road into the shade of some cottonwood trees. Zack followed him. As soon as he stepped out of the cab of his truck his cell phone rang. It was Libby.

"Hey, we can see you down there."

Relief flooded over Zack. Now that she was close and nearly safe his anger with himself for exposing her to this skilled proven killer dissipated and he felt only thankfulness. He looked up the large wash that stretched into the hills above them. Near the top a tiny figure waved. Zack waved back. He waited with Donner in the cool shade, leaning against the broad fender of the SUV and watching the figures grow larger as they scrambled down the wash. They listened to the radio chatter of the agents on the FBI teams as they moved into place.

"Uh oh!" Watching Libby approach less than a hundred yards away Zack saw her release Big Blue from his lead and now the dog rocketed down the slope toward them. Moments later Zack was pinned against the truck by two large paws while his face was liberally washed by a huge wet tongue. Donner laughed heartily.

Then Eagle Feather and Libby and Agent Tibbs were all there, hot and sweaty and happy. Libby's outer shirt was tied around her waist and her sleeveless tank top was dirt streaked and long strands of dark brown hair stuck to her moist face, but she didn't seem to notice. Everyone was chattering at once. Zack walked over to his pickup and pulled a cooler out of the bed. He smiled at Eagle Feather, who looked comfortable despite the heat, and shook his head.

"No, sorry, no margaritas, not just yet; but I've got lemonade and it's cold."

Eagle Feather grinned back at him. "You just can't get things right without me to help you, can you, white man?"

"I guess not."

Libby was there now. "I'm sorry we lost him."

"Don't be. I fully expected that to happen. I'm just happy that you're down and safe."

Libby's face softened and she let the moment stretch out before she bent to pour herself a drink.

Eagle Feather leaned against the truck near Zack. "It's not for me to tell you what to think," he said slowly. "I consider myself a very good tracker, maybe one of the best." He looked back up the wash. "But this guy, this Bear Man, his skills are way beyond mine."

Zack waited.

Eagle Feather's voice dropped almost to a whisper. "You've felt it, I know. You've sensed that this man is different somehow, powerful. Maybe even with capabilities that the ancients once had, powers that we've long forgotten and now live only in the oldest part of our brains. For you white people, that memory is buried deep, maybe too deep. But I feel it. And I think maybe you feel it too."

Zack listened to Eagle Feather's words. "Yes, I've felt it, my friend. You know me better than most. I've not spoken to you of eyes that glow red in the dark or of the smell that comes when they appear or of the way the air thickens when he's around. We've all seen him do what it shouldn't be possible for him to do. He's fixed his thoughts on me and I don't know why. At times he seems actually to be inside me, drawing me toward him."

A flash of triumph flew across Eagle Feather's face. Then it was replaced by a look of concern.

Zack smiled at him. "I belong to my world, not his. The tools that I use to fight him must be the tools that I know. It would be useless for me to dwell on things I can't control. He must be defeated and I believe I'm the one who must do it. My best weapon is the faith I have in myself and the belief that I do what must be done."

Then Zack's voice lowered and became gruff. "And if you mention this conversation to anyone - and I mean anyone - you'll never see a margarita from me again."

Eagle Feather grinned as he walked away.

THIRTY-TWO

Donner and Zack drove east down Fifty-eighth Avenue toward Thermal in the SUV. They had left Libby and Eagle Feather at the safe house relaxing comfortably in patio chairs with frosty drinks while Big Blue splashed around in the cold pool water, much to everyone's amusement.

Zack was more confident than at any other time during this long investigation. It made a huge difference that Libby was out of danger. He knew that his judgment was affected when she was exposed and vulnerable. But now he felt entirely whole, his thinking was clear, he was ready to put his entire mind toward the enigma that was his adversary.

What were the killer's intentions now? He would be expecting them to raid the business at the airport, Zack was certain. He must keep in mind that whatever they found during their search of Pemtemweha Industries it was what they were intended to find.

In the driver's seat next to him Donner was speaking into his headpiece to the men already at the airport, checking off each agent, making certain that everyone was in place. Their vehicle turned off Fifty-eighth Avenue directly onto the airport service road, then they drove toward the end of the northwest runway heading to the terminal buildings beyond. Donner was still talking into his headset but he included Zack as he spoke.

"All flights today are in and out of the east runway. The agents are keeping the departing planes in a queue. There's two there right now."

Zack nodded that he understood. The GPS map on the truck's

console showed the road they were on bending east to a crossover road, then heading on to the airpark business building that housed Pemtemweha Industries. At the intersection Zack saw a white SUV with dark windows parked there.

"Those are our boys," Donner said.

They could see the airstrip now and the queued aircraft waiting behind another white SUV. The airpark building grew near and Zack saw several more SUVs and then a group of men bunched near one of the loading docks. Donner pulled up and stopped.

"Nobody in or out?" he asked, leaping out.

An agent nodded affirmatively and handed Donner some bolt cutters and the agents took their positions with drawn weapons. Donner snipped the lock and as the door rolled up, they swarmed in. Someone flipped on a light. Suddenly an interior door swung open opposite them and guns were raised and there were shouts of "FBI" and "clear" as the men recognized the other agents coming from the front.

But the building was empty.

Zack took a good look around. A dusting of salt crystals coated the floor and reflected the bright light from the open warehouse door with a million twinkles. Large wooden crates were stacked all the way up the wall to the low corrugated-metal ceiling. A crate lay open on the concrete floor exposing half an inch of salt residue coating a plastic vapor-barrier lining from a shipment recently removed. Other crates in the rear of the space were being constructed. Large burlap sacks were stacked against the opposite wall and glistened with salt.

"Open every one of those crates," Zack ordered. "Search every single one of those sacks."

The agents went to work. Donner pulled out his cell phone, punched in a number and said the single word; "Go."

The Gonzales compound search team had been set in motion.

Zack noticed a room built into the rear corner of the warehouse with controls and gauges on its door.

"What's that?" he asked a nearby agent.

"My guess? It's a refrigeration room."

"Can you get us in there?"

They walked over there and the agent pushed down on the thick door handle. It moved easily. He pulled the heavy door open. Frosty white clouds of vapor billowed out into the hot room.

Donner joined the two men at the door. "Maybe it's to keep the meat fresh until it can be salted and cured."

Zack went inside. The room was closet sized and very cold. The vapor from his breath obscured his view at first. As it cleared he saw a single deer carcass hanging from a hook, gutted and headless. There was wild game on shelves on both sides; a fowl of some sort, a rabbit, some unlabeled packaged meat. Everything was frozen solid. On the rear shelf he saw a row of Mason jars with scribbled labels. The entire floor of the little room glistened reddish black; most likely it was frozen blood.

Zack instructed an agent to take samples of all the blood on the floor and walls of the room. He set another agent to opening all the Mason jars to identify their contents. Then Zack stepped back out into the heat.

"Where's the forensics team?" Donner was yelling.

"They've just arrived," someone shouted back. Zack saw two agents enter staggering under the weight of their large kits. He recognized George Flood right away. He looked at the other agent and immediately his face creased into a smile.

"Linda! You made it!"

"Hi, Zack." She came over and set her gear down on the concrete floor, then looked around her at all the crates and salt covered burlap bags.

"You always did know how to show a girl a good time." Trickles of sweat ran down her face.

"Apparently the owner didn't waste his money on air conditioning."

Zack waved Donner over. "Agent Ray Donner, meet Agent Linda Whittaker, Tuba City's finest forensic specialist."

"Tuba City's only forensic specialist," Linda amended, shaking Donner's hand.

"Well, what have you boys got lined up for me here?" she asked.

Zack took the initiative. "Well, as a start, I'd like to compare the salt here to the natron residue you found in the tissue of Roundtree's victims." He pointed to the growing mound of the mineral where agents were slashing open the burlap bags. "Then we'll want to know if there is human blood anywhere on this floor or in that freezer room."

Donner chimed in. "We have an agent searching files out in the office. But we need to dust for prints everywhere remotely possible. And don't rule out footprints. Who knows? This character might well go around the office barefoot from force of habit."

Zack nodded his agreement. "Basically, Linda," he said, picking up the thread, "we need you to find anything you can that connects this warehouse to the Arizona crime scenes or to the crime scene here or to any of the victims."

"In other words, sample everything here?" Linda watched George Flood head into the refrigeration room with his kit. "We're going to need some help with this," she said.

Donner immediately assigned an agent to assist her.

As she turned away, Zack's cell phone rang. He looked at it and saw it was his boss, Luke Forrester.

"Zack, I've got some news for you. We weren't getting anywhere identifying Roundtree's victims with local missing persons files. We increased the range of our search to the national file but still no luck. We thought maybe we were missing something or going about it wrong. Here we have fourteen victims, all of them white girls, all juveniles. There should have been a hit somewhere. Then just before she left for Palm Springs Linda suggested we try Interpol. She was thinking of the salt angle, the use of salt as a preservative when transporting... well... meat."

"And?" Zack felt growing excitement.

"And we had a hit almost immediately. It was for the first victim Blue found buried behind the Roundtree house, the first one the team dug up. She came up as missing from Sweden, from a city named Akarp at some place called Blekinge Lan near the coast. Her name is Agda Adelsteinn. She disappeared from a local food market after her mother left her with the grocery cart and went to find another item. She returned to find the little girl gone; there's been no trace of her ever since, until now. That was four years ago, Zack. And then we got more hits. So far our victims have gone missing from countries in Europe, South America, and one came from Hong Kong."

Zack was silent, waiting.

When Luke continued his voice was low and solemn. "Here's the nub of it, Zack. This case is much larger than we all thought. I had to kick it upstairs to the boys in Washington. The long and short of it is they'll be taking over the investigation, alongside the CIA. As of now, they want you to continue your work there on the ground in Palm Springs until the regional office in LA can get in touch with Donner and issue new instructions."

"Yes, sir." Zack was stunned. He felt a sudden rush of disappointment and anger.

"And Zack, after that I'll be bringing you and Linda home. I know your heart and soul have gone into this investigation. You've opened some eyes at the Bureau, I can tell you that right now. But you'll have to let it go and allow the big boys to finish it. I know how hard that'll be for you. I wanted to prepare you in advance."

"Sir, I appreciate that. You're right. I am personally involved. Maybe it'll be a good thing for me to step away and get this case out of my head once and for all."

"Excellent." Forrester attempted to sound hearty. "Absolutely the right attitude. Good luck with your final operations out there. Any results yet?"

"Nothing yet, sir. Pemtemweha Industries has revealed nothing new."

After a few more sympathetic words Forrester ended the call.

Disappointed as he was, Zack's head buzzed with the news from Interpol. So. The killer wasn't skulking around airports looking for girls at all. The girls were coming to him from all over the world, already dead, crated and preserved in salt like a side of beef, in shipping crates, like these very crates that surrounded him now.

Zack saw Linda glance inquiringly at him from across the warehouse floor. He walked over to her.

"So you heard," she said, reading his face.

"Yes. It's incredible. This turns all of our thinking upside down. He's not molesting or killing these little girls. They're already dead when he gets them. But why? What does he want with them? What's in it for him?"

"That's the question, isn't it?"

"Maybe the answer is here somewhere. Let's turn this place upside down to be sure don't we miss anything. We've got to find evidence to connect this salt and these crates to the girls. And it would help if Donner's man searching the office out front can identify the owner of this place."

Donner came toward them, a finger on his earpiece, talking as he approached. He signed off when he reached them. He looked anxious.

"That was our team at the Gonzalez lease. They're taking heavy fire from unknown numbers somewhere at the rear of the compound. They were taking fire before they could find anyone to serve with their warrant; they had been going house to house when they were pinned down. I've called in a chopper to help locate the position of the shooters but I need to go over and direct that effort personally. Can you finish up here, Zack?"

"No problem. Keep me posted."

After Donner left, Zack settled in to direct a thorough search for evidence. Nothing would be overlooked. The hot desert air flowing in the open garage door gradually raised the temperature in the warehouse. Zack was pleasantly surprised when he went to the tiny office out front and found it air-conditioned. The little office was sparsely furnished, just a desk and two chairs. A pair of brown coveralls stiff with sparkling salt was draped over one of the chairs. An agent bent over a drawer at a file cabinet against the wall. The only other object in the room was a huge shredder.

"Anything interesting?"

The man paused and stretched his back. "Not much. Whoever runs this office must have shredded everything, like he knew we were coming. There's no shipping bills, no invoices, no notes, no labels on the files, nothing that you would expect to find in a shipping office. This place has been sterilized. I've located some state and federal certificates and some permits but they don't tell us anything we don't already know. Beyond that, there's just the maintenance manuals and guarantees for the forklift and the aircraft, but-"

"Aircraft?" Zack's head swung up.

"Uh, yes, its a..." -the agent took a file from a different drawer, looked at it and read it- "Cessna Corvallis TT. It's a single engine aircraft, cruising range twelve hundred nautical miles, cruising speed two hundred and thirty-five knots…"

Before he finished Zack had run out of the office to the warehouse. He grabbed the first agent he saw there. "Have we located any aircraft associated with this business?"

"No, Sir."

"Well, there is one. Get a description of it from the agent in the office and then go find it. Go to every tarmac area and every hangar. We need to know if it's here. If you find it, appropriate it."

"Yes, Sir."

Zack shook his head at his own carelessness. Of course a shipping company would own an aircraft. With an aircraft that could travel twelve hundred miles at two hundred and thirty-five knots this monster could fly to Mexico to buy the drugs he needed and be back in Arizona with them in just hours.

Then Zack had another crushing thought. Their quarry might be in that aircraft right now, slipping through their fingers yet again, off into the blue. He ran back into the small office and interrupted the two agents exchanging information about the aircraft.

"Get that aircraft's identification number and send it out to every airport west of the Rocky Mountains," he ordered the agent with the file. "I want to know everywhere this airplane has ever landed."

Zack took the agent's place at the file cabinet and peered into a drawer. The agent had been right; there were far too many empty folders, and the files that did contain documents weren't labeled. Zack pulled one out. It held official permits. Zack saw that the company described itself as a 'meats and perishables' shipping company, with a permit that allowed the company to import and export said meats and perishables. Zack glanced at the coveralls draped over the chair. The business must be a one-man operation. The man would come in to the office, throw on the coveralls and go unload the plane with the fork lift and then stack the crates in the warehouse, doing it all himself.

And then what? Zack guessed he'd pry open the crates with the pry bar he remembered seeing against a wall and unpack the salted meats or fruits or whatever was in the crate. Maybe there'd be a false bottom. All of the victims were small; they could fit easily in a small section of these crates. Maybe they were sandwiched in between layers of salted meats. That way security X-rays wouldn't distinguish between the body of the victim and the body of the deer or mountain goat packed on either side. Yes, he decided, they probably were packed in the middle; no need for a false bottom. Thermal was a natural first stop on a flight up from Mexico. Most likely Customs would check the crates before the plane departed Mexico. A bribe here, a bribe there; it could easily be done that way.

But what did he ship? What about that deer hanging in the refrigerator room, for instance? How could he have time to run a business, to salt, preserve and ship meats for hunters and still spend time off in Arizona on the reservation burying all those girls and doing God knows what else?

Zack had a sudden thought. He went back into the warehouse and over to the refrigeration room and found George Flood scraping frozen blood samples from the floor.

"George, did you ever determine the origins of the salt in the victim's skin tissue?"

George looked up at Zack. "Actually, no. The natural salt from our local beds lacks the purity of the natron samples we took from the girl. What we found in her skin was an industrially refined natron powder. It might be possible for someone to refine the local lake-bed salt to that degree but it would be a hell of a chore, and why bother?"

"I've got some samples coming your way," said Zack. "Would you be able to tell me if any of them come from the identical location?"

"Yes, we can analyze them based upon carbonate and silicate intrusion percentages to a fairly high degree of accuracy. I can't do it in my lab, but I can send it out and have it done. Once it's been refined, it requires nanotechnology to dissect the samples to compare them. The geology lab at the University can do that."

"Thanks. Keep me informed."

As Zack turned away, his cell phone rang.

"Hello, Agent Tolliver, this is Melissa Mann, reporting for NBC UNEWZ TV, the Flagstaff affiliate. I'd like just a moment of your time- "

"How'd you get this number?"

Zack heard bubbling laughter. "The same way I got it the last time, from Ms. Fitzgerald at the Navajo Police Station in Elk Wells. She tends to be careless with the notes on her desk. If you really don't want to be reached, I'd suggest you change your cell phone number now and then."

"I'll go you one better," said Zack, angry now. "If you ever use this line again, I'll cite you for interfering with an FBI agent in pursuit of his duties."

"Yes, sir, I'll behave, sir," came the demure answer and another little giggle. "But first I thought you might want to make a comment for an upcoming story which will state that you blew the John Roundtree case and as a direct result of that ineffectiveness another child has died out here in Palm Springs."

Zack was shaken. How could anyone think that he had failed in the Roundtree investigation? He wasn't even the agent in charge. In fact, he hadn't even been there at its conclusion, he'd been in a hospital bed when Ben Brewster and Jimmy Chaparral had wrapped it up. Furthermore, if he had been consulted he would have recommended that the investigation be continued. Zack was ready to respond angrily when he realized the trap.

"I have no comment," he said through his clamped jaw, and he ended the call.

An agent approached him from the open garage door. "We've found the plane," he announced. Zack felt a surge of relief at the news. At least the killer hadn't used the aircraft to disappear. "It's parked out there on the apron with the other aircraft," the agent said. "We're going over it now. There's salt residue on the floor of the cargo area, as you'd expect, but the plane is empty."

"Be sure to test for blood, check for fingerprints, and sample any DNA possibles. Also check the carpet for foreign fibers and soil samples. Find out where it's been. There must be a log of some sort. And sample the underbelly for soil samples as well. Do the whole enchilada."

"You got it."

The agent walked away and Zack felt growing frustration and anger. If they couldn't find a way to link Pemtemweha Industries to the Arizona crimes or even to the murdered little girl here in Palm Springs what would prevent the press from blaming him for this failure as well?

Zack forced a deep breath. Got to get hold of myself, he thought. If I'm right, and I know I am, sooner or later we'll find the link.

Back in the shipment office the agent was finishing a conversation on his cell phone. He looked up as Zack entered.

"I just spoke to someone at the State of California Franchise Tax board. They have a business listing for Pemtemweha Industries Inc. organized as a Limited Partnership. It was started up ten years ago by a man named Chet Gonzalez as the general partner with a second limited partner named Alex Gonzalez."

Zack raised an eyebrow at this information. So his intuitive guess about the Gonzalez compound had proven correct. That was big news.

"They had no useful information beyond that, not even Social Security numbers and that sort of thing because the partners belong to an Indian tribe. They wouldn't have been registered with the tax office either if not for the fact that the airport isn't on a reservation," the agent explained. "But here's the interesting part. About six months ago, Gonzalez filed for a change in ownership, naming a different person and removing himself as the general partner."

Zack felt a sense of anticipation. Now, finally, they would have a name. He saw the agent looking at him strangely.

"And who did he name?"

"The new owner's name is Zack Tolliver."

THIRTY-THREE

Zack's jaw dropped. "What...? How did he...?" He could not comprehend what he had just heard. He tried again. "Isn't owner verification required in this state?"

"According to this tax guy, all signatures, all social security numbers, everything that was needed to make the change was in order."

Zack's mind raced to understand the implications of this. "Well, that certainly answers the question of whether he expected us to find this place or not."

Zack pulled out his phone and called Donner.

"Agent Donner."

"It seems our man has once again anticipated our every move. There can be no doubt now that he expected us to find this shipping firm. Where are you?"

"I'm at the command center."

"Are Libby and Eagle Feather there with you?"

"Yes, all safe and happy."

"Okay, look. I've just learned I'm to be called off this case once the L.A. boys show up, probably tomorrow. There's no longer any reason to keep Libby and Eagle Feather in Palm Springs. Please tell them to take my truck and go check out of the hotel and go home. They can leave the truck there; I'll pick it up later. Tell them I said they should get their stuff and just go. Right now. I want them out of the picture.

And please tell Libby I'll bring along anything that's left behind when I leave in a day or two. I'll call her when I'm on my way home. And Donner...?"

"Yes?"

"Be very, very careful. I think we can now assume that he knew we would be coming to the Gonzalez compound as well."

"Copy that. What evidence have you found out there?"

"Precious little real evidence yet. Despite the fact that he literally told us of his connection to this place, we still have no way to prove the fact. But thanks to his games, and his ego, at least we know to keep looking."

"Well, that's good, anyway. I've got to go. There is still gunfire being exchanged out at the compound. We'll talk later."

Zack walked back out to the warehouse. An agent came over to him, checking his notes as he walked.

"We've just checked the Cessna's log," he reported. "We compared the destination airports it lists against the records of the National Transportation Safety Board. The aircraft has made a lot of trips to Mexico, mostly to Baja California and various locations down there. It flew most often to San Felipe, about a hundred twenty-five miles south of the border where it picked up salt loads, according to the records. It also made stops at Guerrero Negro, where there's a big salt refinery, but it made most of its stops in Tijuana from both directions. It left off and picked up cargo there. The cargos they list are preserved game in both directions and salt on the return, just as advertised. Immigration inspection occurs in Tijuana, but everyone agrees it can be sketchy there, due to an overload of work and being under-manned. And the agents are looking for drugs, not little girls. Even so, a lot of money changes hands there. The plane destinations of record here in the U.S. are LAX and Thermal, naturally, and the Palm Springs airport, but that's about all. Nowhere else."

"Nowhere else? Have you checked records at all the Arizona and southern California airports? And what about Nevada, Utah and New Mexico?"

"We've got people working on that right now, but so far nothing."

"Get me the results of the soil samples from the Cessna's underbelly and its tires as soon as possible. We need to make a liar out of those records somehow."

Zack watched the agent walk away. It made no sense. The man would not have risked driving the dead girls great distances in his truck. But the short flight to Tuba City and then the short drive to Elk Wells in the middle of the night? That made more sense. There had to be evidence.

As Zack struggled to fit the puzzle pieces together he felt his frustration grow once again and now it was accompanied by a new feeling of restlessness, a feeling of being trapped. Suddenly he had become a temporary overseer of his own case, a mere caretaker of a case that would soon belong to others. In his last few hours of responsibility he wanted to be where the action was, to be at the command center with Donner or at the Gonzalez compound. He wanted to have his finger on the pulse of the investigation, just as it had been from the very beginning, not waiting here in a backwater sifting through files while the real action passed him by.

And yes, he wanted to see Libby safely away from Palm Springs. He knew that as long as she was here this assassin would see her as Zack's weakness and find a way to use her as he had done once already. At least Eagle Feather was with her, Zack reminded himself. She couldn't have better protection. And who knows, the man might indeed be trapped at this very moment at the Gonzalez compound, pinned down by FBI rifle fire. Yet despite his best hopes, Zack couldn't shake the doubts. It was probably just Gonzalez and his son Alex firing those shots at the FBI in the compound; their quarry might not be anywhere near there.

Well, they could get lucky. The man had anticipated that they'd find Pemtemweha but how could he possibly imagine that Zack would find the Gonzalez lease so quickly? That had been a real guess and hopefully a good one. Buoyed by that last thought, Zack went to check on Linda's progress.

She saw him coming and spoke up first. "I've got a good news, bad news situation for you," she said, cheerfully.

"I know. Which do I want first? Go ahead, you pick the order."

Linda wiped sweat from her forehead. "I had a call just now about the Cactus spines we sampled. They were able to find DNA on one of them, as we had hoped. That's the good news. But when they put the DNA code into the FBI database they couldn't get any matches. So they expanded their search to the CIA database and finally to Interpol but still no good. That's the bad news. This guy either has never had a sample taken or he doesn't exist."

Zack wasn't all that surprised. "This perp is very careful and has the patience of Job. He's always managed to avoid leaving DNA traces before this. But at least it's on file now."

He looked around the warehouse. Salt was heaped everywhere and all of the crates were dismantled. "Any luck with the blood trace search?"

"None," Linda replied. "Not a drop of human blood. We've found blood from lots of other mammals, though."

Zack thought about that. "The absence of blood may support our theory that when the girls arrive here they've been dead a long time, maybe even deep frozen somewhere and then preserved in salt for shipping. In that situation there wouldn't be any fresh blood to lose. That blood trail up on monument Mesa? Real genius. Splashing Roundtree's blood around left the impression of a fresh kill in everyone's mind even if it was later disproved."

Zack' was interrupted by his cell phone. "Zack, it's Donner. We've got a situation over at the Gonzalez lease. I'm going to have to go over in person and I need you there, too. Are you at a place where you can leave someone in charge and meet me there?"

"I'm on my way," Zack replied eagerly. He knew this summons

must mean that things had gone badly in some way but despite that realization he felt new excitement to be in the action at last.

By the time Zack was driving west along Fifty-eighth Avenue the sun was sinking toward the jagged peaks of the fin-like mountain ridge in front of him. He opened his window and felt the cool edge of the evening on his face. If the gunfight at the Gonzales compound remained a standoff it would soon turn in favor of the bad guys, he thought. Darkness and their knowledge of the local terrain could well allow them to escape. As he drove his eye drifted along the ridge in front of him, every feature of it sharply outlined against the lighter canvas of the yellowing sky beyond. Suddenly he exclaimed aloud. A thin column of smoke, a dark rope against the glowing sky, was rising right where he was going. Now he thought he understood the reason for Donner's urgency. *It can't be a coincidence*, Zack thought, pushing down hard on the accelerator.

It took Zack just ten minutes to reach the vicinity of the park. He turned off the pavement at Jefferson Street and bumped across the berm to Cahuilla Park Road, kicking up dust, then squealing back onto the pavement accelerated hard past the trailer park. Zack could see across the lake from here; he was sure now that the fire was at the Gonzalez compound. When the road swung north and straightened out he increased his speed even more. As he grew near a carnival of blinking red and blue lights flashing on dark trees greeted him and he found the road ahead blocked by police cars. Zack turned on his own flashing light and the vehicles shifted just enough to allow him through. Beyond the roadblock Zack turned onto a track leading into the grounds and entered a forest of red and blue blinking lights reflecting on nearby buildings and trees like a flashing neon sign. He slid to a dusty stop and jumped out. An agent appeared at his side.

"Special Agent Tolliver? Follow me, please, Sir."

Zack ran with the agent among sparse trees and past dark and silent buildings. Their feet crunching loudly on dry leaves. The crackling roar of fire grew louder and its red-yellow glare replaced the police strobes dancing on the treetops. The agent led Zack through more trees and then they were in front of a large two-story house. Tongues of flame licked out of the lower floor windows and undulated up the sides of the building. The upper floor and roof were already engulfed. A fire truck was there, parked at an angle to the building and dark silhouettes of firemen struggled to drag a hose toward the structure. Zack found Donner standing as near to the building as the heat would permit, a rifle in his hand.

"Where are the shooters?" Zack asked, shouting over the roar.

Donner acknowledged Zack with a grim look. "Inside. The team insists that no one left the building before the fire started."

"How did it start?"

"No one is sure. There was an explosion inside somewhere just before it started. They must have been storing ammunition or explosives in there."

As if to underscore Donner's words another explosion shook the frame of the house and sent a large billow of flame out the open door and windows, scattering the firemen. Zack and Donner were pushed back by the hot blast and took shelter behind a truck.

"It's going to be damn hard to identify any bodies even if we do find them," Donner shouted to Zack over the roar.

Zack cupped his hand around Donner's ear and shouted back. "All we need is a little DNA. There's got to be enough left for that."

Donner looked back at Zack quizzically. "I didn't know you had any."

"I just learned that we do."

The fire burned out of control, now enveloping the upper floor. The roof to collapsed in places with increased roar and showers of sparks. More fire trucks were responding but it became clear that there was not adequate water for them all and it was more than an hour before the firemen gained the upper hand. It was another hour before the building had been watered down sufficiently to allow entry. Most of the roof was gone and only a shell of the building still stood.

The FBI had maintained a perimeter around the house throughout the fire to prevent any escape and now at Donner's suggestion a second much wider perimeter was established to guard against the possibility of hidden tunnels or any other secret exit; nothing was to be left to chance.

Zack and Donner were allowed to enter the structure with the fire inspectors but only under their guidance and outfitted in full heat protection suits. The pungent smells of burnt synthetics and still smoldering damp wood assailed their nostrils as soon as they entered. The heat was still formidable. The floor had been built directly over the earth and was mostly intact and supported their weight. The house interior was a black shell. Large holes gaped in the ceiling above them draped with long melted carpet strips dripping water. The walls were burnt through in places and hacked by fire axes in others. The first body they found was leaning against a wall near a large blown out window, burnt beyond any chance of recognition. Several partially melted handguns lay on the floor near the ashen body and rifles with scorched stocks and warped barrels leaned against the wall or lay on the floor.

"This fire burned hot and fast," one of the firemen said, his voice muffled behind his mask. He pointed toward the center of the building where a lot of debris and blackened pieces of furniture lay scattered about. "That large explosion must have come from around there somewhere."

They moved cautiously over toward the area. After a few steps one of the firemen pointed at his feet. A blackened cylindrical object lay there and Zack bent for a closer look then recoiled when he recognized it as an arm torn off at the elbow, the shirt fabric melted into the flesh. Donner placed a bright orange tag near it and they moved on. At the blast center they found a charred body. It was missing part of an arm and both legs and was partially hidden under a pile of smoldering debris. The flesh of the face was stripped away and charred and only bits and patches of scalp remained. The thick torso indicated a large man. Zack and Donner stared at the body. Identification would be difficult. Donner tagged it.

A fireman at a far wall waved his arms and Zack went over to him.

The fireman showed him a leg that had been ripped off just below the hip, still dressed in a blue jean leg with a bare foot protruding, the latter curiously unaffected by the fire. Along the same wall they found a second leg, broken and twisted and deeply burned.

"This guy must have been right on top of the explosion when it happened," the fire official mumbled through his mask. "The explosives were probably in some sort of box on the floor and must have ignited when he was right on top of it. That could explain his arm being over there" -he pointed- "and his legs over here."

That made sense to Zack.

Donner came over. "What would cause this kind of explosion?" he asked.

"Probably an ammunition box, maybe a sack of black powder for packing bullets. A lot of people do that around here. But there must have been something stronger as well, like Semtex. The PETN in Semtex would have been ignited from the powder blowing or from ammunition going off - it reacts to shock."

They went back to take a closer look at the body. Donner tugged off melted fabric at the shirt pockets hoping for identification of any sort. His fingers touched a thick matted substance beneath the fabric where it had been partially protected from the flames. Chunks of it came away freely when he tugged.

"Looks like hair," Zack said.

"A lot of it," agreed Donner. "And look here." He pointed to the sole remaining arm where the fabric had pulled away. There was more of the thickly matted substance.

"Hairy son of a bitch," remarked the fireman.

"Just my point," said Donner, looking at Zack. "We have his DNA."

Zack's reply was firm. "If this is him, it will match. We can't be certain without a match. John Roundtree had a very hairy body but it turned out to have been caused by synthetic HGH administered over months or maybe even years until he became hairy as an ape, apparently just to make him look like a Skinwalker and set him up for the killings. That's the level of detail and foresight this guy uses. The only thing that will convince me that this is our man is a DNA match."

"I get your point."

The moment they were out of the building Donner sent for a forensics team to have the bodies removed to the lab.

"We'll have an answer soon," he told Zack. "But meanwhile we'll take nothing for granted. We'll keep a guard around this building and we'll search the entire area for prints and signs of any other person. But I've got to tell you, Zack, I've got a feeling that we got lucky this time."

Zack smiled at his colleague's optimism, hoping he was right. He caught himself in yawn. There was nothing left for him to do now. It had been a long, long day since Eagle Feather and Big Blue had awakened him at five thirty that morning. He decided it was time to head back to his hotel room and get some sleep. He said as much to Donner.

"You go ahead. We can check in with each other in the morning. With luck, you'll be all done here and free to go back home to Arizona. I'll stay and supervise the scene until the bodies are removed and forensics has gotten everything in hand."

Back at the Desert Sun Resort Zack took a very long hot shower. Donner had called him just after he'd reached the hotel, sounding upbeat. He was downright cheery about the progress they were making at the compound. A team was combing every inch of the house by torchlight and the bodies and parts of bodies had already been removed and taken back to the lab. The site would be well guarded over night and would be inspected yet again in the light of day. Donner remained convinced that they had their man. His confidence was contagious.

"I know, I know," Donner had teased. "You'll believe it only when we get a DNA match."

But once again mysteries remained, Zack mused, toweling off. But they could wait until morning. He saw with satisfaction that all of Libby's things were gone. There had been a little note near the soap telling him that she was on her way and to be careful and to call her first thing in the morning. It was a huge relief to have her far away and safe, no matter how optimistic Donner might be. Zack climbed in between the cool sheets and was asleep before he could have another thought.

THIRTY-FOUR

Zack awoke with an aching head and foul tasting mouth wishing he could sleep another eight hours. Instead he rolled over and grabbed his cell phone from the night table to call Linda.

"Anything new from Pemtemweha Industries?" he asked without preface.

"A girl likes to be asked how she is first thing in the morning," Linda complained.

"I was planning to," Zack lied. "I just got my questions out of order."

"Well, the answer to your intended first question is I'm fine, but tired. I was just trying to find my lost coffee when you called. And the answer to the second question is no, nothing new. In terms of blood residue we still have nothing other than animal blood. Our salt samples from the warehouse are in Flood's lab and we should have info on those later today. All the evidence we found at Pemtemweha seems to support just what they say on their permits: they pack wild game in salt and ship it out of Thermal in their little aircraft. They sometimes contract a carrier for larger shipments. That carrier is located in the same building, called UShip. You'll need to talk to Agent Browne for more about them but he ran a check on them and seems to think they are legit. Pemtemweha imports crates of salt and game animals to be prepared and preserved. We sent soil samples from the tires and the underbelly of the aircraft to the LA lab but we have no word on that yet."

"I'll bet they cleaned up that plane," Zack said.

"I would agree. I just have this feeling the whole place was tidied up for us." Then Linda said, "Now I get to ask a question. Since the entire forensic team from Palm Springs is working this case and soon will be joined by a big team from LA, can I go home?"

"That's partly why I'm calling." Zack's voice was somber. "Linda, I need to ask you to stay on here for just one more job. I need you to follow the DNA testing from the bodies of the men who died in that house last night at the Gonzales lease. I need you to supervise that testing all the way to the final results before you leave there. No slip ups. No mislabeling or lost samples. Linda, I trust you. This case won't ever be over for me until I'm convinced we have a positive DNA match from the cactus spine to one of those bodies."

Zack gave a short laugh. "And I'm pretty sure you want me to believe this case is over."

"I sure do." Linda sighed. "Okay, I'll stay. But move me into that fancy hotel where you're staying. I need a little pampering that this Motel 6 can't provide. And Zack?"

"Yes?"

"You owe me."

Zack laughed again and hung up. He knew he owed Linda and he knew she wouldn't forget it. He called Donner at his office. When the connection was made he heard the noise of many voices in the background and knew that the big boys had arrived from the L.A. office.

"Hey, Zack, glad you called. You got your TV on?"

Zack felt a sudden churning in his stomach. "Not yet."

"Go to Channel 4, NBC. This lady doesn't seem to like you very much."

Zack found the remote and clicked it and flipped through the channels until Melissa Mann appeared standing before a familiar backdrop of palm trees, oozing charm, "...and despite the failure of

FBI Agent Tolliver to catch this man in Arizona, FBI agents here in Palm Springs appear to have wrapped up the case in only two days. According to my sources, one of the two suspects killed in the deadly shootout and house fire at Cahuilla Lake State Park near Thermal, California, last night was the man responsible for the serial rapes, kidnappings, and murders of over two-dozen girls across two states. No law enforcement personnel were injured in the gun battle. The second suspect killed was alleged to have been involved in the crimes. Now, behind me…"

"Two dozen?" Zack asked as he clicked off the TV.

"You left too soon last night," Donner replied. "We set up some flood lights and searched behind the house, looking for tunnels, actually. We found several earthen mounds and some were quite fresh. When we started digging we began to find the bodies of those little girls you had prophesied. We're still digging them up. Zack, it looks like your guy had managed to operate here and in Arizona simultaneously all these years. He must have moved in with this Chet Gonzalez the same way he did with John Roundtree out on the reservation. Very clever. Find the weak and disenfranchised, build them up, give them drugs, and make partners out of them. He must have gained an almost hypnotic hold on his partners. That's the only way he could have operated in two places at once; he had to have partners he could absolutely trust."

"The girls you are finding now, are they…?"

"Yes." Donner knew where Zack was going. "They're all blonde and fair skinned Caucasian girls. I don't doubt we'll find that they are imports, just like the others. Not all the bodies have been dug up yet nor do we have any lab results, naturally, but it sure does look like the exact same pattern."

"So now all we're missing is motive," Zack said. "Why? Why is he doing this? Does anything you've learned tell us why this guy imports dead girls from all over the world only to bury them here? Where does he get them? Why does he want them? What could he possibly be doing with them? Is he doing some weird experiments? Is this some kind of fetish that I don't know anything about?"

"*Did*, Zack. Why *did* he import them! The creep is dead. We don't have DNA proof yet but we will. And no, the motive is still unclear. But we've got profilers working on that one. You and I have done all we can. In fact, we've just been officially relieved. The L.A. boys are here in the office right now and they've taken over. You can go home, Zack. I have to connect some dots and write up some reports but then I'm done too. As a matter of fact, this case is pretty much wrapped up now except for a final body count. So enjoy your life, Zack. And next time I call you, hopefully it'll be just to have a fancy umbrella drink and talk about old times. Thanks, Zack. Got to go."

Zack felt empty suddenly. It really was over this time. Even if it turned out they didn't get their man, even if he had somehow managed a substitution and pulled off another amazing disappearing act, he would still be long gone and he wouldn't be back.

Zack pressed another number in his cell phone. It was time to call Libby. She answered on the first ring.

"Zack, I've been watching the news. Did you really get him?"

"So it appears," Zack replied. "We haven't got a DNA match yet and we know that this guy never seems to stay dead very long, but for me, it's all over regardless. I'm coming home."

"I'm glad," Libby said simply. Zack could hear the relief in her voice. "When will you get here?"

"I'm just going to throw my things in the truck, check out, and come home."

"That's great. Eagle Feather and I drove through the night to get here so I haven't had much sleep yet. I'm going to catch a few hours right now but please call me as soon as you get here. Promise?"

"I promise." Zack felt the warmth in her voice. The thought of seeing her soon suddenly felt very good.

He packed quickly and departed right away, electing to start his drive fueled only by coffee and a donut. Alone in his truck with only the hum of the tires and the steady throb of the motor hour after hour, cooled deliciously by the AC, Zack felt wonderfully alone and at peace and let his mind wander where it would. He didn't stop until he had driven all the way to Phoenix and there he pulled into a pancake house for lunch. He had settled into a booth and was sipping a cup of reheated coffee and waiting for his pancake order when his iPhone rang. It was Linda.

"Hi, Zack, I've got some good news." Zack sat up immediately to listen. "First, you should know that because both DNA samples we wanted to compare were in hand, and maybe also because I know a guy, we were able to avoid the backlog at CODIS. They used the standard FBI Short Tandem Repeat technology for the comparison so we got a strong preliminary response much quicker. Zack, of a possible thirteen matching sites for absolute identification we were able to obtain nine sites with our fast and furious approach. There wasn't all that much DNA on the cactus tine but we'll try to collect enough for another test and send that along to CODIS as well. This still may not seem final enough for you, I know. But Zack, a match on nine sites in a quickie test tells me that we can be pretty darn sure it was our man who died in the house fire last night."

Zack sat stunned. The silence at his end was so long that Linda began to think something was wrong.

"Zack? Zack? Is everything Okay?"

"Everything is more than Okay," Zack said. "Everything is great. Everything is so great that I just can't quite comprehend it. After all this time, all our disappointments, all the threats, I...Linda, thanks for rushing that test. It means more to me than you may ever know."

"I think I do know, Zack." Linda said quietly. "It's my pleasure, believe me. Oh, and Zack, I'll be sure to collect my favor..."

"I'll be ready for you when you do," Zack affirmed. But his brain raced on. "Do they have an ID on the other gunman yet?"

"We're not doing the down and dirty DNA test on him so the results will take longer. But we have ample forensic evidence and it all points to him being the Chet Gonzalez fellow we had thought."

The remainder of the trip back was as pleasant as Zack could have imagined. The colors of the arid landscape grew more vivid and the smell of the air sweeter as he neared home. He felt a deep satisfaction within himself, a renewed sense of justice, as if he had just had a prison sentence reversed. He also felt the deep feeling of relief that came with the removal of the sword that had constantly hung over him for so long, the sword that threatened him and then had turned to threaten Libby.

When Zack arrived near the Tuba City turnoff he decided to bypass it and drive directly up to Page. He would catch up with Forrester and Jimmy Chaparral on another day. Right now he wanted rest and a chance to get away from all thoughts of the case. There remained unanswered questions in Zack's mind, questions that he wanted to think about at his leisure, but not now. Right now he wanted to enjoy the moment.

The drive north along the edge of the plateau to Bitter Springs was dramatically beautiful. Zack never tired of the vivid layers of yellows and tans on the face of the cliffs along the river and the sharply contrasting emerald green of cottonwood groves on the banks of the blue green white-frothed waters. He rolled his window all the way down to enjoy the smell of the sage and the warm fresh breeze. The heat here surrounded and comforted him, womb-like; it didn't attack him like the sudden dangerous heat of the California desert. At Bitter Springs he took a right and drove up and over the plateau rampart and at the junction of Route 98 near Page turned south again to his small ranch and home.

Zack creaked up the wooden porch steps with his overnight bag in his hand and his garment bag slung over his shoulder and nudged his way in through the screen door. The house was wonderfully cool and comfortable as it always was this late in the afternoon, a time of day when the westerly breezes through the rear window stirred the cooler air of the shaded interior. But wait. He hadn't left any windows open when he left for Palm Springs almost a week before. The air should be stale and close, not fragrant and familiar as it was now.

"Libby?" Zack dropped his bags on the sofa and walked through the living room to the kitchen. "Libby?" The room was clean and tidy, just as he had left it. But on the bare kitchen table there were two glasses of lemonade. Near them was a folded note propped up against the napkin holder. He opened it.

Dear Zack, I decided I couldn't wait for your call and came over to be here when you arrived. But the beauty of the afternoon called me to our favorite place on the plateau. I took the mare and a bottle of your wine. Meet me there. Love, Libby.

Zack grinned, thinking this idea was typically impetuous of her. He took a long cool drink of lemonade and looked at his watch. By the time he changed into riding clothes and saddled Diablo it would be well after five when he arrived on top of the plateau. He decided to bring an extra sweater for Libby and some bread and cheese for a light dinner.

After making his preparations Zack walked out to the barn. He saw that Libby had parked her ancient station wagon behind it. No wonder he hadn't known she was here, he thought to himself. She usually parked right in front after pulling up in a large cloud of dust. He went into the barn and saw that the mare and the mare's tack were indeed gone. Diablo whinnied his pleasure at seeing Zack. Before saddling him Zack looked him over. The stallion appeared to have been well cared for. He would leave a nice tip for the hostler. Both man and horse were eager to ride and it wasn't long before they were saddled up and Zack was leading the horse out the rear of the barn. Diablo shied when they approached Libby's station wagon.

"What's the matter, boy? Have you forgotten what Libby's car looks like already?"

Zack was puzzled by Diablo's behavior. It didn't fit, in much the same way that Libby's car parked back here didn't fit. Zack sighed. He'd probably developed the habit of looking too closely at unusual behavior in these past few months. He had to let go. Then he thought about seeing Libby again and he pushed the thoughts out of his mind and mounted Diablo. They soon settled into their familiar canter, moving at a fast pace up the trail that ascended the steep face of the butte. As they climbed Zack looked down at the sandy river bottom with its tortuous turns that formed his little valley snuggled between steep sided buttes that the angled sun was painting in reds and yellows.

This scene was never repeated in exactly the same way, Zack had found. Somehow it appeared slightly different each time they came here.

They climbed steadily up the trail, Diablo scrambling sometimes but strong and surefooted. The steepest part of the trail was the final stretch up onto the plateau surface and as they neared it Zack became conscious of a strange yet somehow familiar scent. He struggled to identify it, realizing now that it had been there all along but very faint, mingled with other scents along the way; the smell of pinion pine and fresh dank earth just turned over by horse hooves, the dank aroma of exposed roots near the trail. It smelled of all those earthy smells but now Zack knew it was different because suddenly he knew what it was. Fearing what he might find when he reached the top he urged Diablo faster up the last stretch of trail.

They burst over the top and galloped across the flat grassy surface toward the tree, the solitary tree that was their special place, and then Zack pulled back hard on Diablo's reigns, stopping him so abruptly that the horse sat back onto his hind legs. He froze in the saddle and stared at the tableau in front of him; the blanket spread out under the tree, Libby sitting there with her legs tucked under her, a wine bottle and two glasses on the blanket next to her, the slight whispering breeze stirring her long brown hair and reflecting sparkles of light.

Libby looked at Zack, a strange mixture of hope and dread on her face, a look he had never seen before. On the blanket beside her sat a hooded figure, cross-legged, bare feet protruding from worn buckskin pants, straight backed and unmoving with hands in lap, head down, features hidden under a dark hood.

The instinct that caused Zack to reign in Diablo before approaching too near caused him to dismount slowly, keeping his eye on the seated figure and dropping the reigns carefully. Then slowly, slowly, his gaze never shifting he pulled his rifle out of its scabbard and holding it ready in his hand, pushed Diablo clear and faced the scene before him. He waited. The sun was low and in setting would angle its brightness into Zack's eyes. Along with his fear he felt admiration for the detail of the man's plan, his admiration coming even as Zack understood that his own life hung in the balance. No one moved. Time was no longer meaningful. Zack was unwilling to move or speak, not wanting to upset some unknown precarious balance. He knew only that at this moment Libby was alive and that he must wait and keep it so as long as he could. Near him Diablo crunched loudly on the dry grass, unaffected by the drama and affairs of men. It was Libby who finally broke the silence.

"Zack, I am so sorry." She said this quietly, soulfully, almost in a whisper. The silent figure remained motionless.

"Don't be," Zack said to Libby softly. "This is how it was meant to be all along."

Libby didn't reply. Zack sensed that an unseen force emanated from the unmoving figure, as if it had allowed Libby to speak and now commanded her silence.

Zack waited.

Again the slight breeze gently moved Libby's hair and flipped and turned the small leaves of the tree branch above them and still they waited. Then Libby's mouth moved to speak. But now her face became contorted and hard and when she spoke the voice that came from her was coarse, deep, and malevolent.

"You have interfered with my plans," it said. This was no longer Libby.

Zack felt fear clutch at him, for himself and even more for Libby. He replied quietly. "I followed the trail you placed before me."

"I see you are aware of it," the voice responded coarsely.

The hooded creature still had not moved. Zack remained silent.

Libby's mouth moved again. "And now you will see the power of the being that you have pursued and this woman will be our witness."

Zack still did not move or respond.

After the silence Libby's mouth moved once more. "And you have no questions before the end?"

"I do. But you already know what they are."

"Yes." This last word came in a long breath, almost the hiss of a snake. "And I will answer them all for you, because it is my purpose that you understand before you die. You will be privileged to know what no one else knows and I teach you not to fulfill your needs but my own. I live a solitary life and my knowledge cannot be shared with those unlike me. After so many years even I grow tired of walking among men but not being of them. Even I feel the need to talk of these things to another being and so I select a man, a man like you who might for at least the most fleeting moment understand what I have to say. I test my choice and when I am satisfied I tell him these things and then I kill him. And now I will tell you."

The sun sank lower and came into Zack's eyes. The two figures on the blanket dissolved into black shapes with fiery bright auras, their features erased. Zack felt the creature turn his hooded head and look at him directly. All he could do was stand and listen.

"We begin. First I will answer those mundane questions in your head and tell you why I buried the little girls here on Navajo Land and on the land of the Cahuilla People in California, and in other lands and places about which you do not know. As you had guessed, I am not a sexual deviant nor am I a serial killer. I would become either if it served my purposes but this time it did not. It may surprise you to know that I have killed but one person while engaged in the business into which you intruded yourself. Nor would I have killed that reporter had he not flashed a bright bulb in my eyes at a difficult moment and annoyed me. As to John Roundtree, he killed himself. He had been involved in the lengthy process of killing himself long before I found him and he begged me for the drugs that I could supply him and he was more than eager to assist me in my work. In the end, he asked for everything that he received.

My work, Zack, is contractual. Even I must find the means to live when I am among men and so I market myself for hire around the globe and I contract myself to men who need things done that no one else can do and who are able to pay the high price for my unique services. I travel the world to perform these services and I never fail. My price increases as my reputation grows. It is very lucrative.

In this case, the powerful men who hired me needed to dispose of certain little girls from time to time whom they had secured from around the world to meet their singular and specific lusts and if the girls met with accidents or they disappointed their masters or in other ways lost their appeal or usefulness they would be terminated and preserved by the time honored method of embalmment with salt. Then they were shipped to me at my place of business in crates that also contained exotic animals preserved in a similar way and were passed into the country at an immigration point in Mexico where the exchange of large sums of money could secure everything anyone might need. At my import business I would then unload each little corpse from its salty sarcophagus and transport it to one of several places for burial. In the locations that concerned you, I either drove the body in the back of my truck to the Gonzales lease for Mr. Gonzales to bury or I flew it to the Tuba City Airport at night and loaded it into the vehicle that Mr. Roundtree would kindly have waiting there for me. He would then drive to his conveniently isolated home where he would have a little grave already dug and ready for it.

I carefully select my accomplices not just for their weak wills, their neediness and strong backs, but for the solitary lives they live and the suspicion and fear that tends to grow around such people. It is important, you see, Zack, that people fear my accomplices and therefore stay away from them so that we can operate undisturbed. I chose the Navajo lands and the Cahuilla reservations for the simple reason that native people are more aware of the ancient ones and their powers and so they respect them. They do not need proof that some among them can walk as a bear or fly as an eagle. They know it to be so and they leave us to ourselves."

Zack found his voice. He realized that the creature had been reading his thoughts to choose which questions to answer. Zack asked his own now.

"Where else have you buried these girls?"

The voice laughed, a short deep evil laugh that contorted Libby's features. "The needs of men are many and the lusts of the powerful are extravagant. I had more business than I could handle in Elk Wells or in Thermal alone. And we will leave it at that.

But now time, even for me, moves on. I will answer your final remaining question. I will tell you about my kind. I am what the ancient tribe in Mexico that you call the Mayans called a Mestaclocan. But my clan pre-existed those people, for the origins of my kind stem from the earliest days that humans walked the earth, when survival came from gathering fruits and nuts and killing and eating those smaller creatures that they could catch, but in turn remaining eternally vigilant and prepared to run and hide from the beasts that were larger and stronger. The swiftest runners and the smallest and most clever hiders and the most alert and intelligent thinkers survived. Eventually your genetic predecessors learned that survival could come from working together and that communication had power, and most importantly, they learned to control fire.

But a handful of others had a different gift; they had learned to understand the thoughts of animals. For them a different door to survival had opened and they learned the things animals knew: where to find water, where to find nutritious vegetables and healing grasses and herbs, how to open the senses fully to smells and tastes and feelings that would protect and nurture them. My people grew in that knowledge and honed their animal-like skills and grew to prefer the night to the day and to walk in it unafraid. The discovery of fire pulled your people a different way. Your people chose the fire and its warmth and protection instead of guile and swiftness. Your people grew to fear the night and huddled together in caves next to their fires letting their senses stagnate while my people roamed freely in the forests, growing close to the animals and becoming swifter and stronger. Over the centuries your people became caring, empathetic and emotional instead of predatory and practical. But to you we had become outcasts and you feared us for our superior powers and so we learned to conceal ourselves among you by day and to celebrate our powers alone at night.

We have always been here. Your kind has given us many names around the world. But the cultures that are most attuned to their pasts and to their ancient predecessors and whose histories are kept alive; those people know that we walk among them and they know our powers. Your Navajo friends know this; some tried to help you to know. But you remain the offspring of your ancestors, huddled in your shelter by your fire at night and denying your senses by day. And so you refuse to believe the evidence of your eyes when you see tracks of a man becoming a bear and then a man once more, and you refuse to believe your senses when you detect the red eyes of the night hunter in your camp. But now you know it is true, for I have selected you to know just before you die."

The sun had begun to slip behind the distant mesas and the bright rays that had blinded Zack now became diffused and in dying spread fading rainbows of color above the far rim of the land. He could see the hooded figure now as it slowly stood to its full great height and faced Zack. Red eyes glowed from beneath the hood.

"I'm so, so sorry, Zack," Libby said softly in her own voice.

Zack knew that he must act or die. He must raise his rifle and shoot this thing. But he could not. He was transfixed by the power of those eyes. He struggled in silent desperation to move as he watched the monster slowly raise a small cylindrical object to his mouth and point it at him. Zack knew what it was, and even as he continued to try to raise his rifle he prepared mentally for the impact of the cactus thorn and the feeling of helpless oblivion that would follow. He heard the hissing sound of the reed blowgun and he waited for its sting.

But what came next was not the bite of a needle into his flesh but a terrible hoarse cry of anguish. The creature turned his head violently to face something in the tall grass behind him. Zack felt the power that restrained him weaken in that instant. He quickly raised his rifle and fired twice in succession and saw at once that both bullets had found their mark, ripping into the hooded head of the monster. The creature staggered once and stood unmoving, then bent over as if in disbelief, snarling a low beast-like growl. Behind it a familiar figure had risen from the tall grass; the figure of Eagle Feather, fully dressed in Navajo ceremonial clothing with a small cylinder in his hand.

The creature let its blowpipe drop to the earth and raised both arms skyward and as it did its fingers turned to claws and its arms thickened and grew long and its legs shrunk to become thin and long and scaly and feathers grew out of its arms and shoulders. The dark hood fell back as a leathery down-covered head thrust forward out of it and became a crowned head with a huge curving beak, its red eyes sparking and glowing. The transformed thunderbird took a step toward Eagle Feather and then turned and with two staggering steps on clawed feet stretched out its enormous wings and rose hesitantly up into the air. The strong winds of the plateau caught it then and supported it, and it soared higher and higher and flew off toward the blood red sky to the west.

Then abruptly it faltered, its wings no longer sustained it and it struggled. It hung momentarily suspended there like a rocket at the apex of its flight and then plunged earthward faster and faster, turning and twisting helplessly until it disappeared from sight somewhere beyond the plateau.

In the long minutes of silence that followed the three friends stood like carved statues, their faces reflecting the blood-red hue of the sky from where the giant bird had gone down. Then as if a spell had been broken Libby turned and ran to Zack, tears streaming down her face and she reached for him and pulled him as close to her as she could. Eagle Feather walked toward them and they all stood close, seeking the comfort that they could share with each other. Diablo munched contentedly on the tall grass nearby.

"I won't soon doubt your beliefs again," Zack said to Eagle Feather in hushed tones.

Eagle Feather broke into a rare smile. "I see a bottle of wine over there that shouldn't go to waste, white man," he said.

EPILOGUE

The beer glasses sat half full in front of them and beads of condensation described a path to and from the empty pitcher in the middle of the slick laminated tabletop. It was early afternoon and the bar was not yet crowded. Zack and Eagle Feather sat back in their chairs to enjoy the moment and the company.

"You heard about Lané Shorter?" Eagle Feather asked suddenly, a slight slur to his words from perhaps a bit too much ale. "They found him lying dead in a canyon up north of your place, shot twice in the head."

"I did hear about that."

Eagle Feather pondered that for a moment. Then he had another thought.

"What does Libby remember about that day?"

"She doesn't remember very much," Zack replied. "She seems to know that she's missing a lot of details." He laughed, remembering. "But she can certainly remember that bottle of wine that we enjoyed later. But I'd say you're probably the only one who remembers what really happened."

"Except you."

"Except me," agreed Zack. "As far as everyone else is concerned the case concluded with the deaths of the two men in the burning house in La Quinta. The Bureau is satisfied with that outcome, the press is singing our praises for once, and Ray Donner is up for a promotion. Even Libby believes it all ended there."

"And you?"

"I don't know what I think. I have a clear memory of what I thought happened and what I believe I saw happen on the butte. But did drugs alter my reality? Libby told me later she wasn't the one who poured the glass of lemonade that was on the table. Later I had Linda analyze residue from the glass and she found traces of peyote. I do remember feeling a bit nauseous but put it down to anxiety over Libby. Did the peyote distort my reality and change my understanding of what happened up there? Did the drug slow down my responses? I don't know. Maybe none of it ever happened."

"Oh, it happened, white man. You'd better believe it."

"That reminds me. I've been meaning to ask you what brought you up on the butte that day. How did you know we would be up there?"

"Let's just put it down to a well developed spiritual sense. It's the difference between you and me, white man. When Libby and I drove back from California that day, I had a sense of being followed. I never did set store in the idea that the killer had died along with that Gonzalez fellow in the burning house. It didn't seem likely he would let himself get cornered like that. He's always been ahead of us by several steps, as if he could read our minds. And," –Eagle Feather shot a glance at Zack- "I was starting to suspect what he was."

Zack looked around at the other tables. Only a few people were at the bar. He had bumped into Eagle Feather in town and they'd agreed to a drink. This was the first time since then that they'd spoken of the events of that day. It was still hard.

"What did you think he was?"

Eagle Feather ignored the direct question. "When I dropped Libby and Blue off at her ranch I felt his presence. But when I drove away toward Elk Wells the feeling faded. I was ready to shrug the whole thing off but that night I had a dream. My spirit guide came to me in the dream and led me to a sacred place and there he showed me how to prepare a powerful potion in the old way. It was a protection against all manner of witches. I never question my spirit guide. And so as soon as I woke from the dream, even though it was dark I went to the place I had been shown and prepared the paste according to his instructions. Then I cut a small section of a bamboo pole for a blowgun and I made a dart from a large needle and feathers and cotton wadding. Then I painted the needle with the paste.

I was ready, but my spirit guide hadn't told me what to do next. I had to be patient. So I waited. Later that day, I felt myself drawn back to Libby's ranch. I followed that feeling and brought the blowgun and dart with me. But when I neared her ranch I saw her old station wagon pull out of the drive and turn north. I saw that she wasn't alone. I began to understand then why my spirit guide had come to me.

I figured she must have been going to your ranch so I went there the back way along the old fence line road. I cut over to the plateau and climbed up to a place where I could look down on your ranch."

"So you were already up there," Zack exclaimed.

"Yes, not far, just far enough to see your house and Libby's station wagon parked behind the barn. I guessed Libby must be in the house so I hunkered down to watch. Before long she came walking out the back door and toward the barn and then this person covered by a hood came out of the house and followed her and I knew my spirit guide had not mislead me. Pretty soon the hooded man came out of the barn leading your mare by its reins with Libby in the saddle. They started up the trail. Then the mare broke into a trot and the hooded man jogged on ahead of it as easily as a hawk floats on the wind."

Eagle Feather paused to drink down the last of his beer. Zack waited, hanging on every word. Eagle Feather wiped his mouth and continued.

"I knew I had to get out of there. I couldn't let them get ahead of me and I didn't want that creature to catch my scent. But where were they going? Then I remembered what Libby had told me about your special place up on top of the butte. I realized then that the monster had come for you, not Libby, and that he planned to wait for you and to use Libby as bait. So I circled around the back of the butte along a game trail and climbed up on the downwind side. I hid in the tall grass and waited. I never saw them arrive but I felt his presence. I stayed as still as a hunted deer and blanked my mind in case he could hear my thoughts and waited for my moment. I believe he still might have sensed my presence if he had not been so intent upon you. I could feel his energy pouring down the trail after you. In that situation you became his weakness."

Zack let out a long breath and looked at his friend with astonishment. "You beat him at his own game."

"I was lucky, and so were you," Eagle Feather pointed out. "But there's another mystery and it's your turn to tell me the answer to that one."

"And that is...?"

"Why did he die? My dart was true but my potion, as powerful as it was, should not have killed such a creature by itself. I had hoped to stun him or possibly disable him to buy time to help both of you escape. And yes, your bullets were accurate. But again, even the most perfectly placed rifle bullets shouldn't have killed the creature. Yet they did. How?"

Zack smiled softly. "I find many of your beliefs hard to accept, as you know," he said. "But I don't entirely discount those things that my friend believes so earnestly. I remembered you saying that a man who can accept some things even though he doesn't understand them will never be taken by surprise. Despite my doubts, your words made sense. That very day I dipped my rifle bullets in white ash powder, which I was told was the only way to kill a Skinwalker. Perhaps that is what made the difference."

It was Eagle Feather's turn to look at Zack with surprise and respect.

"There, white man," he said. "Right there. That's the kind of thinking that sets you apart from other white men. And it's why the creature decided to challenge you. And that's why he was so intent upon demonstrating his powers to you that he jeopardized his own safety."

Zack grinned back. "But he couldn't have known when he picked me that he was challenging not just one man but two: a white FBI agent and his Navajo friend."

Zack laughed. "And that was his last mistake."

Coming Soon

Another Zack Tolliver and Eagle Feather Mystery Thriller

In MESTACLOCAN Zack and Eagle Feather pursue an elusive mystery killer through the streets of San Francisco. He kills by night. His victims are found the following morning, always young and active women, always with a single wound to the throat, and…he leaves no clues. Don't miss this exciting sequel.